COLTON'S RESCUE MISSION

Karen Whiddon

HARLEQUIN® ROMANTIC SUSPENSE

Special thanks and acknowledgment are given to
Karen Whiddon for her contribution to
The Coltons of Roaring Springs miniseries.

ISBN-13: 978-1-335-66225-5

Colton's Rescue Mission

Recycling programs
for this product may
not exist in your area.

Copyright © 2019 by Harlequin Books S.A.

Printed in U.S.A.

www.Harlequin.com

Remy grimaced. "I think so. I'm sorry to have disturbed you. I'll come back and talk to Seth in the morning."

She regarded him, her gaze steady. "He and I are supposed to go ski Pine Mountain in the morning before he goes to work. You might want to call him instead."

Again, the stab of envy. Though Remy wasn't a skier of Seth's caliber, he enjoyed a few runs up on the slopes as often as he could, time permitting. Though knowing his brother, he doubted Seth would feel much like skiing tomorrow. He'd be way too hungover.

Saying none of this, he nodded. "Thanks. I'll keep that in mind. Again, I apologize for waking you."

She waved him away with a sleepy smile. "No worries. I guess I'll be seeing you around."

Damn, he hoped so. And once more, that odd combination of guilt and longing assailed him. Swallowing hard, he gave her a quick nod and left.

All the way home, he called himself every kind of fool. He'd just met the woman, for Pete's sake. And while he could definitely understand the lure of physical attraction, he wasn't the kind of man who'd even consider making a move on his brother's lady, no matter how alluring he found her.

* * *

**The Coltons of Roaring Springs:
Family and true love are under siege**

* * *

**If you're on Twitter, tell us what you think of Harlequin Romantic Suspense!
#harlequinromsuspense**

Dear Reader,

Whenever I am asked to write a Coltons book, I'm beyond thrilled. I love this family, adore the settings and enjoy the camaraderie with the other authors. It's so much fun telling these tales.

I hope you enjoy *Colton's Rescue Mission*. Writing it took me back to my visit to a Colorado ski resort and the snowy and festive atmosphere there. Writing about the love blooming between Remy and Vanessa was pure pleasure, and bringing the entire family together brought its own kind of satisfaction.

Best,

Karen Whiddon

Karen Whiddon started weaving fanciful tales for her younger brothers at the age of eleven. Amid the gorgeous Catskill Mountains, then the majestic Rocky Mountains, she fueled her imagination with the natural beauty surrounding her. Karen now lives in north Texas, writes full-time and volunteers for a boxer dog rescue. She shares her life with her hero of a husband and four to five dogs, depending on if she is fostering. You can email Karen at kwhiddon1@aol.com. Fans can also check out her website, karenwhiddon.com.

Books by Karen Whiddon

Harlequin Romantic Suspense

The Coltons of Roaring Springs

Colton's Rescue Mission

The CEO's Secret Baby
The Cop's Missing Child
The Millionaire Cowboy's Secret
Texas Secrets, Lovers' Lies
The Rancher's Return
The Texan's Return
Wyoming Undercover
The Texas Soldier's Son
Texas Ranch Justice

The Coltons of Red Ridge

Colton's Christmas Cop

The Coltons of Texas

Runaway Colton

The Coltons of Oklahoma

The Temptation of Dr. Colton

The Coltons: Return to Wyoming

A Secret Colton Baby

Visit the Author Profile page at Harlequin.com for more titles.

To my dog rescue family, Legacy Boxer Rescue. Because of you, so many dogs have found new beginnings. You truly are the heart of the organization and I love you all!

Chapter 1

Snowfall—check. Festive music playing on speakers in all the outdoor common areas—check. Ornate and glittery Christmas decorations both inside and out—final check.

Remy Colton stood on the sidewalk of downtown Roaring Springs, Colorado, and surveyed the merry atmosphere. As director of public relations for The Chateau, the premier luxury destination also known as a little piece of France, Remy couldn't have asked for more perfect holiday weather. With both his family's ski resorts—The Lodge up on Pine Peak and The Chateau, here in the Roaring Springs valley—booked to capacity for the two weeks leading up to Christmas, any snow was always welcome. And they were definitely getting a lot of the beautiful white stuff.

Remy liked to keep busy during the holidays, especially since he'd never really gotten into the holiday spirit. That was never a problem, even though the PR department pretty much shut down until after the New Year. The Chateau attracted a wealthy clientele—sometimes celebrities—and those patrons could be quite demanding. He never minded pitching in, especially on Christmas Eve or Christmas Day, so his employees could spend the holiday with their families.

As for himself, out of necessity, he always made sure to spend a few hours with his own extended family at the elaborate holiday dinner his uncle Russ and aunt Mara hosted at Colton Manor, the 35-million-dollar showpiece of a home they'd constructed up on a hill. While he enjoyed visiting with his cousins and their significant others, he usually hightailed it back to The Chateau as quickly as he could. As far as he could tell, no one ever noticed or minded. If there was one thing his father, Whit, understood, it was the concept that work came before anything else. Clearly, it had never occurred to Whit that Remy might be lonely.

Pushing away the unsettling thought, he forced himself to focus once again on the positives. Nothing like a great snowfall to make the guests happy.

"Excuse me?" A feminine voice, both sultry and with a faintly northeastern accent. Before he could react, she tapped him on the shoulder.

He turned and eyed a tall, blue-eyed woman wearing top-of-the-line ski gear. Not only was she athletic, but she was also strikingly beautiful. He felt a jolt the instant he met her gaze. Probably one of the guests, though he had no idea how he could have possibly missed noticing her. "Yes, can I help you?"

"I asked at the front desk and they sent me out to

talk to you. I'm looking for Seth Harris. I believe he's the hotel manager. I've already been up to The Lodge, but they said he wasn't working today."

Seth. His gut clenched. What had his brother done now?

Normally he would have directed her to the gondola that ran between The Lodge and The Chateau. But she was correct. Seth was off today. Remy caught himself staring and rapidly checked himself. Something about her eyes...

Whoever she might be, she wasn't his brother's usual type. Seth's taste usually ran to leggy, busty blondes.

Since Remy knew better than to let this woman—whoever she was—drop in on Seth unannounced, he simply shrugged. "I believe he'll be working tomorrow, so I'd suggest you check back at The Lodge then."

Instead of nodding and thanking him, she didn't budge. "I've been told you're his brother. I really need to talk to him."

Remy made a mental note to find out which employee had seen fit to give out such personal information. "Are you a friend of his, Ms. ...?"

"Fisher," she stated. "Vanessa Fisher. And I'm not sure if Seth still considers me a friend or not. We were recently engaged, though we're not any longer."

Engaged? This was the woman Seth had wanted to marry? She looked nothing like the shy woman the rest of his family had described. This woman was tall, true. And she did have dark, silky hair. What everyone else must have forgotten to mention was that she was beautiful. Stunning, punch-in-the-gut gorgeous. Her dark blue eyes studied him.

Years of practice had taught Remy how to hide his shock. Nothing Seth did should have surprised him, but when he'd learned his baby brother had gotten engaged, shock hadn't even begun to describe how he'd felt. Sure, Seth had mentioned dating someone named Vanessa. He'd made several trips down to Boulder to visit her. But first he'd gotten engaged and then, in typical Seth fashion, the engagement had been broken off.

Which meant now Remy was actually meeting his brother's former fiancée for the first time.

"Remy Colton," he said automatically, removing his glove and holding out his hand.

She tilted her head before doing the same and slipped her fingers into his. Touching her sent a pleasurable jolt through him, though she appeared completely unaffected. "Remy," she mused. "Interesting name."

Entranced by her smile, he froze. But then the rest of what Vanessa Fisher had said dawned on him. It sounded like Seth had dumped her. Which meant what?

He started to ask, but his befuddled thoughts must have shown on his face because she shook her head before he even got the words out.

"It's not like that." She touched him again, this time on his jacket arm. Remy normally wasn't a touchy-feely kind of person, but for whatever reason he didn't mind *her* touch. "I'm the one that broke things off," she continued. "Seth and I haven't spoken since."

Cocking his head, he considered her. He'd never once in his life envied his younger brother, but for the first time, he did. Something about this woman knocked him off his feet. While he knew none of this was his damn business, he asked, anyway. "And you're now here because...?"

She met his gaze directly. "That's personal. Now can you tell me where to find Seth or not?"

Since he was meeting Seth a few doors down in the trendy faux-Western bar called The Saloon, he shrugged. Hopefully, his brother wouldn't kill him when he walked in with this woman. "Come with me."

They walked along the snowy sidewalks, mingling in with the happy tourists. This time of year, everyone in Roaring Springs seemed to be in a celebratory mood. They came, they skied, they shopped and ate and drank. Since the townspeople earned seventy-five percent of their income in the winter, the locals were grateful for the crowds.

When they reached The Saloon, the line that had formed spilled out onto the sidewalk. Despite this, those waiting laughed and chatted without the typical impatience that moneyed people often exhibited.

"Excuse me," he said, taking Vanessa's arm as he soldiered through the crowd. "I'm meeting someone inside."

The harried hostess working the front desk recognized him and smiled. "Hey, Remy. Your brother's got a booth in the bar," she murmured. "Go ahead back and join him."

"Thanks." Remy glanced at Vanessa, again feeling a strong sense of attraction. She unzipped her parka, then removed her gloves and shoved them into her pocket. As they walked, he leaned in close, taking in her scent, which, unbelievably, seemed to be a holiday mix of peppermint and chocolate—two of his favorite things this time of the year. "Promise me you're not here to make a scene," he said, taking hold of her elbow.

One corner of her lush mouth quirked up in the beginning of a smile as she glanced back at him. "I promise. I'm not the scene-making type."

He spotted Seth in the corner booth, intent on scrolling through his phone. He barely looked up when Remy slid into the seat across from him. "Um, Seth?"

His brother raised his head, his gaze skittering right past Remy to Vanessa. His mouth fell open. Seth had never been good at hiding his emotions, Remy thought. Surprise first, and then anger crossed his face, which finally changed to a sort of sullen resignation. "Vanessa. What are you doing in town? I thought you always skied Winter Park."

"Do you mind if I sit?" she asked instead of answering the question.

"Go ahead." Seth waved his hand, finally eying his brother. "I'm guessing you and Remy have already met."

"We did." Sliding in next to Remy, Vanessa placed her elegant, long-fingered hand on his arm. "Thank you so much for escorting me here."

When she pulled her fingers away from him, he exhaled, wondering why he felt like leaning into her touch. Predictably, the skin-to-shirt contact, however brief, made him ache for more. Damn. His brother's former fiancée.

Remy let out a breath, suddenly feeling like a third wheel. "I'm guessing I should go," he offered, half-hoping Seth would refuse. "It seems you two have a lot to talk about."

"We do," Vanessa replied softly, barely glancing at him. "Thanks for understanding."

Avoiding looking at anyone, Seth simply nodded, then took a long drink from his beer.

Though Remy hadn't eaten dinner yet—that being the reason he'd been meeting Seth here—he started to slide back out of the booth. Vanessa stood and stepped aside to let him pass, her cool, direct gaze revealing nothing.

Again, envy shot through him, along with shame at feeling this way. Remy loved his troubled half brother and would never do anything to hurt him. He'd spent the last several years trying to forge a family relationship with a sibling he hadn't even known he had and wouldn't jeopardize it for anything, especially not for a woman. He might not be able to explain the strength of his attraction to Vanessa Fisher, but he definitely could refuse to act on it. Staying as far away as possible from her would be a great way to start. Assuming she was even here for long. Knowing Seth, he'd send her packing as quickly as possible.

As he made his way through the crowded pub away from the booth, a stool opened up at the bar just as he reached it. Moving instinctively, Remy took it. After all, he needed to eat. He ordered a draft beer, glad he had his back to his brother's booth. Watching Seth and Vanessa would be a form of slow torture. Which made zero sense. He barely knew her, after all.

When Gary, the bartender on duty, tried to hand him a menu, Remy waved it away. He knew what he wanted. "I'll just have the buffalo burger and sweet-potato fries," he said. "Medium well on the cook."

Gary grinned. "I almost went ahead and put in the

order the second I saw you sit down, but there's always a chance you might want something different."

"Not today." Remy smiled back, then took a long swig of his beer.

"Who's the babe with Seth?" Gary asked. "I've seen her up on the slopes over at Sunlight Mountain a few times, though I haven't seen her ski here. She's a real pro."

"She is?" Unable to keep from glancing back over his shoulder, he observed his brother and Vanessa engaged in what appeared to be an intense conversation. "Maybe that's how the two of them met. Skiing."

"You don't know her?" Gary raised his brow, eying the two in the booth. "She's not Seth's usual type."

Since he'd had the exact same thought himself, Remy simply nodded.

"Be right back," the bartender said. "Looks like Seth wants another beer. And I need to see if his lady friend needs anything to drink."

Remy couldn't help but turn and watch as Gary headed over to his brother's booth. Seth had his back to him but Vanessa looked up and met his gaze. Again, he felt that undeniable sizzle of awareness and wondered if she did, too. If so, she did nothing to reveal it. Instead, she dipped her chin in a quick nod, before returning her attention to Gary and Seth.

And just like before, he felt that unfamiliar twinge of jealousy, combined with a longing so fierce it stunned him. What the hell? He forced himself to turn around and focus on his beer.

Vanessa hadn't expected the butterflies in her stomach upon meeting Seth's charismatic and sexy-as-hell brother. Which made absolutely no sense. She hadn't come to Roaring Springs looking for a new relationship. Especially not with the half sibling of the man with whom she'd broken things off.

Pushing the thought of Remy from her mind, she focused on Seth. While initially he'd appeared shocked to see her, he'd visibly relaxed the instant his brother had walked away. Still, something seemed off about him, though she couldn't quite put her finger on what it was. Of course, part of her would now always feel uneasy around him, due to the way he'd handled their breakup.

"So, tell me, Vanessa, how long have you been in town? And more importantly, why are you here?" With his sandy blond hair and hazel-green eyes, when he turned on the charm, Seth could make women melt. Once, when she'd been particularly vulnerable after losing her parents, he'd affected her this way, though they'd been friends first.

"I just got in this morning," she replied, resisting the urge to tell him her trip had been made impulsively. "I'd hoped to stay a night or two and do some skiing while I was here, but it seems every place is completely booked."

"They are." He sat back, the slightly smug tone in his voice at odds with his sympathetic smile. "This time of the year is our busiest. A lot of wealthy, important people spend their holidays with us. They book their rooms months in advance."

"With us?" she echoed, before remembering he was employed as hotel manager at The Lodge.

"But no worries," he continued as if she hadn't spoken. "If you want to ski Pine Peak, you should. You're welcome to stay with me for as long as you want."

She squirmed, once again remembering his out-of-control anger when she'd broken things off. He'd punched a hole in the wall, and the violence of his re-action had terrified her. She'd cringed away from him, startled and afraid, at which point he'd stormed out. Nope. She didn't think she'd be staying with him now. "That's very kind of you, Seth," she replied, choosing her words carefully. "But I didn't come here to see about the possibility of us getting back together. I felt bad about the way I broke things off and realized I owed you an explanation."

"I didn't think you wanted to get back together." His expression darkened. "And, no, you don't owe me an explanation. I get it. I'm over it, Vanessa."

"Maybe so, but please let me talk." Swallowing, she hesitated. "I'd feel much better."

"Fine." He took another long pull of his beer, then set the empty mug on the table with a thunk and gestured at the bartender for another. "Go ahead and unburden yourself. Even though I basically figured it out when you wouldn't sleep with me. Not once, the entire time we were together."

Wincing, Vanessa glanced around, hoping no one had overheard. She told herself she shouldn't blame Seth for being deliberately cruel. She might have been the same way had their situation been reversed. After all, she'd done him a great disservice. Not only had she ruined their friendship, but she'd also let him think she might be able to love him. "Please don't be like that," she began. "You and I were always friends before we were anything else. I hate that we've lost that."

The bartender brought over another beer for Seth and asked what she'd like. She ordered a glass of chardonnay and waited until the man had walked away before continuing. "One of the things I'll always be grateful for is how you were my rock when I fell apart after my parents were killed. Seth, you saved me. I'll never be able to repay that. But…"

"But I fell in love with you," he said, finishing for her. "And you didn't feel the same way."

Was it wrong to feel relieved that she didn't have to spell it out? Sighing softly, she murmured, "Exactly."

"Then why did you accept my proposal?" He searched her face. "I can understand everything else but that. Why would you agree to marry me if you didn't love me?"

Her gut twisted. Not so easy after all. "I didn't want to hurt you," she explained, aware she might be making a mess of this. "And to be honest, I found myself clinging to…" Aghast at what she'd almost said, she stopped, searching for another way to explain she'd chosen what had seemed safe and familiar, and that she'd been briefly afraid of being on her own.

"I get it," Seth interjected, once again inadvertently rescuing her. "To tell the truth, I think I knew all along that you didn't feel the same way I did. I just wanted…" He took a deep breath. "More."

She nodded, aware that acknowledging the pain in his voice might be worse than pretending not to hear it. "I'm sorry, Seth. That's what I came up here to say. I don't think I can love anyone right now with my life in such an uproar. You deserved more. We both do. When you wouldn't take my calls, I felt like I needed to explain in person. Maybe understanding why will help you move on."

"I've already moved on," he informed her.

Her wine arrived. Grateful, she smiled at the bartender before taking a sip. "Perfect," she said. "Thank you."

"No problem." The man moved away. When she looked across the booth, she saw that Seth watched her intently, his eyes narrowed into slits. Again, she felt a shiver of unease, which was ridiculous. Emotions had been high that day. Enough time had passed and she knew Seth would be calmer now.

After all, he'd never raised a hand to her.

Still, she suddenly realized she wanted out of there, away from him. She'd done what she'd come to do and now maybe they both could have closure. Digging in her purse, she extracted a ten-dollar bill and laid it on the table next to her still-full glass of wine before rising to her feet. "Thanks for listening," she said, hoping her smile looked more genuine than it felt. "I'm going to head out now. It was great seeing you."

"Wait." He stood as well. "Please don't run off, Vanessa. I accept your apology." He pushed out a breath from both cheeks. "I'm really hoping we can still be friends." He pinned her with his gaze, his hazel-green eyes earnest. "Can we? We have a long history of friendship. I'd hate to lose that."

How could she resist? After all, that's what she'd wanted. She'd missed their friendship. Slowly she lowered herself back into her seat. "I'd like that," she said, wondering if it was really relief she felt, or more gratitude that he truly seemed to be over her.

"Great." He pushed her wineglass toward her.

"Enjoy your wine. It's been a while since we talked. I'm sure we have a lot to catch up on."

Instead, they ended up discussing only generalities, like a couple of strangers on a first date. The closing of her favorite Irish bar in Boulder, the skiing up at Sunlight Mountain near Glenwood Springs...

"Have you skied Pine Peak yet?" Seth asked. "I like it a lot better than Sunlight. It's got some great black-diamond runs. Of course, I'm prejudiced since I live and work here."

She thought of her skis, still strapped to the roof of her car. "Not yet. I was hoping to do that while I was up here." Taking a sip of her wine, she shrugged. "Maybe another time."

"How about tomorrow?" He grinned at her over the rim of his beer mug. "It's best first thing in the morning, right when the lift opens. I like to go before work. Come with me?"

"I'm tempted," she admitted. "But like I said, there's not an available room in this town. Believe me, I've checked."

"I told you, you can stay with me." He held up a hand as she started to protest. "I have a guest room. You can stay there. Completely platonic. Please, I insist. There's nothing I'd like better than skiing with you again."

Maybe because she really, really wanted to ski Pine Peak, or perhaps because she felt like she owed him at least that much, she found herself acquiescing. "Just for one night."

"Sure." He raised his nearly empty mug. "I'll have another to celebrate."

Her stomach growled, reminding her that she hadn't eaten since breakfast. "How about some dinner instead?"

Remy had just climbed into bed and shut off the lights when his cell phone rang, startling him. Sitting up, he glanced at the digital clock on his nightstand—eleven thirty. Damn it. A call at this time of night was never a good thing.

"Hello?"

"Remy, this is Liam Kastor. Did I wake you?"

Instantly alert, Remy explained he'd been awake. Since Liam was a detective with the Roaring Springs Police Department, he suspected this call involved something his younger brother had done. It certainly wouldn't be the first time.

"It's Seth," Liam continued, confirming Remy's suspicions. "We got a call earlier from The Saloon. The bartender, Gary, said Seth had been there drinking all evening and got belligerent when they cut him off. I headed down there to check it out, but by the time I arrived, he was gone."

"Driving?" Remy asked, horrified.

"No, thank goodness. His car is still parked in the lot. Either someone gave him a ride or he left on foot. Since it's snowing pretty heavily outside, I sent out a couple of patrols looking for him. Being drunk out in freezing temperatures is never a good combination. There's no sign of him, at least downtown."

Remy swore. "I'll go look for him. Thank you for calling me."

After ending the call, he immediately dialed his brother's cell. After several rings, it went to voicemail. Remy left a quick, terse message asking Seth to call him.

Now he had no other option than to go out and search.

He threw on warm clothes, then snagged his coat and gloves and headed out into the frigid cold. In the time since he'd been home, several inches of perfect powder had accumulated. The plow would be by in the morning, but this kind of snow was easy to drive on.

He retraced the route Seth might have walked if he'd decided to head home to his condo from The Saloon. Since it was only a few blocks, it was definitely doable, at least when sober.

When Remy reached the trendy apartment building without seeing any trace of his brother, he parked and considered what to do next. First, he punched redial, hoping against hope that Seth would pick up. When he got voicemail again, he sighed and shut off his engine.

Inside, he rode the elevator up to the third floor and trudged down the hall until he reached Seth's condo. Glancing at his watch and seeing that it was nearly midnight, he winced but rang the doorbell, anyway. While dealing with a drunk Seth was never pleasant, he had to make sure his brother had made it home safely.

When nothing happened, he pressed the doorbell again and again and again. Sooner or later that kind of noise would get through to even a passed-out drunk.

Sure enough, a moment later the door opened a crack. But, instead of Seth, a tousle-haired Vanessa peeked out at him. The sight of her sleepy, sexy blue eyes hit him like a punch in the stomach.

When the implications of her presence registered,

he felt like a fool. Swallowing hard, he nodded at her. "Is Seth home?"

Covering her mouth while she yawned, she opened the door a bit wider and stepped aside so he could enter. She wore flannel pajamas in a plaid holiday pattern with some sort of fuzzy slippers. Somehow, she managed to look both cute and alluring at the same time.

"Is Seth here?" he asked again, reminding himself to focus.

"I'm not sure." Brushing her hair back from her face, she lifted one shoulder in a delicate shrug. "He was earlier. We had dinner and then came back here so I could get settled. He wanted to go back out but I was tired, so I went to bed. In the guest bedroom," she said pointedly. "Anyway, I've been asleep. At least until you started ringing the doorbell over and over."

"My apologies." He thought about explaining and decided against it. Surely, she knew what kind of trouble her former fiancé could get himself into. "I'm just going to check on him," he said. "Make sure he's okay."

"Knock yourself out." She wandered into the kitchen, still yawning.

Seth's bedroom door was closed. Remy knocked— three sharp raps of his knuckles on the wood. No answer. Reluctantly, he turned the knob and squinted into the dark room, hoping he could make out whether or not Seth occupied the bed.

No such luck. Bracing himself, he flicked on the light switch.

An annoyed groan came from Seth, sprawled out, fully dressed, on the bed. "Turn that the hell off."

Instead of complying, Remy eyed his baby brother, trying to judge how drunk Seth might be. Deciding it didn't matter—he'd learned long ago how pointless it was trying to talk to someone while they were inebriated—he turned out the light and backed out of the room.

"Is he all right?" Vanessa asked, her fingers curled around a tall glass of ice water.

Remy grimaced. "I think so. I'm sorry to have disturbed you. I'll come back and talk to Seth in the morning."

She regarded him, her gaze steady. "He and I are supposed to go ski Pine Peak in the morning before he goes to work. You might want to call him instead."

Again, the stab of envy. Though Remy wasn't a skier of Seth's caliber, he enjoyed a few runs up on the slopes as often as he could, time permitting. Though knowing his brother, he doubted Seth would feel much like skiing tomorrow. He'd be way too hungover.

Saying none of this, he nodded. "Thanks. I'll keep that in mind. Again, I apologize for waking you."

She waved him away with a sleepy smile. "No worries. I guess I'll be seeing you around."

Damn, he hoped so. And once more, that odd combination of guilt and longing assailed him. Swallowing hard, he gave her a quick nod and left.

All the way home, he called himself every kind of fool. He'd just met the woman, for Pete's sake. And while he could definitely understand the lure of physical attraction, he wasn't the kind of man who'd even consider making a move on his brother's lady, no matter how irresistible he found her.

His brother's lady. The notion made him shake his

head. Seth never stuck with anyone very long, never mind proposed marriage. Despite the fact that Remy helped his brother any way he could, Seth constantly seemed to be barely treading water. Maybe resuming his relationship with Vanessa would be the thing Seth needed to completely turn his life around.

Remy definitely hoped so. But he couldn't help but think there was something…off in all of this. For one thing, the reconciliation between Seth and Vanessa sure had happened quickly. Especially since she claimed she'd broken off the engagement. Yet they'd had one dinner and Seth had immediately installed her in his condo. Strange. But none of his business.

Except for the insane pull of attraction he felt toward the woman who was once his almost-sister-in-law.

Chapter 2

Back home, Remy shed his clothes and once again climbed in between his sheets, then pulled his comforter up to his chin. He couldn't shake the image of Vanessa in the soft flannel pajamas, wondering what it would be like to slip his hand under them and caress her warm skin. Guilt immediately followed that thought, because he knew he didn't have the right.

Despite thinking he wouldn't, he managed to drift off to sleep. When he opened his eyes again, he saw his alarm was due to go off in five minutes. He shut it off and pushed himself up.

Thirty minutes later, showered and dressed, he drank his black coffee and nuked instant oatmeal for breakfast. When he'd finished eating, he checked his watch. He had a morning meeting with a new advertising firm from Denver, so he wouldn't have time to stop by Seth's.

As he drove to work, he couldn't help but wonder if his brother had felt well enough to ski. He found himself wondering if Vanessa would go by herself, anyway, and wished he had time to head up to Pine Peak.

Wishful thinking. And foolishness, completely unlike him. Remy considered responsibility his middle name and rarely took time off from work.

Though right now, he sorely wanted to. He hadn't been skiing at all this season. Of course, his sudden desire to go now had way too much to do with the intriguing beauty ensconced in Seth's condo. Trouble, any way he looked at it.

Shaking his head at his stray thoughts, he parked and reminded himself to concentrate on his job. When he walked into the elegant lobby of The Chateau, he greeted Mary, the redheaded concierge who was married to Johnnie Web, a firefighter and local hero. She smiled and greeted him back, her cheerful words making him smile the entire elevator ride up to his floor.

As he stepped off and entered the bustling office, the uncharacteristic quiet made him pause. Usually, phones were ringing, people were talking and the hum of various printers or copiers made a pleasant cacophony.

Today, more than half of the cubicles were empty—people taking off for the approaching holiday. He ought to know because he'd personally approved everyone's requested vacation time.

He'd actually been a bit surprised the Denver ad agency had requested a meeting today to pitch their ideas for a new campaign. While Remy had let it be known that he was actively searching for a new company, all the other major players had scheduled meetings for after the New Year.

Since he actually admired this firm for wanting to get a jump on their competition, he'd agreed to the meeting, despite being short several members of his decision-making staff.

Walking into his office, he looked around for his assistant, Heather. She came out of the break room carrying a donut and a cup of coffee, her long, brown hair up in her usual jaunty ponytail. "Well, good morning," she chirped. "Someone brought donuts, if you're interested."

Before he could reply, her phone rang. Heather rushed past him toward her desk, managing to get there without spilling any coffee. "Remy Colton's desk," she answered. Listening for a moment, her eyes went wide. "Please hold." She eyed Remy, her expression carefully blank. "It's The Lodge. You'd better take it."

"Okay, thanks." He strolled into his office and closed the door. He couldn't imagine why anyone up there would be calling, but picked up his phone and answered.

"I'm sorry to bother you," Denise, one of the shift managers, said. "But Seth didn't show up this morning."

Remy glanced at his watch. "What time was he scheduled to be in?"

Denise hesitated. "Nine. However, when he pulls a time slot that early, he's always a little late."

Remy hadn't known this. "How late?" The question came out a bit sharper than he'd intended.

"He's usually in by ten," she said quietly. "But it's after that and he isn't answering his phone."

Remy cursed silently. If he hurried, he could make it to Seth's condo and back before his meeting, which seemed to be running late. "I'll run over and check on him," he promised.

"Thank you." Again, he sensed her hesitation. "If he's…sick, just let us know so we don't expect him."

"Will do." He hung up, gritting his teeth. Almost immediately, his assistant buzzed him.

"Your ten o'clock canceled," she said. "They were driving up from Denver this morning. Since the pass is closed, they have no way to get here."

He thanked her, actually glad. Now he wouldn't have to worry about rushing things with Seth. It sounded like his baby brother needed a good talking-to.

Vanessa wondered for the umpteenth time if she'd made a mistake agreeing to stay in Seth's condo, even if only for one night. When his handsome brother, Remy, had shown up after midnight, worried, she felt a jolt of attraction low in her belly. Again. And she hated drama of any kind. Getting in between two brothers could create chaos of epic proportions.

Still, after Remy left and she'd wandered back to her bedroom, she couldn't stop thinking about him.

When she woke shortly after seven, she hurriedly showered and dressed before heading to the kitchen, where she hoped to get a cup of strong coffee. Seth's bedroom door remained closed, making her wonder if he'd forgotten their plans to ski. Loath to knock, she texted him instead.

What time are we leaving?

No answer, which might mean he was in the shower. She went ahead and made her coffee, glad Seth stocked milk and sweetener. After a couple of sips, warmth flooding her throat, she felt her original optimism again. There was nothing she loved better than skiing and she could hardly wait to try out the slopes at Pine Peak. She glanced at her gear piled over in a corner near the door. Rather than leaving it in the car and taking a chance on it being stolen, she'd brought it inside Seth's condo.

Speaking of Seth... She checked her watch. They'd agreed on early morning, before he had to go in to work. While she wasn't sure what his schedule looked like today, she figured he'd have to start by nine at the latest. Which meant they were running out of time to ski.

She walked over to the window and peered outside. Snow still fell in a steady curtain and judging from the amount piled up on cars, they'd gotten over a foot of fresh white powder overnight. But there didn't seem to be any wind, which was a good thing.

Perfect for skiing. As long as conditions weren't whiteout, the slope would be rocking and rolling. She could hardly wait.

Gathering up her nerve, she went ahead and tapped quietly on his door.

Nothing.

With her heart racing, she turned the knob and

peeked her head in. Judging by the man-size lump under the covers, Seth was still asleep.

Sleeping it off?

"Seth?" she ventured, staying in the doorway. "Seth, are you going to get up?"

A loud groan was his only answer.

Damned if she would go any farther into the room. She wasn't sure what Seth thought this was, but she could clearly see what might happen if she stepped over and attempted to shake him awake. He'd pull her down and start kissing her, likely ignoring her protests that they weren't intimate anymore.

Nope. Not happening. Suppressing a shudder, she called him again. "Seth. We're supposed to go skiing before you go to work. I'm not sure what time you have to be in, but if we're going to hit the slopes, I'm thinking we need to head out now."

"We'll go later," he mumbled. "I'm taking the day off from work."

"Okay," she replied, backing out and closing the door. Drinking the rest of her coffee, she debated whether or not to head out alone. While she could certainly ski an unfamiliar mountain by herself, it was always much more fun with a friend like Seth, who was a damned skilled skier. And whatever else he might be, she hoped the two of them could remain friends.

She decided to give it a few hours. After all, she had no place she had to be.

Since Seth had told her to make herself at home and to help herself to anything she wanted, she rummaged in the fridge in search of something she could make herself for breakfast.

Surprised to find a wide variety of foods, she settled on scrambled eggs and toast, along with a second cup of coffee.

After she ate, she checked the weather app on her phone. While she personally felt there was no such thing as too much snow, she knew ski resorts didn't always agree. If visibility got too poor, they'd shut down the slope and send the ski patrol out to bring in any stragglers. Her heart sank as she realized the snowstorm had caused exactly that situation. Though they hoped for perfect conditions tomorrow once the storm had passed, those in charge had decided it was too dangerous at the moment.

Which meant Seth's refusal to get out of bed had actually been a good thing. With the passion of a thousand purple suns, she hated getting suited up in anticipation of a couple of good runs and being stopped at the base of the mountain as she was about to get on the lift.

Should she go home then, and leave skiing Pine Peak for another time? After all, she'd done what she came to do and hopefully Seth would now have some closure.

Another quick internet search revealed they'd closed Loveland Pass. She could still take the I-70 tunnel, though she wasn't sure of the road conditions right now.

Her motto when it came to snowstorms had always been Better Safe Than Sorry. Which meant she'd be sticking around Roaring Springs at least one more night, maybe longer.

Glancing once more at the still-closed bedroom door, she knew Seth wouldn't mind her staying with him an extra day or two. If she could just get past this uneasiness. Since she'd been here, Seth had been nothing but a perfect gentleman. Sure, he'd gone out and had a little too much to drink last night, but he hadn't come pounding on her door or anything.

A sharp series of knocks on the front door made her jump. Hurrying over, she checked the peephole. Her stomach did a somersault when she saw Remy standing there, all bundled up in a down parka, a light dusting of snow on his broad shoulders.

Hurriedly, she opened the door. "Come inside," she said. "It's freezing out there."

"I know." As he stepped inside, his solemn expression gave her pause. "They closed down the slopes."

"Yes, I saw. Ditto on Loveland Pass, which shouldn't be such a surprise." She took a deep breath. "Would you like some coffee?"

One side of his mouth quirked up, but he shook his head. "No thanks. This isn't really a social visit. Is Seth around?"

"In there." She inclined her head toward the closed door. "Is everything all right?"

"He didn't show up for work." Remy removed his parka and hung it on the back of a chair. "He didn't even call, so they didn't know if they needed to bring someone else in to cover his shift."

Seth had said he was taking the day off. Clearly, he'd managed to forget to inform his employer of that.

Again, their gazes met and held for a second too long. Remy looked away first. "Is he still asleep?"

Feeling slightly dazed, she nodded. "I think so. I tried to wake him earlier but he was having none of it. We were supposed to hit the slopes first thing this morning. Though I guess since they closed them down, it was lucky we didn't."

"True." Remy grimaced. "Please excuse me while I go talk to my brother."

She nodded, trying to decide if she should retreat to her room or not. As he disappeared inside Seth's room, she elected to remain in the kitchen. She couldn't help but find how seriously Remy appeared to take his role of elder brother fascinating. Obviously, Seth could use the help.

"Get the hell out of my bedroom," Seth shouted. "Who let you in here, anyway?"

"Your houseguest," Remy replied, his tone measured and controlled. "I was here last night, too, after Gary called me all worried about you."

A string of curse words followed. "I don't work for you, Remy." Seth stormed out of the bedroom, briefly stopping short when he saw Vanessa. He'd put on a sweatshirt and a pair of wrinkled jeans and shoved his feet into snow boots. "Sorry about this, Van," he muttered, before snagging his down parka out of the front closet. He turned to glare at Remy. "I'm just living my life and trying to have some fun, bro. I don't need you coming in here and giving me a hard time."

Remy started to speak, but Seth cut him off with a furious command. "Don't." He held up his hand. "I'm out of here. Don't follow me, either of you. I need to be alone." With that, he bolted out and slammed the front door, knocking down a picture that had been hanging on the wall and shattering the glass.

Not sure what else to do or what to say, Vanessa went in search of a broom and a dustpan. She located them in the laundry room and went to clean up the glass.

"Here, let me." Remy took them from her and immediately got busy. Surprised, she hung back, wishing she had something to do with her hands. Maybe then she could better resist this unexpected urge to touch him.

Once he'd dumped all the glass shards in the trash, Remy retrieved the vacuum and went back over the area. Vanessa watched him, amazed how he could manage to look so sexy while performing the most mundane task.

Finally, he shut off the vacuum, wound up the cord and put it back in the hall closet. "There," he said, dusting his hands off on the front of his jeans. "All done."

She nodded. "Thanks." Then, because she felt awkward, she checked her watch. Since she'd had such a late breakfast, it seemed a bit too early for lunch. But since cooking was one of the things she loved and did well, she asked Remy if he'd eaten.

"Not for hours." The grim set of his mouth told her food had been the last thing on his mind.

"How about you let me make you something? I can rustle up breakfast or lunch or brunch, if you want to call it that. Seth told me to help myself to anything I wanted in the kitchen."

Though his gaze narrowed, he finally nodded. "I'd like that, thank you. But something simple. I don't want to put you out."

Relieved, she grinned. "Actually, I love to cook. And right now, I'd feel a lot better if I could keep busy."

He followed her to the kitchen. "Again, I apologize

about all that. You just got here. I'm sure you didn't sign up for all this family drama."

Did she hear the hint of a question in his voice? Deciding to ignore that possibility, she began rummaging in the fridge. "So…what are you in the mood for?" she asked.

"Have you had breakfast?"

Slowly, she nodded. "I made myself scrambled eggs earlier. But that doesn't matter. I can whip you up some breakfast if that's what you want."

Watching her, he considered. "It's still early enough for breakfast to be a respectable option. The Chateau restaurant serves it until ten thirty."

"Breakfast it is, then. Bacon, eggs and toast? Or…" She took a peek inside the refrigerator again. "There are enough ingredients for eggs Benedict with ham. Would you like that instead?"

"If it's not too much trouble." He grimaced and glanced at the front door. "I wonder if Seth will be back to eat."

Though she privately doubted that, she nodded. "I'll make extra just in case. As long as I keep the eggs and the English muffins separate, it won't get too soggy."

Humming happily, she got busy. Next to skiing, cooking was her favorite pastime. And privately, she considered herself pretty darn talented at it. Her friends back in Boston had always raved about the meals she'd made. And since moving to Boulder, she'd hosted a couple of dinner parties with the same results.

And now she'd be cooking for Remy. Why that felt different, she wasn't sure.

"Is there anything I can do to help?" he murmured

from behind her, his voice so close she knew if she spun around, she could reach out and touch him.

Forcing herself to continuing stirring the hollandaise sauce, she simply glanced over her shoulder. "Not really. Why don't you make yourself a cup of coffee and sit down and relax? This won't take too much longer."

"Would you like a cup, too?" he asked. "You look like you're about empty."

Though she rarely had more than two coffees per day, she liked the idea of sharing a cup with this man. Maybe they could talk and get to know each other a little bit better. As long as that's all they did, that should be safe.

"Sure," she answered.

"Cream and sugar?"

"Yes, please." She smiled as he did a double take. "I know, black coffee is better. According to Seth, you can best taste the coffee that way."

"I agree with my brother on that." Remy made them both a cup, then carried hers over to her before taking a seat at the table. "You seem to know what you're doing," he commented. "Do you cook professionally?"

"No." She risked another glance over her shoulder. "I've thought about it. Though I'm afraid if I started doing it for a living, that would take some of the joy out of it."

Just then the front door blew open and Seth burst inside. He shook off snow before removing his coat and barreling through to the kitchen. At the doorway, he stopped short, staring at the two of them.

"What are you doing?" he asked as he came up behind Vanessa and gave her a huge kiss on the side of her neck. "That smells interesting. Why are you cooking for my brother?"

At his touch, she froze. Again, she had the sense of barely leashed violence, though she managed to shrug lightly. "He was hungry, so I thought I'd make him something to eat while he waited for you to get back. There's plenty, if you'd like some, too."

Instead of immediately answering, he leaned around her and peered into the pan. "What is that?"

"Hollandaise sauce. I'm poaching some eggs and serving them on English muffins with cheese, topped by this sauce."

"You know, eggs Benedict," Remy chimed in, his tone dry. "I'm pretty sure you've had it before."

Though Seth didn't respond, judging by the hard set of his mouth, he wasn't pleased.

Why Remy was pushing his brother's buttons, she wasn't sure. But she sure as heck planned to stay out of it. She kept busy, putting the English muffins under the broiler now that the poached eggs were in the water. "Seth, why don't you get some coffee and sit?" she suggested. "Breakfast will be ready in a few minutes."

Seth narrowed his eyes and glared at her, then stalked over to the coffee maker. Relieved, she relaxed her spine slightly, though she couldn't help but wonder if coming here for closure might have been a huge mistake.

The eggs were done just as the English muffins turned the perfect shade of brown. She tossed a few thick slices of ham in a frying pan and when they'd begun to crisp, she put everything together and ladled the hollandaise on top. Perfect, she thought, suppressing the urge to snap a quick pic with her phone. Instead, she smiled and carried the plates over to the table.

"Here you go," she said, placing the meals in front of each man. "Enjoy."

"Aren't you going to eat?" Seth asked, eying his food. "Seems like you went through an awful lot of trouble for my brother."

Still smiling, she ignored the snide tone. "I had scrambled eggs and toast earlier, while you were asleep. And you know how much I like to cook. This wasn't any trouble at all."

"Thank you," Remy said, and he dug in.

Seth eyed his brother, using his fork to move things around on his plate. When he finally cut a piece, he got only the egg and ham, leaving the English muffin and most of the sauce on his plate. He chewed and then set down his fork. "You know," he mused, "I think it's time I hired a professional chef."

When he glanced at Vanessa, she wondered if he was actually going to offer her the job.

"One who can really cook." He pushed his plate away. "Nice try, Van."

Stunned, she could only stare. To her horror, she felt tears prick the back of her eyes. She turned away, ostensibly to clean up the pans. The casual cruelty coming from a man she'd always regarded as a friend hurt. Clearly, Seth hadn't gotten over the breakup, and they couldn't go back to being friends. In fact, as soon as the roads were clear, she needed to pack up and go. Maybe a room at either The Chateau or The Lodge would have become available just for one or two nights, so she could ski Pine Peak. Heck, she'd even take a room in one of the chain motels on the edge of town.

She ran the water, then scrubbed out the pans and placed them in the dishwasher. Seth had gone silent, making her wonder if he might apologize. She glanced back at the table, only to find him glaring at her, his expression furious.

"What were you two doing here alone while I was gone?" he demanded, including Remy in his stare. "And come on, Vanessa, why were you trying to impress my brother with a fancy breakfast? We have oatmeal. Scrambled eggs and toast is what you said you had. But no, that wasn't good enough for him. I'm thinking you—"

"Enough!" Remy pushed to his feet. "I don't know what's gotten into you, Seth. Leave her alone. She was simply being kind. She doesn't deserve this treatment from you."

"Really, Remy?" Standing so quickly he knocked back his chair, Seth faced his older brother. His hands were clenched into fists. "You come in my place, hit on my girlfriend and have the nerve to try and tell me how to act?"

Remy appeared as stunned as she felt. "Seth—"

Again, Seth cut him off. "Mind your own business. Vanessa belongs to me. Our relationship has nothing to do with you." He pointed toward the door. "Leave."

Remy took care not to glance her way. Part of her didn't want him to leave. But when she didn't correct Seth, what else could he do?

"Thanks for breakfast," he finally said, meeting her gaze. "It was delicious." He grabbed his parka and left.

Seth dropped back into his seat, muttering under

his breath. Vanessa cleared her throat. "Seth, we need to talk."

"Do we?" He shook his head. "Don't be mad because I didn't like your cooking. I've never been fond of eggs Benedict, that's all."

"It's not that," she said. "Actually, that's only part of it. You were unnecessarily rude, both to me and your brother. Not just that, but I don't belong to you. And we don't have a relationship."

His harsh expression softened. "Then why'd you come here? Come on, Van, I know you missed me as much as I missed you. You didn't drive up all the way from Boulder just to ski."

Even though the lure of skiing Pine Peak had factored into her decision to come to Roaring Springs, she knew better than to bring that up. "Seth, I came here to explain why I broke things off so abruptly. I wanted to give us both closure."

"Closure?" He spat the word as if it left a bitter taste in his mouth. "What is it with women and closure? Who the hell cares? Either you want to get back together or you don't. Which is it?"

Heart aching, she took a deep breath. "Actually, I was hoping we could go back to being friends. But clearly, that was a foolish idea. I'll pack my things and get out of your hair. I'm sorry to have put you out."

She kept her chin up and her back straight as she walked to the guest bedroom. Luckily, she hadn't done much unpacking, so all she had to do was grab her toiletries and put them in her suitcase.

When she emerged, Seth was nowhere to be found. She had no intention of going in search of him to say goodbye. Essentially, she'd already said that.

It took two trips to get her small suitcase and her ski gear loaded back in her car. Seth didn't bother to make an appearance, something that both saddened her and filled her with relief.

At least the plow had been by. She'd put snow tires on her car right before the first snow and she had chains in the trunk in case she needed them. Either way, she wasn't sure she could make it back home in this weather. With snow still falling heavily, she drove a slow and cautious couple of blocks until she reached The Chateau. If worse came to worst, she'd sleep sitting up in a chair in the lobby.

There were no parking spots open in the small lot, but she finally located one on a side street. This time, she left her skis on top of her car, though she grabbed her suitcase and trudged toward the hotel entrance.

Stepping through the ornate glass doors, she felt as if she'd entered a different world. Though she doubted anyone would have checked out since yesterday, she approached the front desk, anyway.

Just as the polite, well-coiffed young woman asked her if she could help her, Vanessa had an idea. "Yes, I'm looking for Remy Colton. I was told he works here." After all, she'd met him out in front of the hotel yesterday.

"I'm sorry, but Mr. Colton isn't taking visitors today," the woman, whose badge announced her name was Tena, said.

"Could you contact him and ask him to call me?"

Slowly, Tena nodded. "I could take your number, yes."

Vanessa rattled off the digits, then asked that Remy call her as soon as possible. "I'll be waiting in the lobby," she said. "Unless you happen to have any vacancies?"

"I'm sorry, we don't. We're fully booked through Christmas."

Which was the same answer she'd gotten when she'd inquired yesterday and clearly nothing had changed on that front.

Choosing an unoccupied, overstuffed chair facing the front door, Vanessa took a seat. She began scrolling through her phone, checking social media and catching up on the news. Barely five minutes had passed when her phone rang.

Chapter 3

After getting a message to call Vanessa, Remy dialed her number immediately. When he heard her soft hello, he exhaled. "Are you all right? I was worried about you," he said.

"I'm fine," she replied, her voice shaking. "But I've left Seth's condo. I'm not sure what to think about his behavior."

Remy wasn't sure, either. In all honesty, his brother's mood swings, heavy drinking and barely leashed rage worried the hell out of him. The breakup with Vanessa must have affected him strongly, though if his end goal was to get her back, he was going about it the wrong way. He couldn't blame Vanessa for being scared off.

"Is there somewhere we can meet and talk?" Remy asked, pushing away the sharp thrill of anticipation that went through him at the thought of seeing her again. He only wanted to make sure she was safe, he told himself. Nothing more. "Where are you now?"

Her answer surprised him. "Well, actually I'm in the lobby of The Chateau. I was hoping a room would miraculously open up, but no such luck. I'm still not sure the tunnel is open yet. I seriously doubt I could get back home to Boulder in this storm." She laughed self-consciously. "And I really was hoping to ski Pine Peak once it opens. As long as I'm up here…"

"I'll be there in five," he replied. He could tell she wasn't the kind of person who enjoyed asking for help from anyone. "We'll go grab a cup of coffee or something to drink and I'll see what I can do to find you a place to stay."

Sounding relieved, she agreed to wait for him.

"Save my number in your phone," he told her. "This is my cell. You can call or text me anytime."

She promised she would.

Hanging up, Remy walked out into the still-too-quiet office and told everyone they could take the rest of the day off. Despite The Chateau being booked to capacity, the PR department took it easy over the holidays. With so many already on vacation or personal days, they weren't getting any work done anyway, and if the snow continued to fall at the same rate, the plows would have trouble keeping up. They might as well go home and stay warm.

His good-natured order was met with cheers. He stood near the door and watched everyone gather up their coats and head out. A few people high-fived him and one of the older women gave him a hug. Hiding his impatience, he wished they would hurry up so he could lock up the office and go spend the rest of the day with Vanessa.

The rest of the... The realization should have shocked him, but he could barely get past his eagerness to see her.

Finally, everyone had gone. He busted out the door with an unusual spring in his step before he reminded himself to slow down. Vanessa needed a friend, not a suitor. Plus, with Seth so volatile, he didn't want to take a chance of doing something to set him off.

Before heading out into the lobby, he decided to get a breath of fresh air. Mostly so he could get a handle on the conflicting emotions that filled him when he thought of spending time with Vanessa.

Stepping outside, he stood for a moment, letting the snow swirl around him, barely feeling the cold. He took several deep breaths, letting the icy air fill his lungs. He'd always found winter exhilarating, which made living high up in the Rockies perfect.

Glancing at the street and the tire tracks left by his employees, he decided he'd go ahead and walk around to the front entrance of The Chateau and go in that way.

As usual, when he strolled around to the front of The Chateau, a sense of pride and contentment filled him. He loved the structure, inside and out, and loved the people who worked there and made it one of the top vacation destinations in the United States even more.

Stepping into the lobby, he stuffed his gloves into his pocket and caught sight of Vanessa seated on one of the ornate chairs under the skylight, sunlight illuminating her dark hair. Scrolling through her phone, she didn't see him until he'd gotten a few feet away.

When she looked up, their gazes met and locked. Once more, something intense flared between them. One-sided? he wondered. Or did she feel it, too?

"Hey." Vanessa stood, greeting him with a smile and an outstretched hand. "Thanks so much for meeting with me."

When his fingers connected with her slender ones, he fought the completely ridiculous urge to pull her up against him. Instead, he managed a civilized handshake and reluctantly released her.

"Let's go get something to drink and see what we can figure out," he offered.

"Here?"

He debated with himself, weighing the chances of Seth walking in, since the last thing he wanted to do was provoke some kind of scene. Deciding that possibility highly unlikely, he nodded. "There's a wonderful little coffee shop right off the lobby," he said.

"I saw it. It was very crowded, though. I don't think there was any place to sit."

Which wouldn't be surprising. "Let's go check it out." But even before they were close, he could tell they'd need to make another choice. "I tell you what," he told her. "Since the slopes are closed right now, everywhere downtown is going to be packed."

She nodded, eying him. "How about we take a walk? Or are you averse to a little snow?"

Unable to help himself, he laughed. "I love to be out in the snow and cold. People are always acting like I'm crazy when I say I want to go out for a stroll in the winter."

Eyes sparkling, she nodded. "I have snow boots in my car. How about you?"

"Of course," he replied. "In my back seat."

Impulsively, she took his arm. "Then let's go."

Side by side they hurried out of the hotel. He felt giddy, as if he was seventeen again and a love-struck teenager. While rationally, he knew he had to get a grip, for now he decided to go with the flow and simply enjoy the day.

She led him to her vehicle first, a practical and sturdy Subaru. "Four-wheel drive," she said, grinning as she unlocked the doors. "She also gets great gas mileage." Grabbing her boots, Vanessa sat down on the front passenger seat to put them on.

"She?" he asked. "Don't tell me you named your car."

"Of course I did." Boots in place, she hopped out and tugged on her gloves. "Your turn."

Her infectious enthusiasm made his heart pound. Slipping and sliding, he took off for his Jeep, hoping he had an extra pair of socks, too, since his were already soaked.

Luckily, he'd had the foresight to tuck a pair into his snow boots. He motioned her to hop inside, front or back—her choice. She chose the front passenger side, which probably was a good thing. He got in the back seat and closed the door to keep the blowing snow out while he peeled off his wet socks and slipped his feet into a pair of dry ones. Once he'd laced up his Sorel Caribou waterproof boots, he gave her a thumbs-up. "Ready."

She hopped out, pulling on a jaunty ski cap with a pom-pom on top. "I'm hoping the storm has driven most of the people inside," she said. "But with this being a ski resort, you never know."

Debating, he gave in to impulse and took her arm. "I'm sure there'll be a few other hearty souls, but I guarantee it won't be anywhere near as crowded as inside."

"Good." Her teeth flashed as white as the snowflakes. For someone with nowhere to stay, she seemed awfully chipper. Maybe she was one of those people who never worried, and simply figured things would always work out. He'd often wished he could be like that. Instead, he planned and scheduled, feeling as if he had to have control over every aspect of his life.

Walking side by side with Vanessa, he realized it felt amazing to be able to let that überpreparedness slide, if only for a little while.

After a few steps, she pulled her arm free, turning this way and that, surveying the picturesque downtown area with wonder. Bright lights shone from inside the shops and cafés, and in most of the eating and drinking establishments, it appeared to be standing room only. Quite a bit different than the normally bustling sidewalks.

The heavy snow and blowing wind had discouraged most of the tourists from venturing out. Those few people they encountered were bundled up so much that they were unrecognizable. Glancing at Vanessa, he saw she'd pulled out a scarf and wrapped it around her lower face. He reached into his pocket and did the same. They needed to talk, but for now he wanted to simply enjoy being with her like this.

When they reached the end of the commercial part of Main Street, she turned. "I guess we can go back down the other side," she said. "Though I wouldn't mind going in somewhere and warming up a bit."

Since the chill had begun to seep into his bones, too, he nodded. "There's another coffee shop one block back on the opposite side of the road. Maybe since everyone seems to be frequenting the bars, it won't be as bad."

She nodded, her long lashes white with snow. "I've reached my limit on coffee, but I can get hot cider or tea." She missed a step and nearly fell. Without thinking, he reached for her hand and took it, helping to steady her. If this surprised her, he couldn't tell.

Gloved hand in gloved hand, they crossed the street. Traffic was almost nonexistent and even the streetlights had taken on a magical glow. The deep, powdery snow had begun to make walking difficult, even though a few intrepid shop owners appeared to have attempted to shovel the sidewalk.

By the time they reached the No Doze Café, they were both out of breath. Luckily, the inside appeared to be only moderately crowded, rather than packed.

The instant they stepped through the door, Vanessa pulled her hand out of his and removed her gloves. "Oh, it smells wonderful in here," she said, inhaling deeply. "And look—a table just opened up over there in the corner!" She made a beeline for it, grabbing a chair and taking a seat before anyone else could. Grinning triumphantly, she beckoned Remy over.

Entranced by her, he went. "Do you mind ordering while I guard our spot?" she asked. Rummaging in her pocket, she pulled out a crumpled five-dollar bill and slid it across the table. "Here. This will take care of mine. I'd like a large hot apple cider with whipped cream."

"I've got this," he said, ignoring her money. "I'll be right back."

At the counter, he waited in line. Finally, he placed their order—the cider for her and a black coffee for him—and paid. The drinks were ready quickly and he carried them back to the table, noticing how a group of twentysomething guys were eying Vanessa. He had to love the fact that she appeared to be oblivious as she scrolled on her phone.

As soon as he approached her, she put it down and reached for her drink. "Thank you so much." She took a deep sip and made a throaty sound of pleasure that had him aching with desire.

Damn. He reminded himself to focus. He sat, wrapping both hands around his coffee cup. "Are you ready to tell me what's going on with Seth?"

Her eyes widened. "Wow, you clearly believe in getting right to the point."

"I do," he admitted, aware he couldn't tell her he'd simply needed a distraction from the way he couldn't stop wanting her.

She sighed. "I came here because I felt I owed Seth an explanation for the way I broke things off with him. I was abrupt and…" Expression rueful, she shrugged. "I was wrong. Not for ending it, but the way I handled it. I wanted closure. I forgot guys don't seem to get that word."

Her comment made him smile. "Truth. We—or at least I—tend to see things a bit more cut-and-dried. Either something is or it isn't."

Considering him, she shook her head. "Despite my best efforts, Seth seems to believe I'm here for another reason—to get back together. He's hurt and angry…

understandably so." She took a deep breath. "He's your brother, but I'll be honest with you. Seth's taking it to another level." Leaning forward, she met his gaze. "He's frightening me."

"Me, too," he admitted gruffly. Then, because he was curious, he asked her how long she'd known his brother.

"A couple of years. We met on the slopes. We were friends, just that, nothing more. Then I went through something…" She bit her lip, her dark blue eyes huge. "Both my parents were killed in a car crash. Seth was there for me. He became my port in the storm."

Surprised, Remy simply nodded, hoping she'd continue. Maybe his brother *had* matured in ways he didn't always reveal. For Seth to stand by Vanessa while she endured her own private hell, expecting nothing in return… That showed the sort of personal growth, the kind Remy had long wished Seth to have.

She fell silent. He didn't press her, and instead drank his coffee in silence.

"I'll be right back," she said, getting up quickly and heading toward the restroom. Right before she reached the short hallway that led to the ladies' room, she turned and looked at him. "Please wait for me." And then she disappeared behind the door.

For reasons he didn't entirely understand, that broke his heart.

Had she said too much? Or not enough? Standing in front of the washroom mirror, Vanessa put her hands to her flaming cheeks. She needed to remember that Remy and Seth were related by blood, while she was merely a stranger who'd come to town for what now seemed to be entirely selfish reasons. Clearly, Seth would have been better off without her attempt at obtaining a respite from her guilt at the knowledge that she hadn't handled their breakup well.

Turned out maybe that had been all in her head. She should have left well enough alone. And she couldn't believe she'd almost revealed the fact that she and Seth had never even been intimate. If she had, then Remy would know what a cold fish she was.

During her brief engagement to Seth, she'd managed to deflect every attempt he made to get her in his bed. At first, she'd chalked it up to her sheltered upbringing, but she'd come to the realization she didn't want him at all that way. She'd seen the way other women looked at him—he was a handsome man, after all. So it had to be her. With that bit of awareness, she'd understood they both deserved better.

But she'd lacked the courage to say that to Seth. Of course, the fact that when she'd called off the engagement, he'd been so furious that he'd punched a hole in the wall might have had something to do with it. He'd scared her so badly, and after he'd stormed out she'd had all her locks changed so he couldn't come back.

He hadn't. He'd hightailed it back to Roaring Springs, which had given her both relief and peace. Until she'd gotten the foolish idea that she needed to make things right with Seth so they could both move on.

All she'd managed to do was make everything worse.

Though she had learned one thing about herself. Apparently, she wasn't as much of an ice princess as she believed. One look from Remy Colton's hazel-green eyes set her on fire. She craved his touch, wondered about how his lips would feel on hers and imagined carnal scenarios she'd only previously read about.

Had she lost her mind? Seriously, she needed to get a grip on this ridiculous attraction she felt toward Remy. Talk about creating a huge mess! That's what it would be if she even considered acting on these forbidden desires.

So nope, nope, nope. Luckily, Remy seemed oblivious to her feelings. Thank goodness. She needed to remember she simply needed his help to find a place to stay for one or two nights and then she'd be out of this town for good. Hopefully before she managed to make an even worse mess out of things.

Once she managed to regain her composure, she left the sanctuary of the restroom and went back to her table. Remy looked up from his phone and smiled. The warmth of it went straight to her heart.

Shaking her head at herself, she sat back down and took a sip of her hot cider. Though it had cooled down significantly, the drink still tasted delicious.

"I've done some checking," he said. "We keep a family suite at The Chateau and since no one is using it at the moment, it's yours."

She stared. "A suite? That's amazing."

"And in case you're worrying about the cost, we're not going to charge you anything. You can have it for as long as you need it, within reason."

Within reason. His caveat made her smile. "Don't worry. I won't be moving in or anything. I'd just like to ski the mountain once it reopens. And then I'll be out of your hair."

Gaze steady, he shrugged. "How long is up to you. No one will be using the suite until after the holidays."

"Wow. Okay, thanks. I confess I'm a bit surprised you don't have family coming in for Christmas, though."

"We do. But they'll be staying at Colton Manor," he replied.

"Colton Manor?" She couldn't help herself. "That sounds like something out of a movie about royalty or something."

He laughed. "That's closer to the truth than you realize. My family has this huge and utterly pretentious mansion where my uncle Russ and my aunt Mara like to entertain. My grandfather, Earl, has a separate suite of rooms all to himself."

"Your father doesn't live there?"

"No. He tends to do his own thing."

"What about your mother?" Utterly intrigued, she leaned forward.

"Cordelia?" His mouth twisted. "She dropped me off on Whit's doorstep when I was five. She has… substance-abuse issues. My grandparents basically raised me. And Cordelia has been out of the picture ever since I got legal custody of Seth."

"That's a lot to take in," she mused. "You must have been so young yourself and yet still took on trying to raise your little brother."

He shook his head, his expression distant. "I didn't have a choice. I simply couldn't leave him in that environment."

She wanted to tell him how much she admired him for that, but kept it to herself. Remy clearly was a good, honorable man, and men like him weren't comfortable with compliments on actions they considered to be second nature.

They finished their drinks in companionable silence while the snow continued to fall outside. She liked the way Remy put her at ease without even trying.

"Would you like another cider?" he finally asked.

"I think I'm done," she said and stretched, even though she was reluctant to move. "Thank you so much for helping me."

Wearing a pleased expression, he nodded. "We've solved your immediate problem. But I'm still worried about Seth."

"I'm sure he'll be fine," she began.

"Oh, he will, once he thinks about things rationally and calms down. But that's not what I meant. I love him—he's family I didn't even know I had until fifteen years ago. But he's had his share of troubles since we reconnected. He's not always successful in conquering his demons."

Intrigued, she grabbed her empty cup and stood. "You know what? Let's both get another drink. On me this time. That's a story I'd really like to hear, if you don't mind sharing."

"I don't mind at all." His steady gaze touched on her and she felt it like a caress. "Though I have to say, I'm surprised Seth never told you."

She was, too, though she didn't voice that thought. "I'll be right back."

Instead of a line, only one other person waited at the counter. She placed the order and paid, waiting just a minute until the drinks were ready.

"Here you go," she said, placing Remy's coffee on the table in front of him. She waited until she'd gotten settled back in her seat before she took a sip of her own hot cider drink. "Seth didn't really talk much about his past. He always said he liked being an enigma."

Though Remy raised one eyebrow at that statement, he didn't comment. He drank his coffee, appearing contemplative, as if trying to figure out the best way to tell his story.

She waited patiently, enjoying the warmth of the room, the scent of fresh-roasted coffee, the delicious drink and the intriguing man seated across from her.

"When I was five years old, my birth mother dropped me off on my dad's doorstep," he began. "Whit Colton has always been a playboy. Still is, even though he's well past fifty. He had no time for a son, but he made sure to take care of me financially, for which I'm grateful. His parents were delighted to have a grandchild to coddle, so they took care of me and loved me."

He looked down, wrapping his hands around his coffee cup.

Unable to help herself, she made a sound of sympathy and reached across the table to put her hand on his. "That must have been hard on you. You were so young to go through such a thing."

Remy grimaced. "It wasn't easy. For years, I was convinced I must have done something wrong for my mother to send me away like that. And when my father didn't seem to want to have much to do with me, well, that reinforced my belief that it was all my fault." He released a ragged breath then went on. "As a consequence, I became very, very well behaved. Straight-A student, outstanding athlete, all of that. My grandparents cheered me on, encouraged me and treated me as if I mattered. Despite their belief in me, I always felt something was missing. So when I was twenty, I set out to find my birth mother."

Vanessa gasped. "Did you have any luck?" Then, as she realized what that meant, she shook her head. "Of course you did. I'm guessing that's also how you found Seth."

"Exactly. My mother, Cordelia, was an ex-model, which is how she met Whit Colton. She became a drug addict, probably before she dumped me off on Whit." He took a deep breath, his gaze faraway, as though he was lost in his memories. "Though she'd gotten married to Seth's father, he also had drug problems and, worse, anger issues. She'd neglected Seth the way she'd neglected me, except he spent his entire life in that environment. Seth's dad was abusive, verbally and physically, which in turn caused Seth to take out his anger on others, even animals. Though he was only fifteen, he started to have problems with drugs and alcohol too."

Stunned, she covered her mouth with her hand. "That's horrible. I had no idea. Seth never mentioned any of this to me."

Remy shrugged. "He says he prefers not to look back at the past. I'm sure he didn't want your pity."

Pity. She considered Remy's choice of word. Maybe he was right. But then again… "Knowing about this might have helped me understand him better. The anger issues. The times he got falling-down drunk."

"Well, now you know." Remy's matter-of-fact tone didn't fool her one bit. Raw emotion shone from his eyes. "I couldn't leave my half brother there. He wouldn't have stood a chance. I took over legal custody of him, even though I was only five years older."

"His parents let you? Just like that?"

"No." Remy drank his coffee. "I got a loan from my father and paid them to relinquish custody. Not surprisingly, they were eager to waive parental rights for some cold, hard cash."

"Yikes." She winced. "But this was a good thing, right? I'm assuming you must have brought him to your grandparents."

"No. I enrolled him in rehab and sent him to counseling. Once he was off the drugs and had learned to deal with his rage, then I brought him home. I loved him the best I could, as much as he would let me. Things were rough between us for a while, but then seemed to settle down." He sighed. "But you've seen him. Something is…off. He's back to binge drinking. And that anger still lurks right under Seth's skin, ready to erupt at the slightest provocation. I worry about him constantly."

Vanessa wasn't sure what to say. She settled on going with the truth. "Well, that explains a lot. The night I broke up with him, he punched a hole through my wall. He told me to consider myself lucky it wasn't me."

Remy's jaw tightened. Fists clenched, he turned away, his breathing harsh. She watched as he clearly struggled to get himself under control. "I'm sorry," he muttered, slowly moving to face her. "I wish I could have been there to protect you."

She took a deep breath. "He scared me to death. And then the way he's acted since I came here… While knowing about his past helps me understand why he behaves the way he does, I still think it's best if I don't see him again. At this point, I don't think we can even be friends."

To her surprise, Remy smiled. "Maybe it's time you make some new friends."

Chapter 4

Though he knew he shouldn't, Remy couldn't help but hope Vanessa took full advantage of the free luxury suite in The Chateau and stayed for a few days longer. Despite her clear worries over Seth, he really didn't feel his brother was a danger to anyone but himself.

Just in case, Remy would personally keep an eye on Vanessa to make sure she was safe. At least that's the reason he told himself, as he gazed at the beautiful woman sitting across from him. Anything else would make things way too complicated.

"What about you?" he asked, aching to both change the subject and hear her story so he could get to know her better. "Tell me about your childhood. Where did you grow up?"

A brief shadow crossed her face, so swift he might have imagined it. "In Boston. I've worked hard to lose the accent. And my childhood was nothing extraordinary," she said. Her tone was matter-of-fact, but he sensed she'd had her own trials and tribulations to deal with. Most everyone did, it seemed. Individuals who'd had a picture-perfect youth were few and far between.

"Tell me, anyway," he prodded. "I'm genuinely interested."

She gave him a sideways glance, as if she found that difficult to believe. "My parents were older and I was their only child. I always felt like an afterthought and I probably was. They sent me away as soon as they could, to an all-girls school in Switzerland."

"I can relate to that," he told her. "I wasted a lot of my younger years hoping if I was good enough, my dad might notice me." The rawness of his own admission left him stunned. He hadn't meant to tell her that. He considered it private, one of his deepest, darkest secrets. Yet on some level, he truly believed Vanessa would understand.

She nodded. "Me, too. I spent all my time trying to please my folks, because I believed if I did well enough at something, at *anything*, maybe they'd love me enough to let me return home to Boston." She laughed, a painful sound. "Pretty silly, wasn't I? Because they never did. Instead, they viewed each success as validation they were doing the right thing, that I belonged in Switzerland. By the time I realized I'd been knocking myself out for nothing, I was about to graduate. I felt like such a fool."

"No." This time he reached out and covered her hand with his. "You weren't. And I felt the same way as a kid." He took a deep breath and then forced himself to remove his hand. "What did you do after graduation?"

She shrugged. "Though I toyed with the idea of taking a year off, I didn't. In keeping with their plan to have me as far away from them as possible, my parents wanted me to go to university in London. This time, rather than falling in with what they wanted, I refused." Her chin came up and she smiled, though a touch of sadness remained in her pretty blue eyes. "I had my own plans, you see."

Intrigued, he waited.

"In Switzerland, I learned to ski. And it turned out I was pretty darn good at it." Her smile widened, inviting him to take part in her joy. "While all the other kids were partying and living it up, I was on the slopes. I spent all my spare time perfecting my skill."

"You must have truly enjoyed it," he commented.

Just like that, her expression turned serious. "Yes. I did. Skiing was the only thing that gave me pleasure."

More than anything, he wanted her to look happy again. "Does that mean you became a ski bum?" he teased. "Can't say I blame you. We get more than a few of those here in Roaring Springs."

"I wanted to, but I'm too ambitious to just drift along, spending all my time in pursuit of pleasure."

Her self-conscious half smile made his chest ache. "Me, too," he said. "That's why I work so much."

Gaze faraway, she nodded. Remy let his own eyes roam her features while she sat lost in thought. He was amazed once more at how beautiful he found her, even though her features weren't classically perfect.

When she didn't speak again, he prodded her, just a

little. "If you didn't become a professional skier, then what did you do?"

"I decided to go to the University of Colorado in Boulder, mostly due to the proximity to the slopes. I had vague dreams of competing."

"Did you?" Intrigued again, he watched her.

"No. My parents would have been appalled. I think they were relieved I hadn't chosen a school closer to home. Once I graduated, I decided to stay in Boulder. End of story."

Except he sensed there might be more. "Now that you're an adult, why haven't you pursued your dream of competing? If you're that good, it seems like a waste of talent not to."

Sorrow darkened her eyes. "Thank you for saying that. Actually, I'd reached the same realization myself. I started skiing a lot—that's how I met Seth, you know. He seemed to understand my drive. Oh, I was fiercely intent on getting ready for my first competition. I'd entered and had my number and everything."

"Did you win?"

She shook her head. "I never even made it to the competition. Instead of spending every waking moment on the slopes, I truly wish I'd have made a trip home to Boston. The day before the big competition, both my parents were killed in a car wreck. I got the news in a phone call."

Aching to comfort her, he tightened his hand around hers. "I'm sorry."

"Thanks." She lifted her face and met his gaze. The pain and grief in her eyes made him long to take her into his arms. Luckily, the table separated them so he settled for holding on to her hand. She didn't pull away.

"Everything was a blur after that," she admitted. "Since my parents and I never managed to have a close relationship, I felt cheated. And was beyond devastated. I went back east to plan their funeral and begin settling their estate. I'm still dealing with all that. Through it all, Seth was there for me, without question. That's partly why I felt like I owed it to him to explain."

Seth. She'd managed to effectively remind him of his brother. Yet he still couldn't bring himself to let go of her hand. A second later, she did it for him, as she gently pulled her fingers free and wrapped them around her cup.

Lump in his throat, he took out his phone and made a show of checking his emails. Nothing work-related or even slightly important.

Once he'd placed his phone back in his pocket, he looked up to find her watching him. "I'm glad you came here," he said gruffly. "It takes a big heart to try and make things right after a breakup."

Taking another sip of her cider, she sighed. "I don't know. Clearly, I messed that up, too. It would have been better if I'd never contacted him. I should have just stayed away."

He wanted to tell her again he was glad she hadn't. Because then, he never would have met her. Instead, he kept his mouth shut and said nothing. Flirtation, even if heartfelt, was the last thing either of them needed right now. Plus, as long as his brother still had feelings for her, Vanessa would be strictly off-limits as far as Remy was concerned.

Maybe forever.

Damn, how that possibility burned.

"Seth will be fine," he assured her. "It's likely he just needs a little more time."

"I hope so." She drank more of her cider. "I really hope he's able to move past this and everything else. Conquering demons is never easy. Believe me, I know."

"I do, too," he admitted, enjoying this feeling of camaraderie that was developing between them. This woman made him feel a lot of things, and he barely knew her. He could only imagine how it would be if they had the luxury of time to get acquainted without complications.

"I'd like to go skiing with you once they reopen the slopes," he blurted, inwardly wincing as soon as he said it.

Her eyes widened, letting him know he'd been right to question his timing. "I'd like that," she finally replied. "As long as it doesn't cause problems between you and your brother."

Before he could reply, her phone rang. Pulling it out of her jacket pocket, she stared. "It's Seth. I'm not sure I should answer it."

Leaving that choice up to her, he simply drank his coffee and said nothing.

She ended up letting the call go to voicemail. A moment later, her phone chirped.

"He's texting now," she commented, glancing at her screen. "He wants to know if we can talk. I just don't know. Part of me feels I've said all I had to say. I don't want to stir things up again."

Once more, Remy held his tongue. That would be her decision. He couldn't let himself get involved in whatever was between her and his brother. Even if it really was over, he wouldn't interfere.

Shaking her head, she shoved the phone back into her pocket. "I'll deal with him later. And sure, I'd love to ski with you. If you can keep up with me, that is." A quick flash of a smile. "I'm going to guess that you're pretty skilled, since you live up here."

"I'm not too bad," he admitted. "I've skied the black diamonds."

Black diamonds were for advanced skiers.

"Double or triple?" Which should only be skied by experts.

That made him laugh. "I've done a few double diamonds but I'm more of an advanced skier rather than expert. I'm good, but not great, if you know what I mean. I don't go often enough to have spent a lot of time perfecting my skills."

Clearly aghast, she stared. "You live in a ski resort but you don't go often? Why not? Do you have an injury or an illness that you haven't mentioned?"

"No." Still chuckling, he shook his head. "I work a lot."

Even he knew how lame that sounded. "Honestly, though, while I enjoy skiing, I don't have a passion for it."

"Then you've been doing it wrong," she instantly replied. "Or going with the wrong people. I'll show you. Skiing is the closest I've ever been to anything resembling heaven."

He couldn't help where his mind went at that. Not anywhere he could actually say out loud.

Staring at him, she blushed, as if she knew his

thoughts. She opened her mouth and then closed it, looking down at her cider.

"Maybe you can teach me a few tricks," he said, deciding to let her off the hook. "Skiing, to clarify."

If anything, her blush deepened. But then, with the dogged determination he was coming to know, she lifted her chin. "Maybe I can," she replied. "As soon as the slopes reopen, let's go. For now, can you help me get checked into my room? I'd like to get settled before this snowstorm becomes a blizzard and the roads become impassable."

Remy nodded. "That's always a possibility." Even though the weather forecast had only predicted heavy snow, this area of the Rockies had become known for its mercurial winter weather. "Are you ready?"

She pushed to her feet and carried her cup to the trash can, then returned to put on her jacket, hat and gloves. "Now I am," she said.

Remy walked with her to her car, then helped her unload and carry some of her belongings, though she insisted on taking her skis. Foot traffic on Main Street had thinned out and the snowfall showed no signs of slowing.

"You might be right about that blizzard," Remy commented.

She squinted at him through the snow and grinned. "I usually am. I have a thing about weather."

"You dabble in meteorology?"

"No." She laughed, joyous again now that they were outside. Snow stuck to her lashes and she blinked it away. "For whatever reason, I can tell when it's going to rain or snow and for how long. It's a special talent of mine."

He stared at her, his expression incredulous.

"You look like you don't know whether to take me serious or not," she commented. "It's okay. A lot of people have told me I'm a little bit weird."

"Weird?" He shook his head. "Not hardly. I'd say intriguing, more than anything."

At that her entire body went warm—not an easy feat with the wind gusting and snow swirling. She barely knew this man, but he made her feel things she'd never experienced before.

When they reached The Chateau, Remy asked her to wait in the lobby while he went to speak with the people behind the counter. It didn't take long. A few minutes later he returned with a key card. "You're on the top floor," he said. "We only have four, but the suite has a wonderful view. This way to the elevator."

Following him, she looked around, awed despite herself by the elegant luxury of the hotel. While in Switzerland, she'd traveled Europe extensively. This hotel reminded her of several places where she'd stayed in France and Germany.

They were alone in the elevator. The piped-in music played Christmas carols, which again made her feel sad.

Pushing away the melancholy threatening to engulf her, she stepped out eagerly when the elevator stopped on their floor. The hallway seemed to extend out forever. Each doorway was framed in ornately carved wood and her feet sank in the plush carpet.

"Here we are," he told her, using the key card to unlock the door and then holding it open for her.

She stepped into a room larger than her first apartment. A leather couch and recliner had been arranged near a stone fireplace, with a flat-screen television over the mantel. Beyond, she could see a bedroom.

"Check out the view," Remy said, drawing aside the curtains proudly.

Unzipping her jacket, she went over and stood beside him, gazing out at the snow-covered town spread below. "This is…amazing." Troubled, she turned to face him. "Are you sure it's okay that I stay here? It seems like you could get bookings for a room like this and make quite a bit of money."

He smiled warmly down at her. "We never book this room. It's reserved for friends and family only."

About to protest that she was neither, he forestalled her with a light touch on her shoulder. Even through the parka, she wanted to lean into him.

"I consider you a friend, Vanessa," he said. "This room wasn't going to be used at all. As I mentioned earlier, you're welcome to stay as long as you like."

She thanked him, half hoping he would stay a while, half hoping he'd go so she could take a nap and get some rest. He smiled at her for the space of a few heartbeats, and then cleared his throat and turned toward the door.

"Have a good rest of your day," he told her. "I'll be in touch tomorrow, okay?"

Nodding her acceptance, she followed him as he let himself out, turning the dead bolt and adding the chain for good measure. Then and only then did she allow herself to truly explore the suite. She'd never stayed in any place this nice. While her parents had always had money, they were frugal travelers, especially on the rare occasions they'd allowed her to accompany them.

Eying her suitcase, she debated whether or not to unpack. For now, she decided to simply leave her belongings inside. A nap might do wonders to restore her flagging energy.

To her surprise, she slept for two hours. After a hot shower, she changed into her flannel pajamas and perused the room-service menu, too exhausted to drag herself downstairs to eat.

Later, warm and fed, she watched television for a while and then crawled between the softest sheets she'd ever experienced. She immediately fell fast asleep.

The next morning, she woke and stretched before padding to the window and peering out.

The snow was still falling, though now instead of a heavy curtain, fat, big flakes fell relentlessly from sky to earth, swirling on the north wind that stirred up snowdrifts and turned them into icy weapons. After getting dressed, then going downstairs and having breakfast, she decided she'd venture outside briefly after stopping at the front desk to find out if Pine Peak had opened yet. When the desk clerk had informed her that conditions were still too bad, she wanted to check it out for herself.

A few seconds out in front of The Chateau and she had to concur. This hotel sat in the valley. She could only imagine what things would be like up on the mountain.

Disappointed, she went back inside and wandered the lobby area of the elegant hotel, allowing herself to appreciate the festive holiday decorations. Her parents had been big on Christmas, and they'd had their servants put up two tall trees loaded down with decorations. Since her boarding school closed for winter break, she'd always traveled to Boston and returned to a bedroom that felt more like a stranger's than her own.

She might have thought reflecting on the fact that this was her first Christmas without them would have sent her into a downward spiral, but to her surprise, being around so many others intent on celebrating raised her spirits.

Seth had never been able to reconcile how she could yearn after people who made no secret of the fact that they found her a nuisance. After learning his story from Remy, she could better understand his viewpoint. As for herself, she'd never stopped hoping for her parents' love. Now, with them both gone, she'd never receive it.

Though she still had misgivings about meeting Seth, she couldn't help but remember all the times he'd been there for her. His strong, silent presence had helped her get through emotional lows that might have decimated her otherwise.

Impulsively, she texted him and asked him if they could meet for lunch. He immediately agreed, inviting her over for a home-cooked meal. Still skittish, she declined to go to his condo and instead insisted they meet somewhere public. Which happened to be the extremely crowded bar and grill at The Chateau. He'd agreed and they'd set a time—two hours from now.

Which gave her a little time to explore the rest of the hotel. She did some shopping in the gift shop and when she finished, she carried her purchases back up to her room. Then she sat down and put on a little makeup. The simple act of wearing mascara and foundation always gave her confidence. While she wanted things to get back on good footing with Seth, she couldn't discount the possibility that things would go south. She'd need all the confidence she could get.

Finally, a few minutes before the agreed-upon time, she made her way downstairs to the bar and grill. Eying the line at the reception desk, she decided to go ahead and wait for a table for two. Luckily, the line moved quickly and she soon found herself sitting at a cozy spot near the window with a great view of the snowy landscape.

She went ahead and ordered a drink, deciding on a hot rum toddy for warmth. When the waiter brought her drink and offered her a menu, she perused it, trying to decide what she was in the mood to eat. Though she'd have to wait to order until Seth arrived, it never hurt to have an idea of what she wanted.

Checking her watch, she took another tiny sip of her drink. Seth was late. Since he often ran behind, she'd expected this, but she'd been nursing her rum toddy for close to thirty minutes now.

If he didn't show up in the next five, she planned to go up to her room. Since Seth didn't know she was staying at The Chateau, he wouldn't disturb her. Remy had registered her under an assumed name, making a joke out of it, winking and smiling and generally making her feel better.

Her phone chimed, indicating a text. From Seth. Reading it, she wasn't sure what to think. I fell and hurt my ankle. Not broken, but swollen. I'm not up to meeting you. I can barely walk. Is there any way you'd consider stopping by here?

Dubious, she felt slightly ashamed that her first reaction was skepticism. She wouldn't put it past Seth to do whatever he felt necessary to get her alone.

But why? What would be the purpose? She'd already done what she'd come to do. She'd offered him her explanation. He'd reacted badly. What else was there to say?

Another text came through before she'd even answered the first. Please, Van. As your friend. I just need to make things right.

That one word made her waver. Friend. Because Seth had been that, first and foremost. She still owed him for always being there for her.

I'll stop by, she finally texted back. If I can even get there in this storm.

The city is plowing the roads several times a day, he texted. You should be fine.

Assuming he was correct, he had a point. She'd check out front and see if there were any cabs. If so, she'd use one of them for transport. Deciding, she texted him. Okay. But I can't stay long.

That's fine, he replied. See you in a few.

She tossed back the rest of her drink, then asked for the check. Once she'd paid, she put on her parka. After walking through the crowded lobby that hummed with activity, she stepped outside and stopped for a moment in wonder at the fierceness of the storm and the purity of the white landscape. All her life, for as long as she could remember, she'd felt this way about snow. As if each time it covered the earth, the pristine, silent landscape signified a new beginning.

Evidently, Roaring Springs taxi service had either been overwhelmed by demand or, more likely, people were staying put until the storm passed. Disappointed, she turned back toward the entrance, debating whether or not to text Seth and reschedule.

The plow went by just then, breaking the silence and sending arcs of snow onto both sides of the street. Since this completely obliterated the sidewalk, at least until it could be shoveled, that meant going to Seth's on foot was out, even if she had considered the possibility. Still, she'd probably have to shovel snow off her car.

Walking up and down the lot, she could no longer feel her feet. By the time she finally located her buried vehicle, she'd begun to seriously rethink the idea of leaving The Chateau. While the plow had just been by, with this rate of snowfall, it wouldn't be long until the street got buried again. And she didn't want to get stuck at Seth's.

It struck her that he hadn't even asked her where she was staying or been the slightest bit concerned about her safety out in this blizzard. When conditions were considered so dangerous that a ski resort closed the mountain, she thought he at least should have asked.

No point in worrying about that now. Since she'd gotten a little stir-crazy cooped up in the hotel, she decided to risk it. After all, Seth lived only a couple of blocks away.

It took her a good ten minutes, but she finally cleared enough of the snow from her car to be able to drive. She got in and started the engine, sitting in the cold seat for a few minutes until the vehicle warmed up.

By the time she got to Seth's condo, nearly an hour had passed since his first text. Her hands ached from gripping the wheel, but the short drive had been un-eventful despite greatly reduced visibility. She'd had to take it slow, watching for icy patches on the streets. Luckily, very few other vehicles were out. It seemed her earlier guess had been correct. Most people must have decided to hunker down by the fire.

She reached Seth's condo without incident. Though she'd only been there once, luckily she remembered the location. He lived in a trendy part of town right off Main Street. His building was one-of-a-kind, with fully restored, modern styling.

After she parked, she walked across the lot, headed inside and rode the antique elevator to his floor. His door had a red welcome mat in front.

Taking a deep breath, she raised her hand and knocked three times, instinctively using the old coded cadence they'd agreed on during her rough times. She hadn't been taking visitors then and Seth had been the one exception.

The door swung open. "Hey there!" Wearing a big, goofy smile, Seth waved her inside.

She could tell he had been drinking the instant he closed the door behind her and awkwardly tried to take her into his arms. More than just the nearly overwhelming odor of whiskey, his red-rimmed, bleary eyes and delayed coordination told her that he'd had quite a few before her arrival.

Chapter 5

Making a snap decision, Vanessa spun around to leave. "I don't need this. Not today." Not ever.

"Wait." He grabbed her arm. "It's okay. I promise. I just needed to take the edge off. I'm not drunk."

While she wasn't sure she believed him, since he seemed to be in a good mood, she relented. "Just for a little bit. I don't want to be gone too long with this storm still going strong."

"Is it?" He seemed disinterested. "I've been holed up here and haven't checked outside at all. Would you like a beer, or a glass of wine? I also have some whiskey I can mix with cola or pour over ice. I'm drinking it on the rocks. Your call."

"I'm good with water," she said. "Or coffee, tea or cocoa, if you have any of those."

He laughed. "I'm sure I do. Come on into the kitchen and you can choose."

Turning to lead the way, he stumbled into the wall. At the last moment, he caught himself and kept going. Not sure how to react, Vanessa eyed the door. Should she leave or simply pretend not to notice?

"Don't go," he pleaded, glancing back at her over his shoulder. Apparently, he was at least sober enough to notice her hesitation. "I promise, I've got this under control."

Despite her instincts, she trailed along behind him into the kitchen. She wished she'd thought to let Remy know that she'd come here.

"What about your ankle?" she asked.

"It's better now," he said, with a lopsided smile.

After getting her a bottle of mineral water, Seth picked up his own drink—something with ice in a tall, plastic glass—and gestured toward his living room. "Want to sit and talk? I want to apologize for the way I acted when you were here last. Plus, since you were generous enough to explain everything to me, I think I owe you an explanation, as well."

Doing a quick mental evaluation—he wasn't slurring his words and seemed relatively focused—she nodded and followed him into the living room. He'd built a fire in the stone fireplace and had the TV on, though the sound had been turned down so low she couldn't hear it. The curtains were open, revealing the wintry wonderland outside.

He still hadn't asked her where she might be staying. She needed to decide how she would answer if he did, since she'd actually prefer him not to know.

Taking a seat in the overstuffed chair on one side of the fireplace, he motioned her to the other one. Relieved he wasn't going to try to get her to snuggle up next to him on the couch, she did.

"Relax, Van," he chided. "I know I was an ass last time. I'm sorry for that. The breakup just hit me hard. Part of me really wanted to believe you'd come here to get back together, even though I knew somewhere deep inside that you hadn't."

Releasing a breath, she watched him closely. Seth's vibe seemed mellow and not the least bit threatening. Maybe now that he'd had a chance to reconcile himself with the truth, she could finally get that closure she'd come for.

Sipping his drink, he eyed her over the rim of his glass. "Sorry we weren't able to hit Pine Peak before they had to close it."

"Me, too," she admitted. "I'm hoping they reopen before I have to head back to Boulder."

He nodded. "It's a good slope. I get up there as often as I can. Have you been keeping up your normal skiing-every-week thing?"

"When I can, yes. I've had to go back east twice since November, which of course meant I couldn't ski. I did manage to get up to New Hampshire once, but most times I was too busy to spend any time on the slopes."

"Speaking of which, when are you going back to Boston next?" he asked. "Or did you just get back?" Seth knew all about her frequent and necessary trips to try to settle her parents' estate.

"I'm due for a trip," she replied. "Though I decided to go after the holidays. I'd rather wait until ski season is over, but since we still can get snow into March, that might be stretching it a bit too much."

"Skiing still comes number one with you, I see." Seth made the statement without judgment. After all, he was one of the few people outside of the competition set who knew just how skilled she was.

"You know it." Access to difficult mountains had been one of her primary considerations when she'd decided to live in Colorado. That, and she liked the natural beauty of the state and the way the air always felt clean due to the lack of humidity.

"Can't say I blame you." Continuing to sip from his drink, Seth appeared unusually relaxed. She remembered what Remy had said about drugs and wondered if he'd taken something and combined that with alcohol.

While she tried to come up with a way to ask, he nodded off, still sitting up, drink in hand.

Afraid he might spill it, she cleared her throat. When he opened his eyes, she smiled at him. "Maybe you should put the drink down if you're going to nap?"

His bleary gaze drifted from her to his glass. He cursed softly, but placed his drink on the coaster on the coffee table. "Sorry," he muttered. "Probably my cold meds interacting with the whiskey."

"I figured," she replied. Though she hadn't even been there an hour, the time had come for her to leave.

"Don't go yet," Seth begged, as though he'd somehow read her mind. "I'm sorry I'm such a poor host, but I really don't want to be alone right now. I need you to be here for me, Van. Just for a little bit longer."

He needed her. And since she'd said virtually those exact words to him in the dark times right after her parents' deaths, she'd be a jerk if she left now.

But what did he expect her to do? Watch him sleep?

Grab the remote and watch some television? Or scroll social media on her phone?

Then she caught sight of Seth's laptop, open on the kitchen table. While she could always wait to check flights until she got back home to Boulder, it wouldn't hurt to check rates now. Especially since she had need of a way to occupy her time.

"Do you mind if I use your laptop to see about flights to Boston next month?" she asked. "It's kind of a pain to do on my phone and I'd like to get a jump on things."

Eyes half-lidded, he heaved himself up and padded to the kitchen without answering, where she could hear him making himself another drink. "Are you sure you don't want something besides water?" he called. "I have some really good whiskey. Or rum, vodka or tequila, if that's your preference."

"No, thank you." She eyed the laptop, wondering if he'd even heard her. Either way, it really wasn't a good idea for him to keep drinking. Gathering up her courage, she spoke up. "Hey, Seth. From one friend to another, don't you think maybe you've had enough?"

At first, he didn't respond. She could hear the sound of him stirring his drink. Finally, he came back into the living room and dropped himself into his chair. The sudden movement caused his drink to slosh over onto his jeans. He didn't appear to notice. "Why are you giving me such a hard time?" he asked, his voice as mournful as his expression. "I'm just relaxing inside my own home. I'm not planning on driving anywhere."

"I'm worried about you," she said, relieved the anger hadn't returned. "That's the truth. It kind of seems like your drinking might have gotten out of control."

He took a long sip from his glass before answering. "I don't have a problem, if that's what you're inferring."

Since she wasn't going to argue, Vanessa simply focused her attention on the leaping flames of the fire. They sat in silence for the next several minutes while she tried to work up what to say so she could leave. More than anything, she wished she could help him, but she understood she couldn't assist someone who didn't want to help himself. Whatever path Seth had now taken, he had to make his own choices.

She just didn't want to be around to watch him crash and burn. It would be far too painful. Whatever else he might have become, he'd been a good man once. He'd been the actual definition of a true friend. And maybe, just maybe, he needed her to be one to him now.

"Is there anything I can do to help you?" she asked quietly. "Anything at all."

He looked at her then, really looked at her. "What do you mean?"

Waving her hand vaguely, she shrugged. "I don't know, Seth. I can tell something is wrong, but you act like you're fine."

"I *am* fine," he protested, then tossed back half of his drink. "Please stop worrying about me. I get enough of that with my brother, Remy."

Remy. Just the mention of his name made her heart skip a beat. Luckily, Seth had never been the most observant of men. Especially now, while more than halfway to intoxicated.

"I'll try not to worry," she promised, leaning forward. "Seth, you were there helping me in one of the darkest times in my life. I want you to know that I will do the same for you. We won't ever be a couple, at least not in a romantic way. But if you'd like to be friends again, I'm open to that."

"We'll see." He drained his glass and awkwardly pushed up out of his chair, clearly on his way to make another. If he kept drinking like this, he'd be three sheets to the wind in no time.

"Wait," she said, desperate to find a way to distract him. "Would you mind letting me use your laptop to look up ticket prices on flights from DIA to Logan?"

Maybe if she could get him using the computer with her, he'd forget about getting another drink, at least for a little while. Seth had always been really into computers. So much so that she'd always wondered why he hadn't looked for a career in that field.

Swerving unsteadily toward the table, he grabbed the laptop and brought it to her. Dumping it unceremoniously on her lap, he shrugged. "Knock yourself out. My password is 'beginagain2020.'"

She blinked. "Okay. Thanks."

"No problem." Seth waved his hand and resumed his journey into the kitchen.

She powered up the laptop, and when the prompt came up, she typed in Seth's password. The usual assortment of desktop file folders came up. One marked "Loves" caught her eye.

She glanced at the kitchen. No sign of Seth. Feeling daring, she clicked on the folder.

Inside were two subfolders. One marked "Vanessa Fisher," the other marked "Sabrina Gilford." More than curious now, she clicked on the latter and found dozens of photographs. Several were of Seth with his arm around a pretty woman. Others were clearly screenshots of typed notes. Apparently, he and Sabrina had been dating while he and Vanessa were also seeing each other.

She glanced around. Still no sign of Seth. Finger poised above the built-in mouse, she took a deep breath. "Are you all right?" she called.

"Yeah." He poked his head around the corner. "I'm going to the bathroom, okay? Don't run out on me while I'm gone."

"I won't," she promised. The instant he disappeared, she returned her attention to the laptop and quickly clicked on the folder marked with her name. Just like the Sabrina one, there were numerous photos of her and Seth together, as well as several of just her. And like the other folder, there were also notes, detailing his thoughts and emotions.

Not sure she wanted to see this, she closed that file and returned to the other one.

A screenshot of an obituary caught her eye. Enlarging it, she realized Sabrina had died. Hurriedly, she read the obituary, and then went back and clicked on some of the notes.

Then, considering the possibility that Seth might return and ask her about airline fares, she opened up a popular travel site and typed in a ticket-price search for a random date in mid-January. Once those selections were displayed, she minimized the file and went back to reading Seth's notes and screenshots of text messages between him and Sabrina.

From what she could piece together, Sabrina had broken up with him in a similarly vague way as Vanessa had. Judging by his text messages to her, he'd been both furious and threatening.

And then Sabrina had been murdered. Vanessa felt sick. If she remembered correctly, there had been some serial killer in Roaring Springs. Sabrina must have been one of the victims.

Since Seth had still not returned, she took a couple of pictures with her phone.

She closed the file and returned to the travel website and took a snapshot of that. Then she powered down the laptop and closed it.

Still no sign of Seth. She wondered if he'd fallen asleep or passed out in the bathroom. Though she in no way wanted to check on him, she'd never be able to live with herself if she left and found out later that something bad had happened to him.

About to get up and go knock on the door, relief flooded her when Seth emerged, once again heading into the kitchen.

"Did you find your flight info?" he asked, using the ice maker to fill a glass. Which meant he was making another drink.

She'd had enough. About to tell him she needed to go, she stood. This might be better to do once she had stepped into the hallway, she thought. Halfway to the front door, the sounds of an awful crash came from the kitchen. Immediately followed by Seth cursing.

"Are you all right?" she asked urgently.

"No. I cut myself. There's blood. A lot of blood. And it hurts."

Hurrying into the kitchen, she found Seth standing in the middle of the room, surrounded by shards of glass and holding his bleeding hand. Blood dripped from between his fingers, pooling on the floor.

"That looks like a bad cut." She grabbed a dish towel. "Here. Let me wrap this around it so we can stop the bleeding. Then I'll take a look at it. It might be a good idea for you to go to the hospital if it's really deep. You could need stitches."

He swayed, appearing as if he might pass out and tumble face-first into the dangerous pieces of glass. Going to him, and wincing at the crunching under her feet, she steered him toward the kitchen table and helped him settle into a chair. "What happened?"

"I'm not sure." Expression bewildered, he looked at the glass and blood as if he had no idea how he'd gotten there. "I was about to pour another drink. The bottle must have slipped, or my glass did, because the next thing I knew, they were both broken. And I was bleeding."

Remy must have checked his phone ten times that morning, hoping against hope that Vanessa would call or text. When the cell finally rang shortly after lunch, relief flooded him. He realized he'd waited all day simply to hear her voice. Except not like this. Breathless, she stumbled over her words, clearly panicked. "I need your help."

All senses instantly on alert, he asked her what was going on.

"It's Seth," she said. "He's been drinking and he fell and cut himself pretty badly. I think he might have mixed something else with his alcohol, though I don't know what. He claimed it was cold medicine, but I doubt that. He's refusing to go to the ER."

Briefly, Remy closed his eyes. "Where are you?"

"Seth's place," she replied, her voice still shaky.

He inhaled sharply. Why the hell that answer surprised him, he didn't know. He shouldn't have expected otherwise. "I'll be there as quickly as I can." He glanced at the window and the blinding swirl of snow. "How are the roads?"

"They're keeping the streets plowed," she said. "I drove here. It was manageable."

"How long ago?" he asked, pinning his phone between his shoulder and his ear as he shrugged into his coat.

"Not long. A little more than an hour."

More relieved than he should have been, he told her he'd see her soon and ended the call.

His Jeep had gotten buried by snow, but after a few minutes, he'd cleared enough off to head out.

The roads weren't awful, though clearly the snowplow couldn't keep up with the swiftly falling precipitation. When he reached Seth's condo, he couldn't find a parking spot and ended up double parking behind another car buried in snow.

As soon as he stepped off the elevator, he saw Vanessa, standing in Seth's doorway, watching for him. Relief lit up her face the instant she spotted him. "I've bandaged him up as best I could," she said, leading the way into the kitchen. "And I cleaned up the broken glass. But he's lost a lot of blood and the combination of whatever he took and the whiskey isn't helping."

In the kitchen, a haggard-looking Seth sat slouched on the floor, back braced up against one of the cabinets. When he saw Remy, he grimaced and glared at Vanessa. "What's he doing here? Did you call him?"

"I did," she replied softly. "You need help, Seth. More than I'm able to give you."

He cursed, stringing together several swear words that would have made a sailor blush. Vanessa didn't react to them. Instead, she kept her gaze trained on Remy. The hope and trust he saw in her eyes made him feel both humble and proud.

He could fall for this woman. Where that thought had come from, he didn't know. What he did understand was that such thoughts had no place in this scenario.

Crouching down near his brother, Remy reached for Seth's shoulder. With a violent move, his brother knocked away his hand. "Don't touch me."

"Fine." Remy stood and pulled out his phone. "I'm going to give you a choice. Either you let me take you to the emergency room, or I call 911 and you can ride in the ambulance. Your choice."

"I'm fine," Seth insisted. "I'm not even drunk. My cold medicine didn't mix well with my whiskey. I just need to sleep it off."

Ignoring the fact that his brother *always* needed to sleep it off, Remy pointed to the rough tourniquet Vanessa had placed on Seth's arm. "I'm talking about your cut. Looks like you may need stitches."

"And antibiotics," she interjected, earning another irate look from Seth. Vanessa took a step back before glancing at Remy. "You got this?"

Remy nodded. "Yep."

"Then I'm going to head out." Snatching up her

coat, she marched toward the front door. "Take care. I hope you feel better soon, Seth."

And then she was gone. Remy felt her absence with the same sort of chill one feels when the sun disappears behind a cloud.

He returned his attention to his brother. "What'll it be, Seth? Ambulance or riding in my Jeep?"

"Jeep," Seth replied, his voice as sullen as his expression. Remy helped him up, noting the strong stench of whiskey. Somehow, he got a coat around his brother's shoulders and a ski cap on his head. "Be careful on the snow," he warned, keeping a grip on Seth's uninjured arm.

Once at the ER, the triage nurse greeted them by name. Once Remy explained the reason they were there, she asked them to take a seat and promised they'd be seen shortly.

Luckily, since the slopes were closed down, the ER was mostly empty. Dr. Reynolds stitched up Seth's arm, and they did some blood work despite his protests. When the doctor came back to discharge them, he asked Seth if he was aware of the dangers of mixing benzodiazepine with alcohol.

At least Seth appeared sheepish. He concurred that he did know, but claimed to have forgotten he'd taken the pills before he started drinking. His words mollified the doctor, though Remy had his doubts. His brother would say whatever felt convenient to get him out of trouble. It had become Seth's pattern recently and Remy had no idea how to break the cycle.

Pen poised to sign the discharge paperwork, Seth asked if he could have some pain medication.

Incredulous, Remy met Dr. Reynolds's gaze and gave a half shake of his head. "I think ibuprofen will take care of any pain," the doctor said. "Take two before you go to sleep tonight."

Seth frowned, then opened his mouth as if he meant to argue.

"He'll be fine," Remy said, forestalling him. "Come on, Seth. Sign the paperwork so we can get you home before the storm gets any worse."

A surly Seth did as Remy asked. Bundling him up, Remy hustled his brother out into the snowstorm.

They didn't speak for the entire drive home, which was fine by Remy. He'd actually expected his brother to issue a litany of complaints.

Only when they reached the front of Seth's condo building did Remy address his brother. "I'm just going to drop you off here. Please do as the doctor said and try to stay out of trouble."

Seth turned to look at him. The flatness of his gaze matched his voice. "Why did Vanessa call you? How'd she even get your number?"

"She called The Chateau and left a message for me to call her. When I returned the call, I used my cell and told her to save it to her contacts."

"I knew it!" Seth exploded. "You have the hots for my girl."

Remy shook his head. There were several possible responses to that statement, each of which would only add fuel to the fire. He decided to go with a simple version of the truth. "Look, Seth, I like Vanessa. She seems like good people. However, leave me out of whatever is going on between the two of you. I'm only trying to do what's right."

"Of course you are." Seth rolled his eyes. "Mr. Goody Two-shoes, walk-the-straight-and-narrow, black-and-white Remy Colton. I'm thinking it would never occur to you to hit on Vanessa Fisher, especially considering who she is."

Refusing to allow himself to be insulted, Remy focused on the last part of Seth's statement. "What do you mean, 'who she is'?"

"You really don't know? Google her. She's the only daughter of Clive and Celeste Fisher."

The names sounded familiar, but Remy still couldn't place them. Not wanting to prolong this discussion with his brother, he simply nodded. "Take care of yourself."

"I will." After exiting the Jeep, Seth slammed the door. Remy watched until he'd disappeared inside the building, then drove back home in the snow.

Once inside, he did a quick internet search. As Vanessa had mentioned, her parents had been killed in a car accident six months ago. What she hadn't said was that her father, Clive Fisher, was the well-known, wealthy investment banker and author of several self-help books. Vanessa truly was an heiress, with a fortune that rivaled the Coltons'.

As if thinking of Vanessa had somehow summoned her, his phone rang, caller ID displaying her name. Despite everything, his heart skipped a beat.

"I've been meaning to call you," he answered. "I just dropped Seth off at his condo."

"How is he?" Vanessa asked.

"He'll survive." He sounded grim, revealing his frustration. "The doc said his blood pressure was dangerously low, and the tox screen revealed he'd taken a high dose of a benzodiazepine. He finally admitted it, though he claimed it was an accident."

"Did they keep him overnight?"

"No." He dragged his hand through his hair. "They stitched him up, gave him a prescription for antibiotics, told him to take ibuprofen, and sent him on home. I debated whether or not to stay with him, but he didn't want me to. And he's an adult, so I left."

"I can't blame you." Her soft voice felt like a balm to his soul. Suddenly, he ached to see her.

"What are you doing for dinner?" he asked before he could stop himself.

"I'm not sure. I've been debating whether to use room service or go eat by myself in the restaurant."

Taking a deep breath, he decided to go for it. "Do you like steak?" he murmured, deliberately keeping his tone light.

She laughed. "Who doesn't?"

"The Lodge has a great steak house called Del Aggio," he continued. "How about I take you there?"

She went silent for a moment, making him wonder if he'd made a mistake. "That sounds wonderful," she finally said. "But won't you need reservations?"

"They'll fit us in," he told her. "I'll just need to make a quick call. Would seven work for you? If the tram was running, we could ride that up to the resort. But since I believe they shut it down due to the storm, we'll have to take my Jeep. As long as the roads are passable, we'll be good to go."

"Seven is perfect." Though a tinge of hesitation still colored her voice, she also sounded happy. That sent an answering warmth through him. "I'll see you around what...six forty-five?"

He agreed and ended the call. Filled with anticipation, he called up to The Lodge and let them know his plans.

Chapter 6

Del Aggio, in keeping with the general decorating scheme of The Lodge, sported a combination of Western and down-home, country decor. A huge two-sided fireplace sat right in the middle of the restaurant and the crackling blaze they had going did much to keep the diners warm and cozy.

Vanessa and Remy waited in the bar until their table was ready. Though she'd been inside The Lodge lobby a few times, she hadn't taken the time to really check out the interior of the restaurant. Now she realized she much preferred The Lodge's rustic comfort to The Chateau's old-world-style elegance.

"This place makes me feel right at home," she mused, sipping from her glass of Shiraz.

"That's because you're a skier," Remy replied, smiling. "My family did a ton of research and decorated this place accordingly. The Chateau is more for those who like the idea of a ski vacation, but prefer to spend more time shopping and getting pampered."

His comment made her laugh. "You hotel moguls think of everything, don't you?"

"We have to." He gave a modest shrug. "Research matters if you want to be a success."

And The Colton Empire definitely was a success. Seth had gone on and on about his brother's family. Being her father's daughter, she'd checked into them. Seth had been right. The Colton businesses were definitely fiscally solvent and growing.

Remy's name was called. He took her elbow as they walked toward the hostess. At his touch, her entire body warmed. Honestly, she felt as if they were on a date instead of two acquaintances working toward a possible friendship.

Due to Remy's status, they were given a secluded table near the fireplace but with a floor-to-ceiling window on the other side. Outside, the snowflakes danced in the decorative lanterns that circled a large, snow-covered patio with a seating area that must be popular in the summer and fall.

Vanessa perused the elaborate menu that featured every cut of steak, as well as a few token chicken and fish entrées. There was nothing she loved better than good prime rib, cooked medium rare. A well-cooked T-bone would be a close second.

Closing her menu, she saw Remy had already done the same. "You decided quickly," he commented.

"It was an easy choice." Smiling, she sipped her wine. She truly enjoyed being with this man, despite the push-pull of attraction that constantly simmered between them.

The waitress arrived, blushing when she saw Remy. She asked if they wanted another drink. Vanessa asked for a second glass of wine, plus water. Remy did the same.

Once the waitress walked off, Remy leaned forward. "Service is a bit slow here, on purpose. It's a deliberately unhurried dining experience."

Vanessa had to grin. "I'm not in a rush to go anywhere. Are you?"

This made him throw his head back and laugh. "I like you, Vanessa Fisher."

She blushed as deeply as the waitress had. "Thanks. I like you, too."

They placed their orders—Remy got the T-bone, and if she'd known him better, she would have definitely asked for a taste.

He told her about his job in public relations, which had always interested her. In return, she told him about Boston and how her passion for the New England Patriots had now been relegated to second place, behind the Denver Broncos, which her old Boston friends would consider sacrilegious if they knew.

"But I'm still a Red Sox fan," she said breathlessly, as if that made all the difference in the world. "Though the Broncos come first in my heart, I also watch the Pats."

"You like football?" Remy asked, sounding as surprised as if she'd just admitted to belonging to a secret society or something.

"Love it. I try not to miss any games. I actually

DVR them so I can watch them later if I have to miss them."

He laughed again. "This is going to sound so weird, but I do that, too."

"Wow." She eyed him, not sure if he might be pulling her leg. "I've never met anyone else who did that."

"Well, now you have." He turned the conversation to other topics, ranging from the snowfall forecast to what Roaring Springs was like in the summer.

"Is it empty?" she asked.

"It's less crowded than during ski season, but we get different kinds of tourists. Hikers and bikers, people who want to train for endurance bike rides and such. And people who like to shop. For the first two weeks in July, Roaring Springs hosts a film festival similar to Sundance. It's been a tradition for the last ten years."

Intrigued, she made a mental note to check that out. "I'd be interested in attending something like that," she said.

"Great. I'll keep you posted on the details." His easy reply sounded as if he took it for granted that they'd stay in touch.

She realized she liked that idea a lot. But she knew he might change his mind once she revealed what she'd discovered on Seth's computer.

Since they hadn't ordered appetizers, their steaks came just then, perfectly cooked. She cut into hers, anticipation making her mouth water. Remy did the same.

She waited until they'd both eaten most of their meal before bringing up what she'd found on Seth's computer. She wasn't even sure she should. After all, she'd been snooping on Seth's computer. No matter how she tried to spin it, what she'd found had been none of her business. So what if Seth kept computer files on his previous girlfriends? Despite being creepy and a little weird, doing that wasn't illegal.

Still, it bothered her. A lot. Maybe because Seth had never mentioned Sabrina at all, even when she'd been murdered. She really wanted to see what Remy thought about all of it, even if telling him changed his opinion of her. Which shouldn't have mattered, but it did.

A lull had occurred in the conversation. Now or never. She took a deep breath.

"What do you know about Sabrina Gilford?" Vanessa asked, aware her casual tone might be at odds with her intent expression.

In the act of eating a piece of his steak, Remy stilled. "She is—was—my cousin, on my father's side. She was murdered, strangled just like the other victims. We all believed she'd been killed by the same serial killer—the Avalanche Killer—but when Curtis Shruggs was brought into police custody, he said he didn't kill her."

"Maybe he lied?" she suggested, her heart beginning to pound.

"I thought that, too. The only problem is he confessed to all the other murders. Why not claim that one? He said he only wanted credit for his own work. As far as the police are concerned, Sabrina's killer is still out there."

She took a deep breath, unsurprised to realize her hand was shaking. "Remy, please don't think I'm crazy. But do you think Seth might know anything about her murder?"

Inwardly cringing, she waited for Remy's reaction.

She wouldn't blame him if he stormed out, after accusing her of being crazy.

Instead, he eyed her and chewed, seriously considering her question. "As far as I know, he didn't even know her. So I doubt it. Why?"

Debating whether or not to simply drop it, Vanessa pulled up her photo albums on her phone. She clicked on the first shot she'd taken of the pics on Seth's laptop and slid her cell across the table to Remy.

"I was looking at airfare to Boston on Seth's laptop— with his permission. I saw a folder marked 'Loves' and it intrigued me, so I clicked on it. Inside, there were two subfolders, one with my name and one with Sabrina's. Both had lots of pictures. Take a look and see for yourself."

Picking up her phone, Remy studied the images, scrolling from one to the other. His frown deepened as he read Seth's typed notes, and when he came to the newspaper clippings, his mouth twisted in pain.

When he finished, he wordlessly slid her phone back to her. "I wonder why Seth never mentioned he dated Sabrina," he mused. "That doesn't seem like something he would want to hide."

She shrugged. "Did you know about his engagement to me? Or even that he was in a serious relationship?"

"I heard about it." Eying the last bite of steak on his plate, he finally popped it into his mouth and chewed slowly. Once he'd swallowed, he took a drink of his wine. "I wasn't able to make the party when Seth announced his engagement."

"I know," she replied in a soft voice. "I would definitely remember meeting you."

Looking dazed, he started to apologize for not making more of an effort to meet her. "Work had been crazy and I took off for a bit of a mini-vacation. By the time I got back in town, you'd already gone. And then Seth said you'd broken up. I have to say, I wasn't surprised."

"It was all very sudden. Both the engagement and the breakup. I realized it wasn't going to work out, Seth and I getting married." Slightly embarrassed, she sighed. "Seth is—or was—my friend. While I don't recognize the man he's apparently become since we separated, I have to believe he still has a good heart."

Expression relieved, Remy sipped his wine. "Thank you for that."

Not sure how to respond, she stirred her food around on her plate and simply nodded. "I'm sorry I brought it up. Heck, I'm sorry I snooped. I just saw the folder and my curiosity got the best of me. I know it was wrong."

"It's okay." Unbelievably, he seemed to be attempting to comfort her. "You're only human. I think most of us would have done the same thing."

Would he? She wanted to ask, but decided not to. Remy Colton seemed like a pretty black-and-white kind of guy. She doubted he'd ever intrude on anyone's privacy like that.

"Look," he continued, "my brother has been having issues recently. I'll be the first to admit it. And lately, with the drinking and whatever else, I think his addictive tendencies might have gotten the best of him once again. If I can convince him to get help—"

"I think that would be awesome..."

Tilting his head, he studied her. "But? I can tell there's something you're not telling me."

"He's your brother. And my friend. But the Seth I've seen since I've been here scares me. I'm more than a little afraid."

Gaze locking with hers, he finally nodded. "I'll look into this, I promise you. For now, maybe it's best that you make sure you're not alone with him again."

"I don't plan to be."

The waitress returned, bringing with her an elaborate dessert tray. Though Vanessa's first impulse had been to decline, a bowl of berries in cream caught her eye. "I'll have that," she said.

Remy ordered a cheese plate, along with coffee for them both. They spent the rest of the time chatting about inconsequential things, the kind of superficial small talk between two people who had no idea what else to actually say.

She hated it. And wondered if she'd managed to ruin things between them before they'd ever begun.

Remy watched the beautiful woman across from him struggle. More than anything he wished he could reach over, take her hands in his and promise to protect her. From his own brother. That's where things had begun to feel as if he'd stepped into an alternate universe.

Deep inside, Remy had always longed for family, the one thing his self-involved father had no desire to give him. When he'd discovered the existence of a half brother, he'd known he'd move Heaven and earth to make sure the kid was safe.

And so he had. Seth had been his number one priority since the day he'd first seen that skinny, sullen, scared teenager slouching in a rickety chair in their mother's filthy apartment. He'd known right then like a punch in the gut that no matter what he had to do, he'd be getting Seth out of there. Remy never would have guessed that by having his mother dump him off on Whit Colton's doorstep, she'd been doing him a huge favor. He'd wanted to do the same for Seth, and so he had.

And now this. Vanessa's discovery made him question it all again.

Had Seth done something to hurt Sabrina? He wanted to believe that wasn't the case with everything within him. But that one little niggling piece of doubt hung in there, making him question just about everything.

Meanwhile, Vanessa had gone quiet, contemplative. Her long-lashed blue eyes stirred a complicated swirl of emotions inside him. She intrigued him, worried him and made him happy all at once. A combination both dangerous and full of potential.

"I'll do some checking," he reassured her.

Though Vanessa nodded, she seemed distracted, eating her berries one at a time. After she'd finished them, she gazed at the bowl as if she'd like to lick it clean. "I'm sorry if I ruined the evening," she finally said, clearly unaware of her effect on him.

He blinked. "You didn't." Now he did allow himself a light touch on the back of her hand. "I don't blame you for freaking out. To be honest, I'm a little concerned myself. I'm worried about my brother."

"I am, too." She sighed, her pretty eyes going soft. "Maybe I shouldn't have come here."

"I'm glad you did," he told her, meaning every word. He didn't know how a woman he'd just met could manage to make him feel so alive, just by her presence. Every time her gaze met his, his heart turned over and his body stirred.

Remy signaled the waitress for the check. "Well, we aren't going to solve anything tonight. Let me get you back to The Chateau and tomorrow I'll make some phone calls and see what I can find out."

After dropping off Vanessa at The Chateau, Remy continued on to his home, driving slowly in the thick curtain of snow. Once he'd gotten inside, he started up his gas fireplace, poured himself a drink and began flipping through old movies available on Netflix.

When his cell rang, he answered it without looking at the screen, assuming it was Vanessa. Instead, his father's voice boomed at him with his standard greeting. "I'm glad I caught you," Whit Colton said.

"Where else would I be at ten in the evening during a blizzard," Remy pointed out, his tone mild as he sipped on his Scotch.

Apparently feeling as if he'd made enough small talk, Whit cut directly to the chase. "Who is the woman you've put in the family suite at The Chateau?" he demanded. "Are you up there now?"

"No—" Remy replied.

Whit cut him off. "Imagine my surprise when I learn my son has decided to make use of the suite without even checking with me."

The anger in Whit's voice was no surprise. Remy frequently managed to make his father mad, most often without even trying.

"I made sure we weren't going to be using it," Remy said, refusing to allow Whit to make him defensive. "She came up here from Boulder and the storm hit and she had nowhere else to stay. They've closed the tunnel and the pass, so she's stuck here in Roaring Springs until this storm blows over. I let her stay there since she's a friend."

"A *friend*?" Whit drawled the word as if he found it offensive. "Well, I need the suite so you need to get her out of there immediately. Let her stay with you, if she's such a good *friend*."

Remy refused to allow his father to goad him. "No. I'm not going to be waking her up in the middle of a blizzard and kicking her out. That's ridiculous. This can wait until morning."

"It can't." Whit cleared his throat. "You know I use that suite. It's my own personal, private, uh, nest."

"Nest?" Remy repeated, not understanding.

Whit swore. "Are you really going to make me spell it out?"

It took an effort for Remy to keep from groaning out loud. "Let me guess. You're wanting to bring someone up to the room tonight."

"Bingo," Whit growled. "Now get your gal pal out of there so I can have the room cleaned. Pronto."

"Now?" Still disbelieving, Remy scratched his head. "It's snowing like crazy out there and the plows have stopped for the night." He decided not to mention that he'd just gotten home not too long ago.

"Not my problem. You should have thought of that before you used the room without my permission. Just get it done." Whit hung up.

Remy swore. And swore again. Though he hated to call Vanessa this late and possibly wake her, he knew if he didn't, his father would simply go barging into the suite and order her out. That would be infinitely worse.

She answered on the second ring. At least she didn't sound asleep. Remy abandoned all attempts at delicacy and flat out told her what had just transpired.

After a moment of stunned silence, she laughed. "I guess I'd better get packed."

Her laughter puzzled him, but since it seemed infinitely preferable to panic or anger, he'd take it. "I'll be there in a few minutes to pick you up."

"Remy, you don't have to do that," she protested. "I'll figure something out."

"You're staying with me," he said. "I have a guest room, too. And since I got you into this spot…"

"You don't owe me." Her gentle reply made his chest ache.

"Of course I don't. But there's nowhere you can stay in town and it's too damn cold to sleep in your car. Plus—" he softened his tone "—I'd really enjoy your company."

She laughed again, the easy sound spreading warmth through him. "Sold," she said. "I need a few minutes to get packed. I'll wait in the lobby. Just let me know when you get here and I'll run out. There's no reason you should have to park or anything."

Glad he had snow tires on his Jeep, he made it to The Chateau without any problems. Pulling into the circular drive, even now he had to admire the way the warm light spilling out from the windows seemed like a welcoming beacon through the swirling snow.

Under the covered valet-parking area, he texted Vanessa, letting her know he'd arrived. One of the valets hurried over, hunched against the cold, and looked relieved when Remy waved him away.

A moment later, she came out, bundled up and

beautiful, struggling as she tried to balance her suitcase with her ski gear. Remy jumped out to help her, then stowed her gear in the back. Once she'd settled into the passenger seat, she looked at him and grinned.

That grin settled into his heart like a shot of fine whiskey, momentarily knocking the breath from him.

"What an adventure!" she exclaimed, peering out past the light as if trying to see through the swirling snow. "Did you have any trouble getting here?"

"Not really. The plows have stopped for the night, but this Jeep has four-wheel drive."

To his amused disbelief, she appeared excited. "I love four-wheeling," she said.

He drove slowly, his grip tight on the wheel, ready for the slightest skid. Though the snow had filled in any previous tire tracks, as long as it was just powder, the roads would be fine.

"No one else is out," she commented.

"Because everyone has better sense. I imagine they're either in bed under multiple blankets or sitting by roaring fireplaces."

"I hear that. I love a good fireplace."

Suddenly he wanted nothing more than to be cuddling on his couch with her in front of a fire. Blinking, he pushed the tantalizing images from his mind.

Finally, they pulled onto his street. On one side, all of the homes sat on small hills—on the other, the land was flat. He'd always considered himself fortunate to have his little hill with a view.

"Is this where you live?" she asked.

He answered in the affirmative.

Vanessa gave him a sideways glance. "Okay, I'm going to ask you something weird." She took a deep breath, while his imagination went wild. "Could you do a few donuts before we pull into your driveway? I've always loved doing them in fresh powder, as long as there's nothing around to hit."

This made him chuckle. "Are you serious?"

"Yep." She nudged his shoulder with her own. "It's already been a strange night. Indulge me."

Eying her, he shrugged. "I don't know. The streets seem clear of other vehicles, but there are still mail-boxes and evergreens I could hit."

She snorted. "Fine. Never mind then." The amused scorn in her tone made him blink.

The seventeen-year-old boy buried deep inside him responded. Easing up on the gas, he pressed the brake and turned the wheel, sending his Jeep fishtailing. Though he hadn't even thought to try doing donuts since his youth, he hadn't forgotten how.

And the joyous purity of Vanessa's laughter was all the reward he needed.

Back at his house, he pulled into the garage and killed the engine. "You can leave your ski gear in the car for now," he told her. She followed him inside, her expression curious.

"Nice decorating," she said, turning in a slow circle. "Did you hire a designer?"

"No. I'm not much for that kind of stuff. All the artwork came from the last time my aunt and uncle had their house redone. They were going to toss the discards, so I picked everything up. Luckily, all this happened to be in a Western theme, which I can live with. What I didn't use, I donated to Goodwill."

"Interesting."

He crossed the room and relit the gas logs in the

fireplace, instantly sending flames dancing. "Make yourself comfortable," he told her. "Would you like something to drink?"

Shaking her head, she covered her mouth with her hand to mask a yawn. "I'm good, thank you."

"I need to go make up the guest bed. It should only take me a few minutes."

She turned to face him. "No need to go through the trouble. If you'll just give me the bed linens, I can do it. I'm kind of tired and would really like to just get some sleep."

Remy felt his expression soften as he looked at her. Considering she'd been rushed out of the hotel suite he'd promised her she could use as long as she wanted, she seemed to be in pretty good spirits. Most women he knew would have been complaining bitterly. Not Vanessa. She seemed resilient as hell.

This only made him like her more.

"Come this way," he said. "Two work faster than one, so we can make the bed up together."

After making a stop at the linen closet to grab a set of sheets and a blanket, he led the way into the guest bedroom. With Vanessa on one side of the bed and him on the other, they made quick work of getting it ready. He hadn't realized how intimate such a mundane task could be, or how her presence would make the room seem to shrink.

"There you are." He managed to speak normally, despite his supercharged awareness of her.

Her answering smile nearly undid him. "Thank you," she murmured. "I really appreciate you doing this for me."

He nodded and turned to head for the door, intending to tell her to sleep well as soon as he'd reached the relative safety of the hall. But she moved at the same moment and they nearly collided.

Remy froze. Vanessa gazed up at him, her huge blue eyes guileless and shining. What else could he do then but give in to the impulse to kiss her?

The first brush of his lips on hers, meant to be casual, slow and tender, instantly became anything but. As she met him halfway, his hunger flared and his senses reeled. The taste of her was heady, demanding more. When she returned his kiss with reckless abandon, he forced himself to rein in his desire to devour her.

Except she was having none of that. Pulling him down to her, she had them both tumbling onto the freshly made bed.

In that instant, he was lost.

Chapter 7

They locked lips, tongues as tangled as their bodies, the kisses deep and wet and sensual as hell. The two of them touched and caressed and made love with their mouths until Vanessa thought she might combust. Damn. She wanted more. *So much more.* This man— his taste, his touch—drove her wild, made her feel wanton and hungry. Aching, burning, melting, she knew she'd never been so close to losing control.

And she couldn't let herself. Not now. Not yet. Maybe not ever.

"Wait," she said breathlessly, shuddering, barely able to find the strength to pull out of his arms. "We can't. I'm sorry. But—"

Remy looked as shaken as she felt. "You're right," he said, his voice whiskey-rough and sexy as hell. He pushed to his feet, but not before she'd seen the very visible proof of his desire. Her knees went weak. "I don't know what got into me. I apologize."

She wanted to tell him no need, that they'd both been responsible for the kiss. But she didn't, thinking maybe it might be better this way.

"I hope you don't think that this is the reason I invited you here," he continued. "Because I promise you, it isn't."

He looked so miserable, she knew she should say something to ease the tension and make him feel better. But how could she, when every second she spent with this man had her wanting more?

Though she'd never been a risk taker except on the slopes, she decided to take one now. "Remy, I like you. A lot. I think maybe we should just take things slow, but I definitely want to give this a shot. If it goes somewhere, great. If not, that's fine, too."

"This?" He raised an eyebrow. "Do you mean...?"

His hopeful expression made her laugh out loud. "Maybe eventually." She waved her hand vaguely toward the bed. "I mean getting to know each other. I don't know, but I have a feeling that this could be—"

"Something special." His intent gaze told her she'd made the right decision. "I agree. I want you to stay here as long as you like. We can take our time. I'd like to court you, date you and learn everything I can about you."

She laughed. "Sounds like fun. But let's not get ahead of ourselves. We'll just take it a day at a time. Either way, I think we'll have lots of fun."

Slowly, he nodded. "I got ahead of myself there."

"I think we both did." She smiled gently to let him know the encounter had been more than mutual.

He exhaled. "But what about Seth?"

Seth. For a moment, her heart fell. Then she raised her head. "All my life, I've had other people make decisions about what I should and shouldn't be doing. Seth knows exactly how I feel about him. I'd love to remain friends with him, nothing more. Besides that, I owe him." She cleared her throat. "But while I want to be there for him, if he doesn't want assistance, there's little I can do. I've been nothing but honest and up-front with him."

Pausing, she took a deep breath. "All that said, I think we should be careful. Whatever comes of this, I don't want to hurt him. And I never want to cause problems between two brothers."

The smoldering flame in his eyes warmed her.

"Thank you for that. Keeping any sort of relationship with Seth is already difficult enough," Remy said. "And I definitely don't want to do anything that might push him to do anything crazy. Or," he amended, "crazier than he's already done."

Sobering, she nodded. "Agreed. I'm hopeful you can talk him into going to rehab again. I really think he needs the help."

"I'll do my damnedest." Reaching for her again, he pulled her close for a hug, letting her feel the full force of his arousal. She melted, but managed to keep herself still.

After a moment, he released her—reluctantly, she thought.

"Get some sleep," he said. "The weather forecast said this snow should let up by tomorrow afternoon. Hopefully, Pine Peak will be able to reopen. If not, feel free to hang out here. I'm planning to go into the office for a little bit, though not too long. With most of my staff on vacation, I'm not going to make anyone struggle through the storm to make it in."

He stepped back, moving through the door until he stood in the hall. "I'll see you in the morning, Vanessa. The bathroom is right across the hall and I'll put fresh towels in there for you." Then he closed the door, leaving her alone in the small room.

To her surprise, she felt his absence like a cold draft. She shivered, already missing the warmth of his arms.

What had she gotten herself into? She wasn't sure, but the thought of going back to Boulder without giving Remy a chance made her ache with the kind of loss she'd felt when she'd learned her parents were gone. It was damn near unbearable.

Before she could lose her nerve, she opened her suitcase and unpacked it, hanging some things up in the closet, putting others away in the empty dresser drawers. Weird, maybe. But this decision to stay with Remy felt right.

The next morning when she woke, at first she had no idea where she was. Bright whiteness, the kind that only came from a good snowfall outside, came through the window despite the blinds. Stretching, she sat up in bed, and remembered. Warmth and joy slammed into her, along with a healthy dose of trepidation.

The kiss and all the heat behind it had invaded her dreams. She finger combed her hair, thinking that she hadn't felt like this since she'd been a teenager infatuated with the neighbor, a boy two years older than her named Taylor Hopkins. Of course, nothing had come of that. She'd been way too shy and her crush had been complicated by the fact that she'd only seen him on the few occasions when she'd been allowed to go home to Boston. Somehow she'd made it through four years of university in Boulder without getting involved in a serious relationship.

She'd dated, certainly. And a couple of the boys had wanted to take things to the next level, but since she hadn't been feeling it, she never had. Even with Seth, she'd always felt detached, as though she was viewing the relationship from a distance.

This thing with Remy was different. Or could be. Since being with him she felt more alive, more *present*, than she'd ever felt. For the first time in her life, she had high hopes, which might be ridiculous. Who knew?

After taking a hot shower, she blow-dried her hair and applied a little makeup, secretly amused at how badly she wanted to look good for Remy.

Finally, dressed and ready to face the day, she went out into the hallway, following the scent of coffee to the kitchen. She stopped short in the doorway, taking it all in. This room surprised her, too. Instead of being a utilitarian kitchen, Remy's could have been featured in a magazine spread on gourmet kitchens. It featured white cabinets, a beautiful quartz countertop, top-of-the-line stainless-steel appliances and a huge vent hood. She stood for a moment with her mouth open, staring around her in awe.

Remy sat at the kitchen bar, scrolling through his phone while nursing a cup of coffee. He looked up when she entered, his intent gaze locking on hers.

Again she felt that fierce pull of attraction.

"Coffee?" he asked, pointing to his single-cup coffee

maker. "I've got several varieties of pods stored in the caddy underneath it. Pick whichever one you want."

Tongue-tied, she chose a bold coffee she'd had often while in the Pacific Northwest. Once it finished brewing, she fixed her cup to her liking, then took a seat on the bar stool next to him. "Any word on Pine Peak?" she asked.

"Not yet. They sent out the ski patrol at first light to check on conditions. They said they'd update the web page as soon as they knew."

Grimacing, she sipped her cup. "After that much snow, I bet they'll have some cleanup to do."

"Most likely," he agreed. "I'm going to go in to the office for a little while. There's plenty of food in the fridge—eggs, bread, whatever you might want. I have oatmeal in the pantry. Feel free to help yourself to anything. I want you to make yourself at home."

Suddenly feeling shy, she nodded. "Thank you. At some point, I'll need a ride back to The Chateau so I can get my car."

"We can do that." He hesitated, and then leaned over and kissed her cheek. "I'll see you later. Call or text me if you need anything."

She promised she would.

After Remy left, she wandered his house, feeling aimless. The snow had finally stopped falling, but the wind gusts remained in the dangerous category, so Pine Peak remained closed. She'd read on their Facebook page that controlled avalanches were being set off to minimize the risk of a real one occurring and injuring or killing skiers later.

Since she loved snow, she put on her parka and went out into his backyard. Just a few minutes of watching the wind blow the snow into drifts was enough, and she went back inside.

While she was out there, she saw she'd missed two calls and two messages. Before she could even listen to them, her phone rang again. When she saw Seth's number on the caller ID, she let it go to voicemail. A moment later, she heard the chime that signified she'd received a third voicemail. Since she needed to warm herself up, she'd check it along with the others after making a cup of hot tea.

Five minutes later, feeling slightly warmer, she sat down with her hot drink to listen to her messages. They were all from Seth, and with her heart in her throat, she played the first one.

"Hey, Van. Just checking to see where you are and if you're okay. I realized you never told me where you ended up staying. Maybe you made it back to Boulder? If you're still in town, please give me a call back. I need to talk to you about something important."

The second and third messages were repeats of the first, though the tone became angrier and more insistent.

She sighed. Right now, she wasn't in the mood for drama, and the instant she told Seth she was now staying at Remy's, she knew he'd get upset. And that would be putting it mildly.

Barely ten more minutes passed before her phone rang again. Seth. He left a fourth message. She decided not to listen to it just yet. She'd begun to realize he had every intention of blowing up her phone until she gave in and answered. This made her even more determined that she wouldn't. She hated manipulation and games.

During the course of the morning, Seth called eight times more, for a total of twelve. He left messages with every call. Staring at the steadily rising number showing on the message display, she shook her head. Seth had gone off the rails for no reason. She could only imagine what he'd do if he knew where to find her. The thought made her shudder.

Finally, she put her phone on silent mode. She wasn't sure how to deal with all this, and briefly considered calling Remy. But she didn't want to start their first day together by bothering him at work.

Since there seemed no point in going into town, she puttered around the house. Remy had said to make herself at home, so she did. When he called around lunchtime to check on her, she missed the call, but knowing he'd be home soon, she decided she'd wait to talk to him then instead of phoning him back. Seth's constant barrage had given her a major headache. Trying to focus on the positive, she thought she'd see about cooking them both a nice dinner.

Checking in Remy's freezer, she located a package of meat. In the fridge, he had fresh carrots, celery, onions and potatoes—in short, everything she needed to make beef stew. Remy even had a nice bottle of Shiraz they could have with dinner. The only thing missing would be a nice loaf of crusty French bread, but she didn't need the carbs, anyway.

Glad she had something to do to occupy her time and help her ignore her phone, she happily got to work chopping up vegetables, humming as she worked. She felt very domestic all of a sudden, something she rarely ever experienced. Her first home-cooked dinner for a member of the opposite sex. And not just any guy, but Remy. The sexiest, kindest, most generous man she'd ever met.

As soon as he got to the mostly deserted office, Remy called his cousin Molly, Sabrina's sister. "Did you know anything about Sabrina and Seth dating?" he asked, keeping his tone casual.

"I knew she was seeing someone, but she never mentioned anyone specifically," Molly answered after considering his question for a moment. "Sabrina and I pretty much lived separate lives and we hardly ever even talked, except to comment on each other's Facebook or Instagram accounts. She'd been posting some random things just before her death."

As someone who'd always yearned for a family, Remy truly didn't understand when those who were lucky enough to have one didn't appreciate it. But that was just him.

"Okay." Remy cleared his throat. "Anyway, send me what you've got, please." Ending the call, he waited while the texts came in. Molly sent ten photos, three of them from Facebook, three from Instagram and four from Snapchat.

She was right, he thought. They were intense ramblings about the dark side of life and love, not the sort of factual, day-to-day life things Sabrina usually posted. Unless, he thought, she had been high on drugs. Since she'd been a big party girl, that would always be a possibility, but he'd never seen her post anything that weird, ever.

Which meant what? That someone else had been posting to her social media? Maybe even the killer? But why? The only thing Remy could come up with was the possibility the posts had been meant to throw police off the killer's tracks.

He called Molly back. "I got them."

"Weird, aren't they?" Molly said.

"Yes, they are. I agree with you. None of those seem like something Sabrina would have posted. Did you show the police what you sent me?"

"I never mentioned it to them," she admitted. "I've been so overwhelmed by my grief that it slipped my mind, and I honestly never thought it was very relevant to the case."

"I think it's relevant now," he said, feeling certain. "Especially since the authorities have learned she wasn't murdered by the Avalanche Killer. I suggest you get ahold of Daria Bloom, the deputy sheriff in charge of the case, and show her what you've got. I'm pretty sure she'll want to see them."

"Do you think so?" Molly sounded uncertain. "I guess I can try. Do you really think they mean anything?"

"I'm not sure. But the police will know. It couldn't hurt."

After ending the call, Remy sat in silence for a moment trying to gather his thoughts. Why Sabrina? Why had she been singled out? Of course, he and everyone else had wondered the same things about each and every one of the women the Avalanche Killer had murdered. And as far as he knew, the entire town had believed Sabrina had been another one of his victims.

Sabrina had been strangled, just like the others. But the Avalanche Killer, aka Curtis Shruggs, had been eager to confess to his kills after he'd been apprehended last month. Curtis had been proud of his work, defiant in his belief that his actions had been not only necessary, but also justified. He could name each and every one of his victims, in chronological order.

He'd been emphatic that Sabrina Gilford hadn't been one of them.

At first, the police hadn't wanted to believe it. They'd thought they had their killer caught, the case solved and it had all been wrapped up in a neat little bow.

And then they didn't. If Curtis hadn't killed Sabrina, then who had?

Remy shook his head, reluctant to face up to the truth. While in college, Sabrina had been a party animal. She'd gotten worse once she'd graduated. He couldn't help but wonder if her getting together with Seth might have had something to do with that. Seth and his predilection for drugs, combined with Sabrina's never-ending quest for fun, would have been a nightmare waiting to happen. Alcohol, drugs and two people who didn't know when to stop.

But would Seth really have killed her? Was his baby brother even the type of person who could kill? And why would he? Sabrina had been strangled in a deliberate attempt to mimic the Avalanche Killer. Remy thought if Seth had managed to do something stupid while under the influence, it wouldn't be murder by strangulation.

Relieved and a little bit ashamed that he'd even been considering the possibility that his brother could be a cold-blooded murderer, he shook his head. Seth might be a mess, but he wasn't a killer.

He couldn't help but wonder how someone like Vanessa, who didn't seem to be big on partying, had gotten along with his brother. It almost was like Seth might have had two different personalities, showing one side to Vanessa and a completely different side to Sabrina. Especially since it appeared he'd dated both women at the same time.

Had Sabrina been aware of this? Vanessa clearly hadn't.

Now Sabrina was gone. Dead too soon. And the police didn't seem to have any idea who might have killed her. Did Seth?

Uneasy, Remy shifted his weight in his chair. Now that Vanessa had told him about the files she'd found on Seth's computer, he had no choice but to consider the possibility that Seth might have been involved. Even if he hadn't actually taken Sabrina's life, he might know something that could be of use to the police in helping them find the killer.

Remy didn't think the police had even questioned him. Why would they? No one had even known he and Sabrina had been dating. How had that been possible? Had the two of them snuck around, relishing their shared secret?

Seth had even kept this from his own brother. What else had he kept secret? Remy wouldn't have known about any of this if Vanessa hadn't looked at Seth's personal computer.

What a mess. While he didn't want to give away Vanessa, he had to figure out how to best bring up the subject with Seth. It was time he found out exactly what was going on in his baby brother's head.

Checking his watch, Remy saw it was nearly lunchtime. Since the snow had stopped falling and the plow had been through, Remy decided to see if Seth wanted to get together for a bite to eat. He dialed his brother's number. Seth answered on the second ring, sounding both out of breath and furious.

"What?" he snarled.

"Are you okay?" Remy asked. "I'm calling to see if we can get together for lunch. We need to talk."

No response, only by the harsh rasp of Seth's agitated breathing. "I don't know," he finally said, still sounding as if his teeth were clenched. "I'm trying to get ahold of Vanessa. I have no idea where she is. She just up and disappeared when you took me to the hospital."

Not sure how to respond to that, unless Seth asked, Remy knew it would be best not to mention Vanessa at all. "I'm sure she's fine. How about lunch? Getting a good burger in your stomach might make you feel a little better. I can pick you up in ten minutes."

Another moment of quiet, during which Remy prayed Seth wouldn't ask him if he'd seen her.

"Fine," he finally responded. "I could eat. Are you buying? Because I don't have any cash and my credit cards are maxed out."

Though this comment made Remy wince, he kept that to himself. "Of course I'm buying." He always did. Not once in all the time Seth had been working here in Roaring Springs had he offered to pick up the check. Remy figured he never would. After all, that's what big brothers were for.

Before he left, he decided to call and check on Vanessa. She didn't answer, so he left a voicemail, letting her know he was just checking on her and he'd see her when he got home later.

Vanessa. Seth still seemed obsessed with her, and

Remy could understand why. She was special, the real deal. And while he didn't want to skulk around with her behind his brother's back, he also had no intention of setting off Seth.

Swinging by Seth's condo, Remy tried not to think of the last time he'd been here. He pulled up out front, texted his brother to let him know he'd arrived and waited. Seth came out the door a few minutes later, wearing a beat-up down puffer jacket that had seen better days. With his five o'clock shadow and blood-shot eyes, he looked as if he'd just gotten off of a three-day bender.

When he let himself into Remy's Jeep, a foul odor of alcohol mixed with sweat and cigarettes came with him, so strong Remy had to force himself not to react.

"You look like hell," he said, frowning. "What is going on with you?"

"I don't want to talk about it." Seth slouched down in the seat. "You promised to feed me. Let's do that."

While Remy drove, his brother messed with his phone, sending text after text and then waiting for a reply. When nothing came, he texted again. "Why won't she answer me?" Seth finally asked out loud. "What kind of friend avoids me after I was just in the hospital?"

Swearing softly under his breath, Remy glanced sideways at his brother. "Are you talking about Vanessa?"

Seth shot him an aggravated look. "Who else would I be talking about? I already told you I've been try-ing to reach her all day. I know she's not skiing since they haven't opened up Pine Peak yet. So why is she avoiding me?"

"I don't know," Remy drawled. "Maybe because you scared the hell out of her?"

"How?" Seth scoffed at the idea. "I was a perfect gentleman."

"Are you serious?" Remy chided. "You got drunk off your ass and cut yourself badly on broken glass, and then blatantly refused to go to the hospital." He tightened his grip on the steering wheel, trying to keep his temper in check, and a stony silence fell between the two of them for the remainder of the ride to the Honest Slims' Barbeque joint. Despite the weather, or maybe because of it, the small parking lot was almost full.

The instant they stepped out of the Jeep, the delicious aroma of barbeque smoke made Remy's mouth water. Even Seth appeared to perk up. "I thought you said burgers," he protested half-heartedly.

"I changed my mind." For Remy, the decision to eat at Slims' had been spur-of-the-moment. He'd been about to drive past and head to one of the burger joints at the south end of town. Instead, he'd realized he craved brisket and potato salad. Since Seth had always loved Slims', he'd figured it would be a win-win situation.

"You know what? I'm glad. This sounds better." Grinning widely, Seth glanced around and rubbed his stomach. "And I'm starving."

"When was the last time you ate?" Remy held the door open, allowing his brother to precede him into the restaurant.

"Not sure." Seth wouldn't look at him. "It's probably been a while."

Remy held his tongue as they went through the

order line. Both men placed identical orders—brisket, potato salad and fried okra. Seth got sweet tea while Remy chose unsweet.

They carried their trays to a table near the front window. Not Remy's first choice—he'd hoped for a quieter booth but they were all full.

As soon as they sat down, Seth began chowing down, his head bent and completely focused. After a moment's hesitation, Remy did the same, giving himself time to figure out the best way to bring up Sabrina.

Before he could, Seth brought her up himself. "I think I must be bad luck. I dated Sabrina Gilford and she ended up dead. I hope the same thing hasn't happened to Vanessa."

Remy almost choked on his brisket. He fought the urge to bring out his phone and call Vanessa instantly, just so he could hear her voice. Luckily, he got himself under control, aware Seth had no idea where she was staying and would never think to look at Remy's place.

"What do you mean?" he finally asked, in as calm a voice as possible.

"Just commented on bad luck." Seth shrugged. "It just about killed me to learn what had happened to Sabrina." He made a face. "Right after Sabrina and I broke up, she was murdered. And they haven't found the killer. I hope the same thing doesn't happen to Vanessa. Especially since she's hanging around Roaring Springs."

Remy could hardly believe what he'd just heard. "Is that a threat?" he asked quietly, his stomach twisting.

"Of course not." Seth shook his head. "You know me, bro. I'd never hurt a woman I loved like that."

He sounded sincere. Remy relaxed slightly. Seth was his brother, after all. Damaged, true, but not a killer.

Chapter 8

At least Seth had finally stopped calling, though when Vanessa picked up her phone again, now that the stew was simmering, she saw he'd sent thirty-eight text messages to go along with the twelve voicemails.

This scared the hell out of her. Excessive much? The Seth she'd known before would never have done something like this. This Seth seemed to be skirting on the edge of violence.

And the other woman he'd been dating had ended up dead.

Shivering, she shook her head. Seth had been a friend to her when she needed one. She couldn't wrap her mind around the possibility that he might have killed a woman in cold blood and tried to make it look as if she was just another of a serial killer's victims.

Maybe she was looking at this the wrong way. Alcoholism and drug issues did not make Seth a murderer. Neither did dating two women at the same time. She knew Seth, had known him for a long time, and she couldn't imagine him intentionally hurting another human being. *Intentionally* being the key word. What kind of things he might be capable of when under the influence, she didn't know. But surely not murder.

Then why was she so afraid of him?

Tired of questions she couldn't answer and having awful speculations without proof, she stirred the stew and got busy tidying the kitchen. When she'd finished that, she decided to do a load of laundry. Since she'd packed limited clothing for what had been supposed to be a short trip, she needed to wash what she had or she would have to go out and buy herself some more things to wear. Exploring the house, she discovered Remy had built a really nice home gym in the basement. She spent a good hour down there lifting weights and running on his treadmill.

Finally, after taking a quick shower, she returned to the kitchen, double-checked the stew and waited for Remy to get home. Funny, this domestic feeling. She'd never felt like this, not even when she'd purchased her first home in Boulder. She wasn't entirely sure why she did now.

Finally, she heard Remy's Jeep pulling into the driveway and her heart began to race. Smoothing her palms down the front of her leggings, she wondered if she should try to appear busy, as if she hadn't been breathlessly anticipating his return all day.

In the end, she decided the heck with it and raced to meet him at the door.

"Hi!" she greeted him, feeling heat turn her cheeks

pink. He stopped short, his lean frame both casual and serious.

"Hi yourself."

Uncertain how to act, she stepped back so he could come inside. "Did you have a good day?" she asked, aware she might be babbling, but unable to stop it.

"I did. Things are kind of slow at the office, but I talked to Seth today at lunch," Remy said, finally pulling her in for a hug and kissing her cheek. "At first, judging by the way he was talking, I thought he was about to confess to killing Sabrina Gilford." He gave a short, uncomfortable laugh before releasing her. "Instead, to my relief, he shared a few insights with me. They were actually valid. He thinks he might know who killed her."

Feeling both cautiously optimistic and skeptical, Vanessa crossed her arms. "Did he talk to the police?"

"Not yet. He's promised to, later today. I'll follow up with them tomorrow morning." He laughed, a painful sound that matched the haunted look lingering in his eyes. "I can't tell you how much better I felt after hearing that. I'd seriously begun to worry Seth might have been involved."

Lifting his head, Remy glanced into the kitchen at the stove. "Whatever you've got simmering there smells delicious."

"Thanks. It's beef stew. It'll be done in a few hours, just in time for dinner." She refused to be distracted, even if she wanted to kiss him until she couldn't think straight. "Did Seth actually pass along his information to you? Or did he just vaguely mention he had some?"

Remy chuckled. "That's exactly what he tried to do at first, but I pressed him. No way was I letting him off the hook that easily. It turned out Sabrina was cheating on him."

"Like he was cheating on her?" Vanessa interjected. "And me?"

"Yes. He showed me text messages and a few snapshots on his phone of Sabrina and her other boyfriend. Apparently, he accidentally ran into them."

Or he stalked them. Vanessa didn't voice that thought out loud. Though she hated to burst Remy's bubble, she had to point out the obvious. "But doesn't that make him even more of a suspect?" she asked. "Now he would have a motive."

Remy froze. "I can't believe that didn't occur to me. I guess I'm just having difficulty thinking of my baby brother as a killer."

Now or never. Without saying anything else, she handed him her phone.

At first, he stared at the screen, not comprehending. "You have thirty-eight text messages?"

Slowly, she nodded. "And twelve voicemails. All from Seth."

Remy had already opened the text messages and started reading. His frown deepened. "This is crazy."

She kept silent, letting him make his way through them. When he finished, he raised his head and met her gaze, his own tortured. "I can't believe this."

Taking a deep breath, she nodded. "I know. Me neither. The voice messages are worse."

"Worse?" Remy's voice rose. "I just had lunch with him. He mentioned he was trying to get ahold of you, but nothing about blowing up your phone with incessant texts." Clearly stricken, he tried to hand her back her phone.

"Did you want to listen to the voicemails?" she asked, refusing to take it. She hated the way she felt— like she'd just crushed his heart. But none of this was her fault, and if Seth was as dangerous as he had begun to seem, someone needed to stop him before he hurt someone else.

"No. Not right now." Remy dragged his hand through his hair. "I'm not sure I can take it. To be frank, I'm not sure what to think."

"You need to play them," she gently pointed out. "Please. I'm scared and worried."

Still holding her phone, he took a deep breath and then nodded. Gaze locked on hers, he pressed Play on the first voice message.

She stood, silent and still, while Remy doggedly made it through all of the increasingly awful voicemails Seth had left. While he had never come right out and actually threatened her, some of the creepy things he'd said could definitely be construed that way. Hearing them replayed hurt her heart.

Once he'd finished listening, Remy shook his head. His complexion had gone ashen. "I'm so, so sorry," he said quietly. "You shouldn't have to go through this. No one should. This has got to stop now." Then he pressed the icon to call Seth back.

Eyes wide, she took a step back. Though doing so might be ridiculous, she didn't want to be anywhere near Remy when he and his brother spoke. As if Seth's bad energy could somehow reach through the phone and hurt her.

Gaze locked on hers, Remy put the call on speaker.

"It's about time you called me back," Seth answered, his voice flat and eerily calm. "Where the hell are you? And why haven't you been picking up your phone?"

"It's me, Seth," Remy said, the sharp edge to his tone letting his brother know he meant business. "Vanessa just let me see her phone with all the texts you sent, and I've listened to the voicemails, too. I've got you on speakerphone. What the hell is wrong with you?"

"Vanessa is with *you*?" Seth roared. "What the—"

"Stop." The single barked order had immediate results. Seth went silent, and Vanessa nervously twisted her hands, wondering for the hundredth time what had happened to the kind, caring man she'd once known.

"You've been frightening the hell out of Vanessa," Remy continued, his voice like steel. "And quite honestly, after reading those text messages, me, too."

For a moment, Seth didn't respond. When he finally spoke, he'd clearly dialed back his anger and resentment. "You're right," he said, surprising her. "I acted like an ass. Vanessa, will you ever forgive me?"

Remy started to reply, but she held up her hand to let him know that she wanted to handle this herself.

"Seth, I'm not sure an apology is going to do it this time," she said, her voice resolute. "I really feel you need to get some help, whether it's for addiction or anger issues or both. Either way, for the first time since I met you, I felt as if I was in danger from you."

"I would never hurt you, Van."

"Maybe not," she concurred. "But the way you've been acting since I arrived in Roaring Springs is nothing like the guy I know. Nothing."

"I know." Subdued, Seth suddenly appeared to be on the verge of tears. "I need help. Remy, I promise

I'll go back to rehab after the holidays. In the meantime, I can start going back to the AA and NA meetings. Will that be enough for you, Vanessa?"

"Seth, this shouldn't be about me. You have to want to get help for *you*. I shouldn't factor into this at all."

Remy cleared his throat. "She's right," he finally said. "Unless you want to do this for you, it's not going to stick."

"I know, I know." Conciliatory now, Seth sighed. "I'm messed up. I love you both and I appreciate you sticking with me through all of this. Van, I'll try harder to improve on being your friend and, Remy, I know I need to be a better brother. I should have told you that at lunch today. I'm sorry. I'll leave you alone now."

"You're not going to start drinking, are you?" Vanessa asked worriedly. "I know you're upset and that's your default coping mechanism."

A thread of bitterness ran through Seth's self-deprecating laugh. "While I will admit that is tempting, I plan to pour out every bit of any alcohol I have left. Then I'm going to call the guy that was acting as my sponsor before I went off the wagon and talk to him. I won't bother you again tonight. Take care, both of you." And he ended the call.

Placing her phone on the table, Vanessa sat down on one of the bar stools before her legs gave out. Putting her head into her hands, she took several deep, shuddering breaths. When she finally raised her head, she found Remy watching her. His hands were clenched into fists, as if to keep himself from touching her. That's when she realized he struggled with this attraction as much as she did.

"Seth sounds very sincere," she breathed.

"He does." Remy swallowed, still holding her gaze. "I worry so damn much about him. He's really messed up, but there's a good person somewhere inside him, I know it."

"There is." She hastened to reassure him. "He just got a little lost."

Remy lowered himself onto the bar stool next to her, sitting so close their knees touched. "Are you all right?"

The concern in his deep voice warmed her. Slowly, she nodded. "How about you?"

He smiled. "I'm about to be a lot better," he said, right before he leaned over and kissed her.

She melted into him, matching the heat of his lips on hers with a passion of her own. He didn't touch her—not yet—and she didn't touch him either. The only place their bodies fused was their mouths. She wanted to devour him, her tongue dancing with his, every movement searing her. He slanted his mouth over hers, caressing her lips again and again, until she couldn't restrain herself any longer. She pulled back and, quivering, she reached for him. Then, ever so slowly, she slid her hand down his muscular chest. Heart hammering against her ribs, she reveled in the feel of him, enjoying the heat blazing from his eyes as he watched her. Emboldened, she let her fingers explore every inch of his upper torso, stopping just short of his belt.

"Go ahead," he rasped, still watching her with those hot, hungry eyes. She liked that he kept his hands locked on the counter, loved that he let her do this in her own time, her own way.

Body tingling, she continued her lazy exploration.

His harsh intake of breath when she reached for his belt buckle caused a shivery ache inside of her.

When the buckle came free, she undid his jeans, letting his magnificent arousal spring free. Eying him, she licked her lips. She ached to take him into her mouth, but as she bent to do exactly that, he stopped her. "Not yet," he groaned, his voice raw. "I want to be inside you first."

Immediately, blood surged to her lady parts. He kissed her again, his lips scorching her skin as he moved from her mouth to her neck. With one deft movement, he unhooked her bra, helping her remove it and her shirt. Grinning at each other, they both divested themselves of the rest of their clothing, standing naked and unashamed in front of each other.

Now she let her gaze feast on him, loving his lean, athletic frame with broad shoulders and narrow hips. Muscular, too, the kind that came from regular workouts in the gym.

Heat blazed from his eyes as he caressed her, cupping her breasts before lowering his head to taste. His tongue lathed her sensitive nipples and she groaned. Pleasure radiated to her core, and she felt liquid heat flowing through her. She was ready. More than ready.

"Now," she ordered, tugging him to her. Tangled together, they moved into his bedroom and, kissing ravenously, fell backward onto his bed.

Finally, Remy lowered his body over hers. She pulled him close, welcoming him. With one swift movement, he buried himself deep inside her, filling her. Savage, such primal, raw possession. He groaned, she sighed, and again, they paused and grinned at each other. Though he was already hard, she felt him swell even more inside. As he began to move, the pure, explosive pleasure made her arch her back and cry out.

She met him thrust for thrust, as hungry for him as he appeared to be for her.

This, she thought. This was what she'd been missing all along. And then she felt herself ride the crest all the way to the top, before shattering into a thousand stars.

Lying with Vanessa snuggled in his arms, in the aftermath of what had been the most powerful, earth-shattering lovemaking he'd ever experienced, Remy marveled at the miracle that had brought her to him. He breathed in the clean, strawberry scent of her silky hair, with his eyes half-closed, wondering if he'd actually drift off to sleep. Just the feel of her soft skin and lush curves pressed against him had him half-aroused again.

Realizing he'd forgotten to set the alarm, he considered the plausibility of easing out from her arms and walking naked over to the keypad so he could do that. Especially since they had a killer on the loose in Roaring Springs, he would feel safer with the alarm set. He guessed that came from growing up in Whit's mansion. His father had always been an overly paranoid sort, and Remy had come to feel having to set and disarm multiple alarms anytime he arrived or left was normal. Now, in his own home, he had only one, very high-tech system for which he paid dearly.

Best to get up and set it.

No sooner had he reached a decision than he heard the sound of someone unlocking the front door. Or *trying* to. Heart pounding, he leaned over Vanessa to get his pistol from his nightstand. She woke and sat up, her elbow banging him hard in the nose. Head reeling from that, he moved her aside, pushing past the sudden pain to focus on the danger.

The bedroom light came on. Cursing, Remy grabbed his pistol and flicked off the safety. He spun, pushing her behind him as he brought up his weapon, ready to defend Vanessa at all costs.

Seth stood in the doorway, staring at both of them with an expression of shocked disbelief.

Vanessa gasped, yanking the sheet up to cover her breasts.

"I knew it." Seth didn't bother to conceal the bitter hurt in his voice. "The two of you have been getting it on behind my back."

"It's not like that," Remy began. "How did you get in here?"

"You gave me a key," his brother reminded him, his expression dark. "Not once in my wildest dreams did I imagine I'd walk in and find the two of you doing the nasty."

"It's not like that," Remy repeated.

"Oh, really? Because it sure looked like that to me."

Looking from one man to the other, Vanessa shook her head. "We are so not having this discussion right now, right here. Seth, please wait for us in the kitchen. We'll be right out after we get dressed. Then we can all talk like reasonable adults."

For a second or two, Remy actually thought Seth was going to do as she asked. Still framed in the doorway, he actually hesitated. Then his expression crumpled. "You don't want me to see you without your clothes on."

"That's right." Vanessa spoke with a calmness

Remy knew for certain she didn't feel. He knew because her heart pounded under his arm.

"Please close the door behind you and wait for us in the kitchen," she commanded softly. "As soon as we're dressed, we'll meet you there and we can all talk."

Seth slammed out of the room without another word.

Remy let out a breath he hadn't even been aware he'd been holding.

"Oh, wow," Vanessa said, her blue eyes huge. "This isn't going to go over well."

"I agree." Grimly, Remy put the safety back on his gun and returned it to the nightstand drawer. Still wide-eyed, she watched him, but made no comment. He began gathering up their clothes, handing Vanessa hers, and they both got dressed in silence.

"This—us—meant more than what it must have looked like to Seth," he commented, swallowing hard.

"Yes," she agreed. "It was." She tugged her shirt over her head.

When they were done, Remy took her hand. "Are you ready?"

She gave a slow nod. "At least we don't have to hide anything now."

"True." He opened the bedroom door and, still hand in hand, they went out to face the music.

Seth was in the kitchen, slurping up a bowl of Vanessa's beef stew. "Is this your specialty?" he asked her. "Or did Remy make this?"

"I did."

Seth nodded. "This is really great."

Clearly uneasy, she shrugged. "Thanks."

"Get some. Join me," Seth prompted. "Let's all have a meal together like we're one big, happy family."

Remy sighed, his gut twisting. Even though his brother's voice hadn't contained even one ounce of sarcasm, what else could it be? "We'll eat later," he said. "Right now, we just want to talk."

"I'm sure you do." Still cordial and pleasant, Seth grabbed his now-empty bowl and returned to the stove to get a generous helping of seconds. He whistled as he filled his bowl.

Vanessa exchanged a worried glance with Remy. He dipped his chin, trying to let her know he felt he could keep the situation under control. Especially since Seth now appeared determined to kill them with kindness. Though it worried him that his brother now acted as if he had multiple personalities.

Inwardly wincing, Remy waited until Seth sat back down. "I'm really sorry that you had to walk in on us like that. Once we knew what direction we were heading, we'd planned to tell you about it."

"It?" Seth asked sharply. "Just because you two couldn't keep your hands off each other doesn't mean anything serious, does it?"

"We don't know," Remy clarified, willing to overlook his brother's overly simple analogy. "This has been very sudden."

"Yes," Vanessa interjected. "After I left your place, I didn't have a place to stay. Remy let me stay in the family suite at The Chateau. I'd still be there now, but…"

"But *what*?" Narrowing his eyes, Seth glanced from one to the other. "Remy's house seemed a bit more welcoming?"

"My father showed up with one of his lady friends," Remy said. "When he found out Vanessa was using the suite, he called me and demanded that I kick her out. There's not a single vacancy anywhere in town. Would you rather she'd stayed in her car and froze to death?"

Seth looked hurt. "She could have stayed at my condo."

"No, I couldn't," Vanessa replied. "You scared the hell out of me the last time I was there. When Remy called to tell me I had to vacate the suite, he very kindly invited me to use his guest bedroom. I accepted."

Now Seth rounded on his brother. "You invited her here with the intention of getting her into your bed, didn't you? None of this is Vanessa's fault."

"Fault?" Vanessa pushed her hair back from her face. "You're acting like I didn't have a choice here." She took a deep breath. "I'm sorry if this caused you pain, Seth."

Remy swallowed. "We had no intention of hurting you." He dragged his hand through his hair, feeling as if his insides were shredded. "But we—"

"We?" Seth roared. "There is no *we*, not with you two. Vanessa and I, we're the *we*."

Vanessa winced. "Seth, you and I are over. You know this. You even agreed that we could try to become friends again."

"Friends?" he scoffed, looking from her to Remy and back again. "Come on, Van. I know you didn't drive three hours up here just because you wanted to be *friends*. You regretted breaking up with me and you came to see if there was a chance we could get back together. And then you met my brother and decided to go for him instead. After all, he's got much better prospects than I do."

"Prospects?" Remy asked, puzzled by Seth's choice of word.

Instead of elaborating, Seth shrugged.

"It's not a competition," Vanessa said softly. "It never was. We aren't together, Seth. We're never going to be, whether or not I see Remy. You need to understand that."

Remy admired her courage. She spoke in an even tone, clearly refusing to allow Seth to ruffle her.

"I know," Seth finally responded. "But geez, Van. My *brother*?"

Again, the knife to the gut, twisting. Remy knew Seth probably wanted him to say something along the lines of "if it bothers you so much, we'll stop." And he knew, deep down inside, he should. Even if he knew that Vanessa and his brother would never be together again.

Remy considered himself a good man, an honorable man. He knew the best thing to do would be to keep his distance, to back away.

But he wasn't sure he could let Vanessa go. Whatever they'd started between the two of them felt too powerful.

"Seth, Remy knows I'm not staying in Roaring Springs long. This wasn't planned, not at all. We simply got swept away." Vanessa took a deep breath, her expression tormented. "Maybe it will go somewhere, maybe it won't."

Remy somehow managed to keep his face expressionless. While she was absolutely right, he'd managed to get ahead of himself, too. Even though he and Vanessa had talked about it, he could sympathize with

Seth there. Something about Vanessa was damn near irresistible. If he wasn't careful, he knew he might just end up getting hurt.

Expression bored, Seth nodded. "Look, you guys, I know I've been messed up lately. Vanessa, I get it now." He lifted one shoulder, clearly trying for indifference. When he met her gaze, he appeared earnest. "I just figured it was worth a shot." Jerking his head toward Remy, he smiled a tight smile. "I'm sure my brother thinks the same."

Seth pushed to his feet and ambled toward the front door. Hand on the knob, he turned to face them. "No more alcohol. No more drugs. I'm going to walk the straight and narrow, but I'll need your help to do it. Both of your help, okay?" He looked from Remy to Vanessa and back again.

"Of course," Remy said. Vanessa seconded that.

Seth nodded. "Thanks. I'll talk to you tomorrow. And, Remy, remember this—you owe me."

With that, he let himself out the door.

"Oh, my goodness." Vanessa exhaled loudly. "That was…"

"Intense." Remy dropped into a chair. "I feel awful."

"I do, too." Her mouth trembled.

When he met her gaze, her shiny eyes told him she was blinking back tears. His gut wrenched. "Are you okay?"

Instead of answering, she covered her face with her hands. He gave her a moment, then, unable to keep from touching her, he squeezed her shoulder. "It's going to be all right," he promised gruffly. Even though he had no idea if that was the truth.

Chapter 9

Having Seth walk in on her and Remy right after they'd made love had been one of the most surreal experiences of Vanessa's life. She wasn't sure how she felt about it, or how she *should* feel about it.

On the one hand, she refused to be ashamed of the relationship developing with Remy. And it wasn't technically like she'd cheated on Seth. True, clearly she'd made a mistake coming back and trying to get closure with him, but under no circumstances had she left him with the wrong impression of her actions. She'd been clear and up-front and Seth had even agreed that they'd try to regain their earlier friendship.

But to come between two brothers? That was the last thing she wanted to do.

"I'm a grown man," Remy reminded her, when she voiced her concerns. "As is Seth." Despite his definitive statement, he still frowned. "Though I never meant for him to find out this way."

She knew what she ought to do, though the thought of actually following through with it tore at her heart. "Maybe I should go home as soon as the roads are cleared," she offered.

"Why would you do that?" Remy demanded.

"Because I'm thinking maybe you two need to work things out without me being around and getting in the way."

"Vanessa." Remy kissed her cheek. "Ever since I found Seth living in that dump with our mother, I've dedicated my life to helping him." He took a deep breath. "Maybe by making sure life was easy for him, I did more harm than good. Seth hasn't had to stand on his own two feet because he always knew I'd be there to pick him up."

Not sure how to respond to that statement, she stuck to her guns. "Regardless, I don't want to come between you two."

Remy kissed her cheek again, this time lingering a moment. "Vanessa, if you want to run off, there's nothing I can do to stop you. But don't use Seth as an excuse. If he hadn't walked in on us, he would have found another reason to find fault with me."

Bemused, she eyed him. "I don't know what to think."

"Then don't." This time, his mouth found hers for a slow, deep kiss. "Stay and ski Pine Peak. Once, twice, or as many times as you want. Stay until we figure out if this thing between us is going anywhere."

"Persuasive devil, aren't you?" she murmured as his lips moved over hers.

"I try." When they finally came up for air, they were both breathing fast. "Let's go back to bed and try and get some sleep. Maybe we can hit the slopes tomorrow."

The next morning, Remy's alarm woke them. Blinking back her dreams, Vanessa shouldn't have been surprised to find herself in Remy's arms, his aroused body pressing hard into her backside. She stretched, arching herself into him, not even minding the delay when he reached into the bedside table and pulled on a condom.

They made love fast and furious, the kind of rough and primal sex that she'd only read about. Thrilling to each thrust, she climaxed quickly, and then again just as Remy found his own release.

After, he padded to the shower. When he emerged, his dark hair still damp, he checked his phone. "If I can clear up my schedule, I'll go ski with you."

This made her happier than she could have believed possible. She rushed through a shower, emerging to find he'd made them both egg-and-bagel sandwiches. She wolfed hers down as she drank her coffee and checked the resort's website on her phone.

"Nothing yet," she mused. "When will they post whether or not Pine Peak is open?"

"It'll be open." He spoke with great confidence. "I checked the weather and even walked outside. The wind is gone and the skies are clear. I know they were setting off some small avalanches as a precaution, but skiing conditions are perfect."

"Yay!" She wanted to jump up and down but settled for clapping her hands. "I'd already bought my passes and lift tickets. Since they were for the days the resort was closed, I'm pretty sure they'll honor them today."

"They will." Remy checked his phone. "I need to make a call and make sure there's nothing pressing going on this morning at the office, and then we can suit up and get on our way."

After Remy cleared his schedule, he and Vanessa loaded all their equipment in his Jeep and headed up to the mountain.

"We should get there right when the lifts start running," he told her.

Feeling like a gleeful little kid, she nodded.

As soon as they'd parked, she bounded out of the car. She could scarcely contain her excitement. This— the cold air, the perfect powder, waiting in line to get on the lift—was when she felt the most alive. Each mountain had its own personality, and she'd skied many. Some were unforgiving, tempting those daring enough to brave the slope to make it to the bottom unscathed. Others were flirty, at first seeming deceptively simple, before one skied around the corner to find themselves on a treacherous and challenging run.

The first time she skied a mountain, she always waited a moment before pushing off, savoring the anticipation.

"You look so happy," Remy commented, his voice warm.

She grinned and turned to face him. "I am. I've been waiting for this a long time. I've heard such great things about Pine Peak. I can't wait to see if they're true."

His hazel-green eyes sparkled, rivaling the sight of the sunshine glittering off the snow. "I dare to say they are. It's been far too long for me, so I'm excited, too. This is going to be fun."

Fun. While his innocuous choice of word might seem banal, she found a celebratory joy in the contrast of control and freedom while racing down a mountain. In skiing, she'd found both her escape and her salvation. One of the reasons she'd become so skilled had been her eagerness to do it over and over again.

She and Remy took the first run together, choosing a challenging slope labeled as a black diamond. She whooped out loud as she sped down, around turns marked by trees, avoiding large boulders and other skiers.

When she finally reached the bottom, she swirled to a stop and beamed at Remy, who came in right behind her. "Fun was right! I want to go again. Now am I imagining things, or did I hear there's a double black on this mountain, too?

Grimacing, he waved her away. "There is. You'll have to do that one alone, though. I haven't quite got the skill to tackle it."

Though she wanted to make a comment informing him he'd never get better if he didn't practice, she also understood how annoying a comment like that could be. Not everyone was as in love with the sport as she.

"I can do it another time," she said, struggling not to reveal her disappointment. "Let's ski this same one again. Or another, your choice."

"Vanessa." He studied her, his expression patient. "How about you take a pass at the double and I'll wait for you in the coffee shop. I haven't skied in at least a year and I'm already sore."

Again, she bit her tongue. For the life of her, she'd never understand how anyone could live in a ski resort and rarely take advantage of it. "I don't know…"

"I'm serious," he persisted. "Enjoy yourself. I plan to. Come find me when you're done and we'll grab something to eat or we can pick something up on the way home."

Maybe she should have hesitated, but she'd waited way too long to give up after one run. "Okay," she said. "I'll come look for you when I'm done. Are you sure you don't want to have at least one more go?"

"I'm sure. Maybe after I rest up a minute, I'll hit it one more time. Meanwhile, I need to return a few calls."

Work again. While she admired his work ethic, she also wanted to remind him he'd taken the morning off to ski. One turn down the mountain wasn't much of anything. But she didn't want to nag, so she held her silence.

Something must have shown in her face. "All right," he relented. "Let's do this one again. Then I'll take a break and you can go test your skills on the black diamond. How's that sound?"

Instead of answering, she flung her arms around his neck and kissed him. Though their lips were both cold, heat still sparked between them. She grabbed his gloved hand with hers and beamed. "Let's do it."

This time, she asked Remy to go first, mainly because she wanted to be able to see him ski. Honestly, she'd been so caught up in the experience that she had no idea of his skill level.

Remy appeared to be a capable, though cautious skier. He took no chances, stayed right in the middle of the run and appeared focused on simply getting from the top to the bottom.

She caught up with him a few seconds after he'd skied to a stop. "Thank you!"

His gaze went to her mouth and for one breathless moment, she thought he might lean in and kiss her. Instead, he shook himself, as if brushing off snow. "I'm going for coffee now," he said. "Enjoy yourself and I'll see you when you're done."

She liked that he didn't ask her how long she'd be or how many times she intended to ski the mountain. For that, she wouldn't have had any kind of definitive answer since she tended to keep going until she either got too cold or too tired.

"I will." Hesitating, she decided to go ahead and give him an out. "If you have other things you need to do, I don't mind if you leave. I can hang out at The Lodge until you're finished or I can ride the gondola back to The Chateau."

Meeting her gaze, he shook his head. "Nope. I'll wait. Who knows, I might decide to take another run down the mountain later." This time, he gave her a chaste peck on the cheek and turned to walk away.

Heaven help her, she wanted to run after him, grab him by the collar and kiss him senseless. Instead, she knew they'd have all the time in the world that evening, so she simply smiled. "See you later," she said, her voice full of promise.

Back in line at the lift, she waited, shifting her weight from one ski to the other as she inhaled the sharp, clean air. The higher altitudes energized her, made her feel invincible. These days, when she went back to Boston, the combination of being at sea level and the humidity weighed her down and made her feel sluggish.

Finally her turn to get on the chair came, along with an older man with silver hair and a charming smile. He made small talk the entire ride up, not flirting, simply one stranger sharing his love of the sport with another.

When they reached the top, he saluted her before turning away and skiing off. She turned the other way, searching for the sign that marked the double-black slope.

There. Heart pounding with anticipation, she breathed deeply, finding her center. When she felt steady, she pushed off.

The double turned out to be everything she'd hoped for. Challenging, even to a skier as skilled as she, with twists and turns and downhill runs so steep she'd clenched her jaw so hard it hurt.

Three quarters of the way down, a man stepped out of the trees, right in her path. Seth. At her rate of speed, if they collided, bones would be broken. Or worse, one or both of them could die.

She leaned hard to the left, throwing all of her weight into the turn, praying she could maintain enough control to stay on the path and out of the trees.

Luckily, her skilled reflexes enabled her to avoid crashing into him. As she flew past, he yelled something at her. While she didn't catch the exact word, she knew he'd screamed an insult.

It didn't matter. Not now. She battled her furious anger, aware if she gave in to emotion, she'd run the risk of losing control. And that wasn't going to happen. Not on her first double on Pine Peak.

As soon as she reached the bottom, she quickly skied out of the way and bent over to catch her breath. What the hell was wrong with Seth? Why would he try a stunt like that? He was also a skilled skier and knew all too well how dangerous stepping into her path would be.

And then a second thought occurred to her. How had he known where to find her? While she hadn't taken great pains to hide from him, she'd figured he'd be at work at The Lodge.

Instead of meeting Remy at the coffee bar, she called him and asked him if they could go home immediately. He met her at his Jeep, his expression laced with concern. "Done already?" he asked. "You sounded upset. Is everything all right?"

"I'll tell you about it later," she replied, feeling jumpy. Unable to keep from looking behind her, as if Seth might appear at any moment, she hopped into the passenger seat the instant Remy unlocked the door.

Picking up on her cue, he started the engine and drove away without any more questions. She liked how he didn't badger her and could wait until she felt ready to talk.

As soon as they pulled into his garage, she got out and stormed into the house. Remy followed close behind.

"Are you all right?" he asked again, catching hold of her arm.

Surprised to realize she was both shaking and on the verge of tears, she let him pull her into his arms and hold her.

"What's wrong, Vanessa?" He kissed her temple. "Did you fall or something? Are you hurt?"

Grim, she pulled away and faced him, bracing herself as she told him what Seth had done. As she spoke, arms crossed, she couldn't stop rubbing herself on her upper arms.

Remy's expression turned from concerned to furious. "You're sure it was him?"

"Yes. What the hell is wrong with him? He used to be my friend. I could have been killed. We *both* could have. Luckily, I was able to make a hard turn and avoid him without hitting a tree. It's like he wants me dead."

As much as it pained her to say those words, she could tell it hurt Remy more. He swore and reached for her again. "I should have been there to protect you," he gritted out. "I'll have a word with my brother. And maybe you should go to the police."

"I can't," she said, her voice muffled up against his chest. "He's already messed up. If I got him arrested, wouldn't that make things worse?"

"I don't see how they could be worse." Remy swallowed hard. "Seth is spiraling out of control. He needs to be stopped before he hurts you or anyone else."

For whatever reason, his words allowed her to let go and cry. She sobbed, while he kept her close, her entire body shaking with the force of her sorrow. She cried for a jumbled mix of reasons—the fallacy of her good intentions of coming here, her lost friendship with Seth and his clear deterioration. She wept because her feelings for Remy were so new and she didn't want to give him up, not just yet.

And when he put a gentle finger under her chin and raised her tearstained face to his, she knew she wanted him to kiss her before he lowered his mouth to hers.

Watching Vanessa sleep, Remy forced himself to breathe slowly and deeply. Making passionate love had released some of the pent-up fury he'd buried deep inside himself, but he still had to figure out what to do. Seth had tried to hurt Vanessa. She could have been seriously injured or even killed.

Finally, his brother had crossed a line from which there could be no returning. Remy didn't understand why Seth directed his anger at her rather than at him. He'd been so determined to believe that deep down Seth was a good guy that he'd failed to protect Vanessa.

This had to stop. First thing in the morning, he'd be visiting Seth and setting him straight. If he had to have Vanessa take out a restraining order against his brother, so be it. Somehow, Remy must have managed to fall asleep, because when he opened his eyes again, it was 4:00 a.m.

And someone stood at the end of his bed, watching them.

Vanessa stirred, perhaps sensing something. Remy held himself perfectly still, willing her to go back to sleep. Instead, she opened her eyes. Catching sight of Seth, she gasped.

Seth stood for one second longer, then turned without speaking a word and left.

"I'm going after him." Remy pushed back the sheets and swung his legs out of the bed.

"Wait!" Vanessa caught at his arm. "Don't follow him. We need to call the police. That wasn't heartbreak I saw in Seth's eyes. It was malice. He wants revenge."

This time, he couldn't even argue. Because as much as he hated to admit it, she was right.

With Vanessa wavering between leaving or staying, he instructed her to keep all the doors locked. Since he hadn't had time to get his key back from Seth, he asked her to put chairs under both the front and back doorknobs.

"Why?" she'd asked, her eyes going wide.

"Just in case. I don't think Seth will actually try anything—but we can't take the risk."

She sighed, but finally agreed to do as he asked. He kissed her cheek, aching for more, and headed into the office early. As soon as he was there, he began calling all his cousins for help. Family stuck together and no matter how embarrassing the situation felt, he knew they wouldn't judge.

If Seth turned out to be the one who'd murdered Sabrina, he wanted everyone on full alert. There was no telling who his brother might decide to hurt next.

The first person he called was his cousin Trey, the Bradford County sheriff. Since it went straight to voicemail, he had to settle for leaving a message. He didn't worry, since he knew Trey would return his call. The sheriff took his job seriously and he was the most by-the-book man Remy had ever met.

Next he called Wyatt, asking him to put them on a conference call with Decker, Fox and Blaine. Wyatt ran the Crooked C Ranch, Fox bred quarter horses, while the other two worked at The Lodge. Blaine managed The Lodge's extreme-sports division, something he excelled at since he was ex–Special Forces, and Decker was The Lodge's director of operations. Both were sensible men, and although he felt slightly disloyal talking about his brother, Remy knew he needed all the reinforcements he could get.

Once all four were on the line, Remy outlined the events of the past few days. He held nothing back, including what Vanessa had found on Seth's laptop. Once he'd finished, Fox swore. "I wasn't going to mention this to you, but Sloane's husband, Liam, swears it was Seth's car that followed them back from Denver the night Sloane was almost killed."

"Did you tell Trey?" Remy asked, his stomach twisting in knots. It was one thing to have all these suspicions about his brother and quite another to have other people come up with more.

"I did," Fox said. "Trey's been looking into it. He's also learned that the person who threw a brick through Bree's gallery was not the same man who took a shot at her. It's possible it could have been Seth, but without proof, Trey's hands are tied."

Wyatt spoke next. "Phoebe found out that Seth was at the same premiere where someone threw water on her. She thinks it was him, but again since she has no concrete evidence, she didn't want to make it an issue."

"I have more bad news," Decker interjected. "I've recently learned that some of The Lodge payroll accounts have come up short. The books were doctored. I've been keeping this quiet until I get a full report from my CPA, but Seth had access to them as the hotel manager."

Remy swore.

"Now, I have no proof it's him," Decker cautioned. "And until I do, I won't be pursuing criminal charges. But since you've brought all this other stuff up, I thought you should know."

"I don't usually pay attention to gossip," Blaine chimed in. "But there's been a lot of talk among some of the other employees about Seth and money. Again, like Decker said, there's no proof. But I agree you should know."

"I've got a call in to Trey," Remy said. "Is he aware of this?"

"I've alerted him to my suspicions," Decker replied cautiously. "That's all they are at this point—suspicions. However, if I obtain evidence, I will be pressing charges."

"I don't blame you." It was almost too much for Remy to process. His phone chimed, indicating another call.

"Trey's calling me," he told the others. "I'm going to have to let you go."

Instantly, they all agreed and he clicked over. It took him a few minutes to fill in the sheriff, and some of what he mentioned Trey already knew, but he had to get it all out.

Some of his panic must have shown in his voice. Trey listened and when Remy finally wound down, he told him to take a deep breath. "How about we just go over and have a talk with Seth?" his cousin offered. "I can swing by your office and pick you up in about fifteen minutes."

Remy agreed and ended the call. He deliberated whether or not to phone Vanessa, but in the end, decided he'd rather tell her in person. No sense in getting her all freaked out while home alone.

He went down to the lobby to watch for Trey. When the sheriff's cruiser pulled up five minutes early, Remy hurried outside. As usual, Trey appeared competent and unruffled—Remy felt grateful since he felt like such a mess inside.

"It's not your fault," Trey said, once Remy had

buckled himself in. "You did the best you could with that kid. No matter how this turns out, you need to know that."

Tight-lipped, Remy didn't even try for a fake smile, knowing the other man would see right through it.

When they got to Seth's condo, he wasn't home. Though Remy didn't see his pickup truck in the parking lot, he and Trey went inside the hall and knocked, anyway.

No one answered. Just in case, Remy tried the doorknob. To his surprise, it turned easily. "It's unlocked."

Trey raised an eyebrow, but didn't comment.

"I'm going inside," Remy said. "Are you with me?"

"Do you honestly feel as if your brother's life might be in danger?"

Hesitating, Remy nodded. "I do. He's not himself. Who knows what we might find if we open the door."

Jaw tight, Trey considered. "I don't have a warrant," he told him. "I'd need probable cause."

Remy pushed open the door. What he saw just inside made him stop short, his heart in his throat. On the table just inside the door were several firearms—pistols and shotguns and AR-15s. What the actual hell?

Turning to look at Trey, Remy opened the door wide enough so his cousin could see, too. "I don't know about the laws, but is finding a cache of weapons enough of a probable cause?"

"I'd say yes. Exigent circumstances," Trey explained. "That means I have a reasonable belief that evidence may be destroyed in the time it would take to get a warrant."

Once inside the condo, the sheriff called in for backup. While they waited, he meticulously photographed each weapon. "These will be bagged for evidence. Even though there hasn't been a crime yet that we know of, we'll need to see proof that your brother legally purchased these guns."

Still in shock, Remy grimaced. "I'm going out on a limb and saying I'm guessing he probably did not."

Two deputies arrived and Trey stepped aside to let them take over. "Bring them back to headquarters and we'll store them in evidence," he said. "Seth will have to come in and claim them if he wants them back."

Remy could imagine how little Seth would like that. He dreaded telling Vanessa. Like him, she'd jump to the inevitable conclusion that Seth had been planning something deadly.

"We've got to find him quickly," Trey said, no doubt sharing Remy's silent speculation. "We don't know what other firepower he might have on him or what he's planning. It's imperative we stop him before someone gets hurt."

Worried, Remy dialed Vanessa. After three rings, the call went to voicemail. He left a detailed message, hoping she was all right.

Chapter 10

At the sound of the front door opening and then closing, Vanessa froze, the flow of her graceful movement interrupted. On the YouTube video she was streaming, the yoga instructor continued giving instructions in her soothing, serene voice, though Vanessa's calmness had instantly gone right into panic mode.

She'd forgotten to wedge the chair under the doorknob as Remy had instructed. Heart pounding, she wondered if her carelessness would result in yet another unwanted, angry confrontation with Seth.

Maybe not. *Hopefully* not. Remy could have simply decided to surprise her at lunchtime.

"Remy?" she called out, willing him to respond. Instead, nothing but silence answered her. Tense, her stomach twisting, she looked around for something she could use as a weapon in case she needed to defend herself.

Coming up short, she wondered if she should hurry into the kitchen and grab a knife, just in case. But she'd read that more people are hurt by the weapon being used against them by their attacker, so she stayed where she was. Frozen, heart hammering in her ears, she waited for whoever, whatever, to make their move.

When nothing happened—no noise, no movement, no furious Seth jumping out to confront her—she wondered if she'd imagined the sound of the door. She'd been in a half-meditative trance, but still...

Finally realizing she needed to pause the video stream, she did that. Definitely not Remy, since he hadn't responded to her when she'd called out his name.

Moving slowly, she went to check the door. Still locked. Which meant either she'd imagined everything, or the intruder had locked the door after gaining entrance.

What to do, what to do? Part of her shouted "run," ordering her to head for the door as fast as she could, and get out, right *now*. The other, more skeptical part chastised her for letting her imagination get away with her and for overreacting.

Had she? Eying the paused yoga stream longingly, she wished she could simply return to her session, where she'd been stretching and posing and pushing herself to the max. Truth be told, all along she'd been hoping Remy would come home and surprise her. She'd actually allowed herself to daydream, in love with the idea of him walking in and watching her move her body in ways that felt both sensual and empowering.

She wavered too long, stuck between gut instinct and feeling foolish.

There. Another sound, this one barely discernible, as if someone was trying to move quietly but a misplaced foot and a random squeak of the floor betrayed them.

Damn it. The back of her neck tingled. She hadn't been wrong—someone *was* in the house, and she needed to get out immediately.

She spun, nearly tripping over her own feet as she raced for the door. But before she could, Seth stepped into the foyer, between her and the door, his expression impassive.

"Seth," she gasped, putting her hand to her throat in fright. "You startled me. What—"

His arm came up. He held a pistol pointed right at her. "Hello, Vanessa."

Think fast. Maybe she could talk her way out of this.

"Seth." Despite her best efforts, her voice quavered. She slid her phone into her yoga pants pocket and tried to compose her expression into something she hoped appeared neutral.

"In the flesh," he mocked, his expression as cold as his gaze.

She swallowed hard. "Why are you here, Seth? And what are you doing with that gun?"

"What I should have done a long time ago," he drawled, his eyes narrow as he glared at her. "Driving the karma bus straight for you."

Part of her wanted to ask if he had taken something—some drug judging by the way his pupils looked—but she knew a less antagonistic approach would be best. For the first time she understood that the Seth she'd known and loved like a brother had vanished completely. This Seth, with the flat stare and mean twist to his mouth, was not only lost to her, but also deadly. She and Remy had known he was spiraling out of control, but they hadn't grasped how far gone he already was.

He wanted to kill her. She shivered, trying to hide the stark terror that realization brought.

"Seth, let's sit down and talk," she offered, schooling her expression into one of concerned politeness. "Please. Put the gun down. There's no reason for you to act like this."

Sneering, he let loose a string of profanities, calling her every name in the book and some she hadn't ever heard of. She felt each word rain on her like a blow and it took an effort not to hunch over from the pain of hearing a man she'd once considered her best friend talk to her this way.

Fear turned her blood to ice as she waited, silently, for him to finish. He hated her—the contempt and disgust in his voice was testament to that.

"I'm going to kill you," he declared once he'd run out of expletives. "You understand that, don't you?"

Somehow, she found her voice. "I really wish you wouldn't."

He laughed at her and came closer, his gun still aimed directly at her.

"Would you please put that down," she asked, her legs going weak from fear. She couldn't help but wonder how quickly she'd die. Would it hurt? If he shot her in the head, she hoped she'd be killed instantly.

"You want me to put the gun down?" he asked,

smiling a shark's smile. "I guess you want to die in a more personal way. Maybe I should strangle you with my bare hands."

Though she wanted to tell him she didn't want to die at all, she couldn't seem to push the words out of her frozen mouth.

He came closer, still smiling. Because the sight of that patently evil smile chilled her to the bone, she closed her eyes.

"Look at me," Seth demanded. "I want you to look at me while I kill you."

A shudder snaked up her spine. Slowly, she opened her eyes and did as he asked. He stared at her, that same malicious smile turning smug. "You deserve this," he declared. "You know that, don't you?"

She gave up the idea of even trying to formulate a response. There was no reasoning with him, anyway. Eying the gun and Seth's dead, cold eyes, she decided she'd take a chance, anyway, and make a run for it. At the worst, he'd shoot her. Maybe she'd make it out. She had to try.

Taking a deep breath, she braced herself. And then Seth launched himself at her, slamming her up against the wall so hard she saw stars. With his hands around her throat—what had he done with the pistol?—he choked her, his grip tight. Painful. Deadly.

Wheezing, she fought back, primal instinct taking over. But she refused to die, craving air, needing to breathe. She brought up her knee and got a lucky shot right between his legs, and he gasped and released her, cursing, and doubled over. She squirmed away, ready to go for his eyes if need be, too panicked to try to find the gun. Sprinting for the front door, she nearly made it, but Seth caught hold of her shirt and spun her toward him. Luckily, the fabric tore.

Free again, she ran outside onto the front porch, screaming at the top of her lungs. She jumped over the stairs, intent on getting away, praying Seth wouldn't shoot her in the back.

An elderly man came out three houses down and called to her so she ran there, letting him usher her inside and ordering him to bolt the door.

Once he'd done so, she asked him to call 911 before she broke down into a blubbering mess. Where was Seth? Would he shoot out the windows, bash down the door, come after her and kill her, anyway? She couldn't stop shaking, couldn't talk to the police dispatcher, and finally had to hand the phone to her rescuer so he could tell them to come help her.

Still no sign of Seth. Did he know where she'd gone? At any moment, she expected him to crash through the window or the door and finish what he'd started.

She wanted Remy… She wanted her parents. She wished she'd never come to Roaring Springs. All she could do was cry while the elderly Good Samaritan awkwardly patted her shoulder and waited for the police to arrive.

Finally, she asked for a tissue and blotted her face and blew her nose. She took a deep breath, dug her phone from her pocket and dialed Remy, but the call went straight to voicemail. That's when she saw she'd missed a call from him. When? She hadn't even heard the phone ring.

He'd left a message. She played it back, trying to draw comfort from the steady sound of his voice, but he sounded worried. Though he didn't say why, he'd asked her to call as soon as she could.

Had he somehow known what Seth was going to do? Surely not, or he would have called the police. Right?

Two deputies arrived and the elderly man—his name was Chris, she remembered him saying—let them in. When she haltingly told them what had happened, they immediately called for backup. The second set of deputies went to search Remy's house while the first two took her statement.

"You need medical attention, ma'am."

"No." She shook her head. "I want to go to the station and make a report. I'm pressing charges. And I need you to make sure he can't get to me again."

"We will," the young deputy assured her. "But I really think you should at least get checked out. Those bruises on your neck look bad."

"I'll live." Then, at his incredulous expression, she relented. "I'll go after I make my report. I want to make sure Seth is arrested and charged. He's off the rails and dangerous."

"Let's take you down to the sheriff's office," the older of the two said. "I'll have Dispatch put in a call to Trey. We'll get this thing straightened out."

Though she wanted to snap back that there was nothing to straighten out—that Seth needed to be arrested—she held her tongue. She'd save everything for the sheriff, including her wrath if they tried to sweep this under the rug.

Trey's police radio crackled as he and Remy got back into the cruiser. "Sheriff, you'd better get back to the station pronto. We've got a young lady here who says Seth Harris attacked her. She's pressing charges. We've got men out looking for Seth to bring him in, but so far no one has been able to locate him."

A young woman? Remy swallowed hard. Vanessa? Who else could it be? "What's the woman's name?" he croaked.

"A Miss Vanessa Fisher," the dispatcher replied. "She's refusing medical attention."

Which meant she wasn't seriously injured, didn't it? Remy opened his mouth to ask, but the dispatcher spoke again, this time to Trey. "What do you want me to do, Sheriff?"

"Put out an APB immediately," Trey barked. He turned to Remy. "What kind of vehicle does Seth drive?"

"Ford F-150 pickup," Remy answered, his heart racing. "Black with oversize tires."

"Did you get that?" Trey asked the dispatcher.

"Yes, sir. I'll get the APB out immediately."

As soon as Trey replaced the radio, he turned to Remy. "You okay? You're looking a bit pale."

As soon as Remy managed a nod, Trey grimaced. "Then buckle up and hang on."

After flipping a switch that turned on his police lights and siren, Trey sped away from Seth's building.

"She was at my house," Remy said. "The woman Seth attacked. Her name is Vanessa Fisher."

"The one you've been telling me about?" Trey asked. "She used to be engaged to Seth?"

"Right."

Trey eyed him. "And what? Since she was at your place, I'm guessing she's seeing you now?"

Remy nodded. "Sort of. Seth's been threatening her, but neither of us realized she might be in any real danger from him."

"But tell me you took precautions, anyway. You said he had a key to your place. Did you at least change the lock?"

Feeling like a fool, Remy shook his head. "I planned to, but I haven't had time yet. I told Vanessa to wedge a chair under both the front and back doors."

"Well, either she forgot or Seth managed to get inside, anyway." Grim-faced, Trey drove with a single-minded intensity.

Though it was usually a ten-minute drive to the sheriff's office, they made it in five. Trey had no sooner pulled up into his designated parking spot than Remy opened his door and bolted from the car. His cousin followed, his pace a bit slower, but not by much.

Inside, Remy started trying to articulate where he wanted to go. Trey shook his head and took Remy's arm, then told the front-desk officer, "He's with me." He led Remy to the back, toward his office. "I'm going to give you some time alone with her," he said. "I'll read over her statement and she and I can talk once you've gotten her settled."

Grateful, Remy thanked him.

The instant he saw Vanessa, head in her hands, her long hair a curtain hiding her face, Remy's legs almost buckled. He went to her, dropped to his knees in front of her chair and gathered her into his arms. "It's okay," he murmured. "You're okay."

Immediately, she burst into tears. His strong, capable Vanessa. The ache that had begun in his throat spread to his chest.

Holding her close, he murmured soothing, nonsensical words. Trey took his place behind his desk, steepled his hands in front of him and waited.

Grateful for this kindness, Remy held on tight, wishing he could take her pain from her and into himself. Part of him wanted to find his brother and beat the tar out of him. But he knew right here, right now, this was where he belonged. With her. Time for reckoning would come later.

Finally, Vanessa's weeping slowed. Taking deep, shuddering breaths, she tried to gather her composure. Trey slid a box of tissues across the desk and Remy handed them to her, waiting patiently until she'd grown calm enough to try to tell them what had happened. What Seth had done.

When she lifted her head, he caught sight of the horrible, purpling bruises around her neck. Damn. He bit back the curse word, his jaw clenching. For a moment, he saw red. "Seth did that?" he asked, letting his shocked disbelief and helpless rage show in his voice.

Tears welling in her eyes, she nodded. "He wanted to kill me," she rasped. "I think he meant to shoot me first, but then he decided to make it more personal."

The thought of what might have transpired sent a chill through him. "Tell me what happened," he said, still holding on to her with both hands. "I'm guessing you didn't block the doors with chairs."

She shook her head. "I meant to, but I forgot. I wish I had." Blinking back tears, she told him everything. By the time she finished, he struggled to contain himself.

Seth had tried to kill Vanessa. Horror and blinding,

all-consuming fury filled him, though he struggled to keep it from showing.

"You're okay now," he whispered, smoothing back her hair from her bruised face, the sight of the purple and yellow marks on her neck making him feel sick.

"I'm guessing this means he probably killed Sabrina," he added, handing her another tissue and waiting while she blotted at her eyes.

"Do you feel well enough to let me take your statement?" Trey asked, his voice gentle. "I heard everything you told Remy, so I just need to ask you a few questions and then we're done. Okay?"

Slowly, Vanessa nodded. With Remy's arms still around her, she answered the sheriff's questions, which were mostly clarifying the circumstances around Seth's attack.

Finally, Trey thanked her and said he had everything. "You can take her home now, Remy. I'll drive you both since I brought you, if that's all right."

Outside, in the crisp, cold air, they all hurried to Trey's cruiser. He offered the front seat to Vanessa, but she wanted to sit in the back with Remy. Gratified, Remy pulled her as close as the seat belt would allow and held her, breathing in her clean, fresh scent and aching down to his marrow. "Are you sure you don't want to get checked out by medics?" he asked. Vanessa simply shook her head no.

On the drive home, she stared straight ahead, subdued. Trey made several attempts at light conversation before finally giving up. When they reached Remy's house, the sheriff suggested Remy get a locksmith there as soon as possible.

"I'm calling as soon as we're inside," he promised.

"Good. Because another blizzard warning has been issued for tonight. I've got as many men as I can spare out there searching for Seth, but if we don't find him before the storm hits, he's going to be looking for someplace warm to hide. Make sure he can't get in."

"I will."

"Let me go in with you and make sure no one's there," Trey suggested.

The thought hadn't even occurred to Remy, but his cousin was right. "I appreciate that," he said. Helping Vanessa out of the cruiser, Remy kept his arm around her as they hurried up to the house after the sheriff.

"The front door is unlocked," Trey commented, drawing his service pistol. "Maybe you two should wait in the car."

Vanessa started to tremble. "I ran out of here screaming. Seth was still inside." She turned to Remy, her expression worried. "I'm sorry. One of the deputies came back to look for Seth and I didn't even think about asking him to make sure to lock up."

"I wouldn't have expected you to." Trey squeezed her shoulder. "You did what you had to in order to stay alive. Let's check this place out. Once we know it's clear, I'll leave. But I intend to have deputies do drive-bys constantly."

"Thank you," Remy responded.

"Maybe we should stay somewhere else." Vanessa's voice trembled. "I wonder if your father is done with that suite at The Chateau."

One look at the stark fear in her eyes and Remy knew he'd do whatever it took to make her feel safe. "I'll call him and find out," he promised. "Don't worry. I'll figure out something."

Trey stepped inside, followed by Remy, who didn't want to wait while Trey cleared his home. Expression panicked, Vanessa joined them. "I can't stay here alone. I'm going in with you."

Remy put his arm around her and kept her close.

Inside, the three of them stuck together as Trey swept every room. Finally, they returned to the living room after he'd declared the place clear. About to leave, the sheriff hesitated at the front door. "Remy, are you armed?" he finally asked.

"Yes," Remy answered grimly. "I have a Ruger I keep in my nightstand, plus a twelve-gauge."

"Good. Hopefully, it won't come to that, but better safe than sorry."

Though the idea of having to shoot his own brother sickened him, Remy agreed. He knew he'd do whatever he had to do in order to protect Vanessa.

As soon as Trey left, Remy wedged chairs under the doors and closed all the blinds. He called a locksmith that he'd used before and they agreed to send someone out that evening. Remy asked for a call when they were on their way. After instructing Vanessa to wedge the chair after him, he ran next door and left a spare key with his neighbor, a trucking company owner named Charlie, and asked if he wouldn't mind letting the locksmith in once he arrived. Since the weather had all but shut down his fleet, Charlie readily agreed, even after Remy offered a halting warning about Seth.

"I'm not surprised," Charlie drawled. "That boy's been a loose cannon for a while now."

Not sure how to respond to that, Remy simply nodded. "I'll pick up the new keys from you sometime to-morrow, weather permitting."

With this accomplished, he returned home, knock-ing and announcing himself to a clearly spooked Va-nessa, who let him in. He told her that his neighbor would be meeting the locksmith for them. Though she nodded, her distant expression made him realize she'd retreated somewhere deep inside herself. As he watched her, she shivered, seemingly unaware that she did so.

"Would you like to get out of here?" he asked. "We can go into town or just for a drive. Whatever you want?"

Blinking, she finally seemed to focus on him. "I had a panic attack when you went next door," she ad-mitted. "I never have panic attacks." She took a deep, shaky breath. "Now that you've gotten the locksmith taken care of, will you call your father and see if we can stay at The Chateau?"

"Of course." Glad of the reminder, he dialed Whit's private cell phone. His dad answered on the second ring.

"I need to use the suite," Remy said, making his request a statement rather than a question. "Today. Right now, actually."

"For how long?" Whit asked, sounding distracted.

"I'm not sure. At least a few days."

"Fine," Whit answered. "I won't be needing it until after the holidays, anyway. Knock yourself out." And he ended the call.

Since Remy had been prepared to argue and insist, his father's easy capitulation surprised him. When he relayed the news to Vanessa, her relief made her entire face light up.

"Let me get packed and change out of my yoga clothes," she said. "Will you come with me? I don't want to be alone, not even if you're in the next room."

"Of course." He followed her and stood in the doorway while she threw her things into her suitcase, keeping out a bulky sweater, jeans and boots. When she'd finished, she peeled off her yoga outfit and put on the much warmer clothes, her back to him. Then she zipped the bag closed and looked at him.

"Your turn," she said. "I'll come watch you pack now."

He made quick work of this chore. At the last moment, he took his pistol out of the nightstand and slipped it into a shoulder holster he could wear under his coat.

"All done." Grabbing his suitcase, he reached for hers but she shook her head.

"I'll carry it. I can swing it like a weapon if someone comes after me."

Since he knew she'd seen him put on the holster, he didn't comment. Whatever it took to make her feel safe was fine with him.

They hurried to his Jeep. Outside, the sky had turned an ominous shade of gray, warning of the approaching storm. "Back-to-back blizzards are unusual," he commented.

Vanessa nodded but didn't reply. Instead, she kept up a constant scan of the landscape, as if she expected Seth to appear at any moment.

They made it to The Chateau and Remy headed around back, using the employee parking lot. The leaden sky hadn't yet opened up, though an icy wind blew down off the mountains, carrying a warning of the storm yet to come.

Once inside, Vanessa stuck to Remy's side, glancing around them constantly. His heart ached for her—and with the knowledge that his own brother had caused this fear.

He got their room key and ushered her into the elevator.

She kept her head down, not speaking, clearly still grappling with everything that had happened.

If she wanted space, he'd make sure she got it. Ditto, if she needed comfort. Whatever Vanessa required, she'd have.

The suite sat at the very end of a long hallway, the dark mahogany double doors tucked in a small alcove. Remy used his key card to unlock the doors, holding one open with his body so Vanessa could slip past him.

Moving like a wraith, she did. Chest heavy, he nudged the door closed, wishing he knew what to do to help her.

"Make love to me," she said, as if answering a question he knew he hadn't spoken out loud.

Slowly, he turned, and she came to him, her soft curves molding to him as he wrapped her in his arms. On fire, she kissed him with an intensity that drove everything but red-hot desire from his mind.

"Are you sure?" he asked, when he came up for air. Though already hard, he had to make sure she knew what she really wanted. "You've just been through—"

"I want to feel alive." With that, she touched him, the insistent intimacy of her caress leaving no doubt. He struggled to regain self-control as she stroked and caressed him, then helped him shed his clothes at the same time as she got rid of hers.

There was an intense urgency in her movements. "This," she demanded, guiding his hand to her core, letting him feel her heat, her wetness. She arched her back as he stroked her there and then, with one fluid motion, she pushed him back onto the bed and straddled him.

More aroused than he'd ever been in his life, he groaned as she settled herself over the top of him, sheathing him tightly. He slid his hand down her taut stomach to the curve of her hips, his gaze locked on hers, his body bucking helplessly as she rode him.

"Too soon," he rasped, trying to make her hold still. "Please. Give me a moment to—"

But she only shook her head, the wildness in her eyes matched only by the way she moved. She took him, claimed him, propelled him to ride the crest of fulfillment in one shattering explosion. As he emptied himself into her, he realized too late that he hadn't used protection.

Then Vanessa shuddered, her body clenching around his as she reached her own peak. The tremors, an aftershock of pleasure, continued through her as she held him fiercely, as if she'd never let him go.

That's when he knew. *He loved her.* This woman, proud and passionate, prickly and stubborn, was meant to be his. He could only hope she felt the same way.

Chapter 11

The snowstorm came with a vengeance, waking up Vanessa from a sound sleep. Her first reaction—instant, wide-eyed terror—subsided as she realized she was at The Chateau and that Remy held her securely in his arms.

Remy. After that first mad, passionate round of lovemaking, they'd gone at it again a couple of hours later. She couldn't get enough of him. And while she knew some of it was due to the adrenaline rush and the need to reconfirm life, that didn't even scratch the surface of how much she'd begun to care for him.

Outside, the wind howled around the building corner. She slipped from the bed without waking Remy and went to the window. Peering out, she could barely make out the light poles below through the swirling maelstrom of snow.

Trapped. Her first thought made her feel slightly ashamed. She shouldn't think that way. Even though she once again couldn't leave town due to a snowstorm, she had Remy. He alone made all of this worth it. If she'd never come to Roaring Springs, she'd never have met this amazing, wonderful man. She only wished he wasn't Seth's half brother.

Thinking of Seth sent a shudder through her. He'd been her friend, then briefly her fiancé, and now clearly her enemy. How had she missed his addiction issues and anger problem? How could the man who'd been a rock and supported her through her parents' deaths have tried to kill her?

While she might never have the answers to those questions, she could only hope he was found and brought in without any bloodshed. Gazing out into the swirling whiteout, she wondered where Seth was. The last she'd heard, the sheriff's department had organized a massive manhunt in Roaring Springs and the surrounding area. They'd hoped to apprehend him before the blizzard hit. She wondered if they had. Doubtful, since they most likely would have let Remy know.

Despite everything, she wanted Seth to get help, not to die alone in the freezing snow. She thought back to the times they'd been together, tried to remember if there'd been something she'd missed, some hint or clue of the darkness hidden inside him.

She'd thought him a bit self-centered, she mused. And he'd always seemed to have a deep-seated mistrust, maybe even envy, of people who were better off than him. For the first time she wondered how much of that stemmed from his involvement with the clearly wealthy Coltons.

She'd always treated Seth more like a brother than a mate, she realized. She'd refused to allow the physical part of their relationship to progress beyond kissing and some heavy petting. This had never appeared to bother Seth. If it made him angry, he'd managed to keep his feelings hidden from her.

Of course, he'd been dating Sabrina Gilford on the side. What he hadn't gotten from Vanessa, he no doubt received from her. She thought of the photos she'd seen on Seth's computer. The dark-haired woman had laughed up at him, her fondness for him evident on her pretty face. She hadn't seemed abused or worried in any way. And Seth, with his arm around Sabrina's slender shoulders, had gazed down at her with the same adoration with which he'd once looked at Vanessa.

How much of that had been feigned? Was Seth really that good of an actor? Why bother to pretend to be in love with two different women? Her eyes widened as she found herself wondering if he'd actually proposed to both of them. Had Sabrina broken off things just as Vanessa had? Was that the reason she'd ended up dead?

Seeing where her thoughts had gone, she wrapped her arms around herself and forced herself to face the truth. The man she'd once considered her best friend most likely was a murderer. If he'd succeeded when he'd grabbed her, would that have made him a serial killer?

Vanessa sighed. She supposed she should consider herself lucky that he hadn't killed her that day at her place in Boulder when she'd given him back his ring.

Some of the chill from outside mixed with her dark

thoughts made her shiver. She turned, went back to the bed and slipped between the soft flannel sheets, squirming just enough to put herself back into Remy's arms without stirring him. This was where she belonged, she knew. But how could she and Remy forge a future with his brother between them?

Morning brought that particular brightness of sun on fresh snowfall. Which meant the storm had ended as quickly as it had appeared. Sitting up in the bed, loath to leave the warmth of the covers, she debated whether or not to go back to sleep.

"Hey there." Smiling, Remy stretched, drawing her gaze to his muscular chest. "Come here."

Unable to resist, she slid down next to him. His morning arousal delighted her and she reached for him.

"Wait." He grabbed her hand before she could touch him. "We didn't use a condom last night."

"Should I worry?" she asked, half teasing. "I'm clean and I'm on birth control. What about you?"

Expression relieved, he kissed the hand he'd captured before guiding it back. "I'm clean, too." He looked around for his jeans, his body already pushing into her expert strokes. "Do you want me to grab one now?"

"No." Her unequivocal answer came straight from the heart. "I don't want anything between us."

After making love again, she dozed, secure in Remy's strong arms. "Do you want the first shower?" he asked. "I've ordered breakfast from room service. It should be here in about thirty minutes."

"Yes, thank you." Happier than she had a right to be, she dashed for the ornate bathroom and took a hot shower.

Blow-drying her hair while Remy showered felt cozy and domestic. If not for her niggling worry about Seth, she might have allowed herself to relax and enjoy the feeling.

They enjoyed a leisurely breakfast. Though he had to be worried, Remy appeared more concerned with making sure she was comfortable. She caught him glancing at his watch a few times and finally asked him if he was due in at the office.

"No," he answered, clearly distracted. "This time of the year things are super slow, so I texted my assistant and had her let everyone know to stay home due to the storm." He took another long sip of coffee before pulling out his cell. "I'm going to check in with the sheriff."

She nodded. "Okay." And then she held her breath while she waited to hear what he found out. Judging by his sober expression, the news wasn't good.

After ending the call, he met her gaze. "They shut down Pine Peak due to the storm, but got word of multiple avalanches." He swallowed hard. "And one of the ski patrol got a call about a man stranded up there. They're not sure if he was caught in one of the avalanches or not. Either way, Trey thinks it might be Seth."

Her stomach twisted. "Are they sending the ski-rescue team out?"

"Yes, but they're severely undermanned. I'm going to go offer to help."

She stared at him, trying to find the best way to divulge her thoughts. "Remy, you're not a strong enough skier. I don't want to lose you."

"Maybe not." Grimacing, he shrugged. "But I don't

have a choice. Seth's my brother. I can't let him freeze up there alone."

"I'll go," she said, surprising herself. "You know I can handle it. I even volunteered on a ski patrol when I was in Switzerland."

Remy started shaking his head before she'd even finished. "Please stay here, Vanessa. If it is Seth, with him being so unstable, there's no telling what he might do if he sees you."

He had a point. Wavering, she let him pull her into his arms. "Can we at least go to The Lodge and sit in with whoever is coordinating the rescue?"

"Yes." He kissed her cheek. "That we can do. It might be a bit of a struggle getting up there—the plow will be busy digging downtown out first, but we'll figure something out."

"How about we ski there?" she asked, itching to get going.

"It's all uphill," he reminded her. "Snowshoes might work better."

She saw his point. "Do you have any?"

"Not personally, but we always keep several pairs in the extreme-sport area. I'll call my cousin Blaine—he runs that program. They should be able to deliver them to our room."

Vanessa nodded, still trying to figure out a way to go along with the rescue team. She had confidence in her skiing skills and knew she would be an asset, no matter what Remy thought. Though he wasn't wrong about a possible bad reaction from Seth if he saw her or caught her alone. After all, he'd tried to kill her once. No doubt if he saw a second chance, he'd take it, regardless of the circumstances.

Reluctantly, she knew she had to stay behind.

Remy finished his call and told her the snowshoes would be delivered in a few minutes. "Go ahead and suit up," he said. "No idea how long getting up to The Lodge might take. We have a tram, but they shut it down until they can get the snow cleared off the rails."

The trek up to The Lodge might have been arduous, but the bright blue sky and sunshine made it actually pleasurable. Though her legs were well conditioned to skiing and snowboarding, using the snowshoes for such an uphill distance made her muscles burn. Beside her, Remy appeared to be feeling it, too, though he made no complaints. Instead, he appeared fixated on reaching their destination.

When they reached the large sign at the entrance to the resort, Remy stopped, his labored breath producing puffs of steam in the frigid air. "They haven't even cleared the driveway," he said, clearly disappointed. "That's usually one of the first things the grounds crew does."

She understood. If the drive had been plowed, they could have taken off the snowshoes and simply walked it. Now they were facing another steep grade they'd have to climb.

"I'm guessing they were busy with more important things," she murmured, glad for the opportunity to catch her own breath. "Just think of this as conditioning for the next time you strap on skis."

Her comment made him laugh. She smiled back, basking in the warmth of his grin. A second later, it faded. "If the snow is this deep at this lower elevation, just imagine what it's like up there on the mountain."

Though he hadn't said his brother's name, she knew

exactly what he meant. Focused once more, they began trudging up toward The Lodge.

When they reached the parking lot, Vanessa stared at the private luxury cabins dotting the mountainside before eying the main building itself. The modern construction managed to look both historic and decadent— *the* place to be if one wanted to stay at the best ski resort in the state. Each time she saw The Lodge, she fell in love with it a little bit more.

Though she'd never booked a room here, she could honestly say that nowhere else could possibly hold a candle to this one.

"This way," Remy said, snapping her out of her thoughts. "We're not going inside the main building. There's a ski-patrol cabin right before the road that leads to the lift."

"Lead the way."

The one-story frame building looked deserted on the outside, though she knew had the lift been open, the place would have been buzzing with activity. But the instant they stepped inside, the small but focused group of people gave off an intense vibe that showed they meant business.

She should have been surprised, but this ski patrol was high-tech. A large computer screen monitored each member's GPS location. Impressed, she slipped in the middle of a group of three men and a woman. "Any luck so far?"

If they were surprised to see her, no one showed it. "Nothing yet," the woman said grimly. "Though our people are just now reaching the area where the stranded man was last seen."

Remy came up behind her and placed his hands on

her shoulders. When the others registered his presence, their eyes widened.

"Hey, guys," Remy said quietly. "I know you'll do your best to locate our stranded guest and bring him back safely."

"Yes, we will, Mr. Colton." A petite young woman, her blond hair in a long braid, regarded him solemnly. "We're all hoping it's not Seth. He's a skilled enough skier that it seems unlikely he'd be in this position."

Vanessa couldn't believe she hadn't thought of that. "If it's not Seth, then who…?"

The young blonde lifted one slender shoulder. "It could be any one of our guests. We have a group of guys from Longmont up here celebrating a bachelor party. They'd been warned several times about taking unnecessary risks. My bet is that it's one of them."

Vanessa exchanged a long look with Remy. If the stranded skier wasn't Seth, then where was he? He couldn't have left town, not with all the roads closed. Unless…

"Does Seth have a snowmobile?" she asked Remy, keeping her voice pitched low.

"No," he replied. "At least not that I know of."

"Maybe he borrowed one, so he could get out of town."

Remy shook his head, taking her arm and leading her away from the others. "He has nowhere to go. No matter how desperate he got, I don't think he'd go back to our mother and that hellhole apartment. Not when he's invested so much time and money creating a nice life for himself here in Roaring Springs."

"They found him!" One of the rescue team shouted. "Alive. They're bringing him in now."

* * *

Remy and Vanessa joined the small group of people waiting to meet the injured man and his rescuers as they came down from the slope. Vanessa gripped Remy's hand so tightly her nails dug into his palm, but he didn't mind. So far, no one had mentioned the guy's identity, so they had no idea if it was Seth or one of the young men from the bachelor party. Though odds were high it was the latter, Trey had joined them just in case. If they brought Seth down on a stretcher, he'd promptly be arrested and charged.

"There they are!" someone shouted, pointing at a speck way up on the mountain. Everyone grew quiet. As the group drew nearer, Remy strained to make out the features of the man on the stretcher.

"It's not him," Vanessa breathed, at the same moment he realized the exact same thing. On Remy's other side, Trey grunted and walked over to the man's group of friends, who'd celebrated with a few unrestrained cheers. They fell quiet the instant the sheriff approached.

"Well." Still holding Vanessa's hand, though her grip had loosened somewhat, Remy tugged her close. "What do you want to do now?"

"I'm not sure," she answered. As she glanced over her shoulder, her eyes widened. "The crowd size has doubled."

Turning, he saw she was correct. Alerted by the ski patrol, most of The Lodge management staff had come out to watch them bring the injured skier down from the mountain.

Catching sight of Remy, one of Seth's counterparts hurried over. "The plow is on the way, with an ambulance right behind it. We've got people working on a press release, too."

"Good. Make sure they run it by me before releasing it."

"Will do." The man moved away.

"Listen." Vanessa tugged on his hand. "That sounds like the plow."

Everyone around them murmured, some craning their necks to see if they could catch a glimpse of it. A moment later, the plow made its way up the driveway, shoving aside snow into great piles on either side.

Another cheer went up as everyone caught sight of the ambulance, lights flashing, following right behind. As the plow made a slow circle to go back down, the ambulance parked and three EMTs jumped out. As they surrounded the young man, whose name apparently was Eric, the ski patrol relinquished custody and vanished into the crowd.

Eric's group of bachelor-party attendees remained at his side, unusually quiet while they watched the paramedics set up. Remy suspected one or two had bad hangovers, but they all seemed genuinely concerned.

"Looks like he's going to be okay," Vanessa said. "Let's go inside and maybe get something to eat or a cup of coffee."

He squeezed her hand. "Great idea."

Hand in hand, they walked toward the side entrance.

As usual, the interior lobby of The Lodge was packed full of skiers. Today, with nowhere to go, they seemed hell-bent on spending money and having fun. The gift shop had a sign up noting they'd sold out of souvenir T-shirts, scarves and knit caps. The bars were packed and it was standing room only.

Remy sensed an impatient vibe. The vast majority of the guests were here for the snow sports. Since the storm had stopped, they were all biding their time until Pine Peak reopened.

If no one seemed concerned about the man who had been rescued from the mountain, Remy knew there was good reason. They didn't know. Per policy, Lodge employees kept the worrisome news under wraps and would continue to do so until a successful rescue had been announced by Decker. He'd be releasing a statement very soon. Luckily, they'd been successful.

If they hadn't been successful, they'd figure out a way to do a press release that wouldn't scare off any of the guests. They had procedures in place for handling fatalities. Even if someone died in a skiing accident, once the slopes were determined safe, the skiing would continue.

Luckily, Eric hadn't died. Remy figured he'd find out later what exactly had led to the young man becoming stranded.

"Each time I see this place, I'm more and more in awe. I notice more and more details, like these absolutely beautiful Christmas decorations," Vanessa breathed, turning her head and trying to take them all in. "It's impossible to take them all in on one visit. I love that they're totally different than the ones at The Chateau."

"They are." He grinned. "The decorator there is instructed to go for an elegant, old-world, European vibe. Here, they strive for a more artsy, outdoorsy feel." Gazing at her, blue eyes sparkling, creamy skin pink from the cold, he wanted to kiss her senseless. Of course, that would have to wait for later. "Which do you prefer?" he asked, gesturing at a huge tree decked out with deer and moose among all the other ornaments.

She took his question seriously, studying the tree. "I like them both," she finally said. "Although, if and when I ever put up my own Christmas tree, I think I'd lean toward a more casual approach, like the rustic look here."

"If and when? Are you saying you've never put up your own tree?"

With a slightly embarrassed grimace, she shrugged. "I always visited my family and my parents had a tree there. Until six months ago, I never had my own place and nowhere to go." She swallowed. "This will not only be my first Christmas alone, but the first in my Boulder house."

"Makes sense." Giving in to temptation, he bent down and lightly kissed her mouth. "There's the café. Let's go get in line."

Relaxing into him, she nodded. "Sounds good, though I can think of something else I'd rather be doing…"

Sorely tempted, he hugged her. "Coffee first. We can always go to the room later."

They joined the line, which seemed ridiculously long, waiting with her in front and him pressing himself into her. Cozy and tempting at the same time. He felt a moment of happiness so pure, so bright, it hit him like a lightning bolt. This woman made everything better. They completed each other. As soon as possible, he would tell her, though he really wanted to wait until Seth was captured and safely locked away.

Just thinking his brother's name felt sobering. Pushing away the entire train of thought, he decided to focus on only what was good and bright about this day. Vanessa was unharmed, and they'd found each other. He had to believe Seth would get caught or turn himself in and finally get the help he so badly needed.

The line moved slowly. There were still five or six people in front of them when a shot rang out. Where? Spinning around, trying to keep himself between the shooter and Vanessa, Remy tried to locate the threat.

Another shot. There were screams, though Remy wasn't sure if they were because someone had been hit or just from general panic.

All hell broke loose. People bolted, running in every direction. Over the roar of the crowd, someone else shouted, *"Run!"* In full panic mode, everyone took off, a confused, terrified, thundering herd of people all scattering in different directions, no one sure which way to go.

Remy eyed the nearest decorative pillar and shoved Vanessa behind it. "Stay down," he ordered. "Don't move, not for anything, you understand?"

"Wait." She grabbed at him, her expression frantic. "Where are you going? Get down here with me."

"I can't." He shook off her grip. "This is my family's hotel. I've got to find the shooter."

Another shot, then two more in rapid succession. More screams, the smell of gunpowder, desperate perspiration and maybe even the coppery scent of blood. The lobby emptied out, despite the melee and crush of guests all running in opposite directions.

Trey appeared at Remy's side, his pistol out. "They're saying the shooter is near the lobby fountain," he growled, glancing sideways at Remy. "I'm guessing you're not armed?"

"No. I didn't see a reason to carry it when Vanessa and I snowshoed up here from my house."

Another shot. And another scream, a long one, trailing off into sobs. Trey cursed. "Stay behind me." Crouching low, he took off and pushed through the crowd going in the opposite direction. "Come on." Remy followed his lead, dodging between pillars and at the same time urging the terrified guests toward the emergency exit.

And then, amid the chaos of the fleeing people, Remy saw him. Seth, standing at the top of the small maintenance staircase that ran up behind and looked over the huge lobby fountain.

Seth surveyed the stampede below him with a smug smile, clearly taking pleasure in the panic below. Even worse, he had his arm around the neck of a terrified young girl, who appeared to be around thirteen or fourteen years old. He must have dragged her up there with him, Remy realized. The teen wept unabashedly, clearly out of her mind with fear.

Trey appeared at Remy's side, dragging him back behind one of the pillars. "Stay out of sight," he warned. "For all we know, Seth could have come here with the intention of taking you and Vanessa out."

"Maybe. Either way, he's shooting innocent people." Remy heard the shocked disbelief in his voice. "Do you know how many people he's injured or killed?"

"I don't know." Grim-faced, Trey clasped Remy's

shoulder. "I'm sorry, I know he's your brother, but I'm going to have to take him out."

"What about the girl? He's using her as a shield."

"Daria's on the way. She's the deputy sheriff and my best sharpshooter." Since Roaring Springs was so small, they didn't have a dedicated SWAT team.

Remy shuddered. "Let me try and reason with him."

"I think he's beyond reasoning."

"No! I refuse to believe it. Come on, Trey. You have to at least try to talk him down. If it doesn't work, then by all means have Daria put a bullet through his head."

"We don't have a skilled negotiator," Trey admitted. "I can try, but…"

"Let me do it." Remy swallowed hard. "I think if anyone can get through to him, I can."

"I don't know about that. I can't let you put yourself in danger."

"Look." Remy pointed. Seth had raised his pistol again, eying the dwindling crowd of people as if searching for his next victim.

Trey swore. "Daria needs to get here now. She's having a bit of trouble because some of the roads are still not plowed."

"I can't let this happen." Jerking away from Trey, Remy stepped out into the open. Just about everyone had fled the lobby, except for two clearly terrified people who were huddled together behind another pillar. Judging by the way the woman wept and the man held her, they were Seth's hostage's parents.

"Let her go, Seth," Remy shouted. "You need to stop this right now."

For maybe two seconds, Seth froze. And then he

laughed. The awful mocking sound seemed to echo in the nearly empty lobby.

"Let the kid go," Remy repeated. "Take me instead."

"I don't want you. But I will take Vanessa. Send her out here and this girl can go free. She's shaking, can you see that?"

"You son of a bitch. I'm not sending Vanessa. She's not here. You're angry with me, not her. Take me."

Narrow-eyed, Seth appeared to be considering. "Let me get this straight. You want to die for Vanessa Fisher. Do I have that right?"

Though he wouldn't have put it that way, now wasn't the time to be splitting hairs. "If I have to, yes. Just let the girl go."

"No. Get. Vanessa." Seth screamed so violently, spittle flew. His young captive closed her eyes and swayed, looking as if she might pass out from terror.

"I'm here." Vanessa's voice, coming from the other side of the fountain. Too far away for Remy to protect her.

"Vanessa, no!" He stepped forward, determined to get to her any way he could.

Ignoring him, Vanessa continued to move toward the staircase. "If I come up there with you, will you let her go?"

"Yes." Glowering at her, Seth kept the pistol pressed up against the teen's head. "But get up here fast, before I change my mind."

Remy made it about halfway across the room before Seth shouted at him to stop. "Take another step and she dies."

Remy froze. He wondered how much longer until

Daria showed up with her high-powered rifle. It didn't seem like he had a chance in hell of talking Seth down, not now. Especially not since Vanessa had revealed herself.

"Do as he says, Remy." Taking deliberate steps, Vanessa never took her gaze off Seth as she moved closer. "Seth, I know you're not a monster. Give me your word that you'll let this girl go once I reach you."

Instead of promising, Seth laughed maniacally, never moving his gaze from Vanessa. The sound echoed—the cackling of a madman. Remy's gut twisted as he realized he'd severely underestimated just how unstable his brother had become. "Don't hurt her," he called, hoping against hope that Seth still had a small shred of decency.

Both Seth and Vanessa ignored him. "I'm here," she said, speaking in the soothing kind of tone one used with irritable small children.

Heart in his throat, Remy watched her as she reached the bottom of the massive fountain. Even now, she'd made herself a perfect target. If Seth wanted her dead, he had a clear shot.

While Seth focused on Vanessa, Remy took the opportunity to move a few feet closer, praying Seth wouldn't notice.

So far, so good.

Vanessa had now climbed up, not on the bottom step of the small staircase which she probably hadn't noticed since it was blocked off with a chain and hidden mostly behind the massive fountain, but on one side of the fountain itself. The same thick concrete edge that kids like to balance on while they tossed their pennies into the water. Seth stood several feet above her, glowering at her while still holding the young girl in a tight grip. Remy noticed he didn't seem sure where to aim his pistol, as he switched from the teenager's temple to Vanessa and then back again.

While Seth was preoccupied, Remy took advantage and moved another couple of steps closer.

"Come up here, Van," Seth ordered. "It's just a few more feet."

"No." Vanessa's voice, clear and certain, rang out. "Bring the girl to me. Once she's here safe, then I'll go up there with you. Or someplace else—whatever you want."

Remy held his breath, praying that her gambit worked. If they could get Seth down from his vantage point, he'd be much less of a danger to any other innocent bystanders.

"Why?" Seth finally asked, squeezing the teenager so hard that she cried out. "Why would I want to go anywhere with you?"

"Don't you have plans for me?" she asked, sweetly reasonable. "That girl hasn't done anything to hurt you. She doesn't deserve to get caught up in any of this. Bring her down and let her go."

To Remy's shocked disbelief, Seth began hustling down his captive…one step, then another.

Head held high, Vanessa waited for him, looking for all the world like a queen awaiting her subject.

Meanwhile, Remy inched a little bit closer. Seth never even glanced his way.

Two more steps, and Remy could see the wide-eyed girl visibly trembling. Now Seth had come halfway down. Still a clean target, should Daria have arrived and gotten set up. But as long as Seth kept that pistol pressed up against the teenager's temple, Remy knew the deputy sheriff wouldn't risk it. Since he didn't want his brother to die, Remy hoped like hell Vanessa could talk Seth into giving himself up.

Movement caught his eye. Trey, moving briefly from behind his pillar, gave Remy a quick thumbs-up before ducking back into the shadows.

Thumbs-up. Did that mean Daria had taken up her position and had a high-powered rifle aimed at Seth?

Chapter 12

Heart pounding, Vanessa struggled to keep her voice steady. Instinctively, she knew she couldn't let Seth see her fear.

As if this was a perfectly normal circumstance, she checked her watch. "Come on, Seth. Bring the girl down and let her go. You and I have unfinished business."

She caught her breath as Seth manhandled the teenager another couple of steps. The girl's eyes locked on hers, the terror in them clear, amplified by her tears. Silently, she pleaded with Vanessa to help her, save her, not to let her die.

One more step. Two. Seth's captive held herself rigid, moving like a robot, clearly afraid to make the wrong move.

Vanessa couldn't blame her. She was pretty damn petrified herself.

Only three steps remained until they reached the bottom. Vanessa took a deep breath. She could do this. She *would* do this.

On the other side of the fountain, she saw Remy, carefully and slowly moving closer. She wanted to shake her head at him and warn him to stop. They didn't need to risk Seth noticing and flying into a rage.

She crossed her arms, tapping her toe in feigned impatience. She wasn't sure why or how she knew this, but somehow she realized the best way to deal with this crazy, out-of-control situation was to pretend everything was fine.

Frowning at Vanessa, Seth hustled his captive down the remaining steps. "Come over here," he ordered, his arm still around the teen's neck.

Heart thundering in her ears, Vanessa complied. She walked until only a few feet separated them. Wondering if she dared, she decided to reach for the girl, hoping to pull her from Seth's grip.

Before she could, Seth shoved the teenager away. She stumbled, too shocked to realize she was free. "Go," Vanessa urged her, watching as the girl half ran, half crawled to a small group of people who must have been her family.

Once she knew the teen was safe, Vanessa returned her attention to Seth. "What now?" she asked, her voice quiet and, amazingly, calm. "Are you going to shoot me in the head, right here, in the lobby of this hotel?"

"No," he answered, the bleakness in his gaze both startling and frightening. "I've messed up, Vanessa. I didn't mean to hurt anyone, except maybe you. So now, I'm going to use this gun to put an end to my misery—to *everyone's* misery."

Shocked, she stared. Unbelievably, Seth was smiling, though his eyes remained pools of darkness and despair. "And if I know you," Seth continued, "you'll blame yourself. My death will haunt you for years to come."

Then he lifted the gun to his head, pressing it against his own temple. Horrified, Vanessa wasn't sure what to do. Several scenarios flashed through her mind. Should she try to jump him, maybe knock away the pistol? Undecided and uncertain, she hesitated a moment too long.

Remy did not. He ran and leaped across the space separating them, landing on top of Seth and sending the gun flying.

Miraculously, it did not go off.

"Stay down," Remy ordered, struggling to restrain his brother. Seth fought him, crying and laughing at the same time, his expression a study in confusion.

"You should have just let me die," Seth cried out.

"Never," Remy responded, his voice heartbroken. "You're still mine to protect."

At that, Seth stopped struggling, his gaze meeting Remy's.

"Why?" Remy asked. "Why hurt innocent people? What brought you to this point?"

"You're a Colton," Seth replied, the anger in his voice matching the emotion in his eyes. "You couldn't possibly understand."

The sheriff appeared, seemingly out of nowhere, and joined Remy. Working together, they got Seth's hands behind his back and then Trey put him in cuffs.

Once he'd been restrained, Trey motioned to two of his deputies to take him away.

"Take him out the back," Trey ordered. "The news vans have started showing up out front. I've got people warding them off, but the last thing we need is them showing video of Seth on the evening news tonight."

For a second, Vanessa thought Remy might go with the two men escorting Seth. But he visibly checked himself and remained in place.

"That was a close one." An athletic woman with short brown hair wearing a Bradford County Sheriff's Department uniform sauntered up, carrying a deadly-looking rifle. Her golden-brown eyes briefly touched on Vanessa. "There were a few times when I had a perfect shot. Luckily, Trey refused to give me permission to take it."

Vanessa realized this woman must be the sharpshooter from the police department. If Seth had made one more wrong move, she would have taken him out. Despite all he'd done, the thought of him dying that way made her stomach hurt.

"I'm glad it all worked out," Vanessa finally said, hoping she sounded calmer than she felt.

"Me, too." The other woman studied her. "You were really brave out there. Good job talking him down." She stuck out her hand. "I'm Daria. Daria Bloom."

"Vanessa Fisher." They shook. Vanessa appreciated Daria's cool, firm grip.

Daria glanced past her, her gaze landing on Remy. "Are you okay?" she asked, her smooth brow wrinkling in concern. "You look a little pale."

"I'm fine." Remy attempted a smile, which clearly

said he was not. "What about the guests? Were there any serious injuries?"

"A couple of minor gunshot wounds, but nothing too bad." The sheriff smiled reassuringly. "No fatalities. I've got paramedics treating everyone now."

Another uniformed deputy walked up and joined them. "We got Seth loaded up out back and he's on his way to the station for processing and booking. The mayor has been trying to reach you. Mayor Dylan would like to get with you to formulate a statement he can give to the press. He's stressed his highest priority is reassuring the people of Roaring Springs that they are now safe."

For a moment Remy raised his head and opened his mouth, making Vanessa think he planned to take issue with that statement. She saw the second it sunk in that his own brother had made the entire town feel threatened. The flash of pain in his gaze made her ache to go to him and offer comfort, but she knew this wasn't the place or time.

"I assume you're going to keep him locked up until the judge sets bail?"

"I think it's safe to say the DA is going to deem him a flight risk. There probably won't be bail," Trey answered, his expression solemn.

"Will you at least try to keep an eye on him? After this stunt, I'm afraid he might try to hurt himself."

"Of course." Trey clapped Remy on the shoulder. "We've already placed him on suicide watch."

"Thank you," Remy said, his expression both defeated and sad. Vanessa knew that he still felt responsible for the acts of his brother. She resolved to talk to him later about that.

A tall, well-built man with wavy brown hair walked up. "Is everything under control?" he asked.

Trey nodded. "Yes, Decker. We've already taken Seth off premises and the wounded have either been tended to on-site or transported to the hospital."

Decker dipped his chin before turning his attention to Remy. "Have you dealt with the press?"

Remy looked stunned. "I...no."

"I've got men keeping them back," Trey interjected. "I know Decker's head honcho at The Lodge, but I'm going to need to take his statement. Is there someone else you could send?"

Remy straightened, smoothing out his miserable expression. "I don't work at The Lodge, but I'll handle this."

"Thank you." Decker turned away, calling out to someone else, his attention already elsewhere.

As Remy visibly composed himself, Vanessa joined him. "I'll go with you, if you don't mind."

Remy took her arm and put a bit of distance between them and the others. "This is not my job, Vanessa, but I'm helping out." His voice shook.

"It's okay, Remy," she insisted. "This involved your brother, for goodness' sake. I don't know who that Decker guy is, but he either doesn't realize what you just went through or he's an idiot."

After a startled glance, Remy laughed. Some of the tension left her hearing that sound.

"Decker is another one of my cousins. Not only that, but he's the director of operations here at The Lodge. He's in damage-control mode right now. I get it."

Abashed, she swallowed. "I'm sorry. I didn't mean to disparage your cousin."

"Oh, honey." He kissed her cheek. "I appreciate you wanting to defend me. Thank you."

Stunned at both his insight and the endearment, she froze. *Honey.* She kind of liked that.

Trey came up. "Hey, Remy. I know you're about to go do your thing with the press, but remember Mayor Dylan wants to do a joint statement. He's on his way here. Can you hold off on helping Decker with the press for a bit longer?"

Though his expression seemed pained, Remy nodded. "Trey, I'll be honest with you. I'm still trying to process what Seth has done. There's no way I can handle a press conference right now. I'll send someone out to let them know. That way they won't get too restless. But I'll probably be delegating the actual conference to someone else."

Trey immediately nodded. "Of course," he said. "I completely understand. Do what you have to do."

"Thanks." Remy turned to her. "I don't know about you, but I need to go somewhere quiet, where I can think."

From the corner of her eye, she saw Trey grab Decker, who appeared to be making a second pass of the room. The two men conferred, heads close together. Finally, Decker glanced at Trey and nodded before someone else claimed his attention.

Trey returned. "It's all set. Decker is going to take care of everything. And he said you could use his office if you need some privacy."

Vanessa watched Remy closely. His guarded expression almost crumbled, but he appeared to wrest control of himself at the last minute.

"Thank you," Vanessa told Trey, taking Remy's

arm. As long as she kept her focus on him, she didn't have to deal with the fact that her legs were trembling so much that she could barely walk.

"Outside," she told Remy. "I need to get away from the people, the sounds, all of it. Let's go for a walk."

"Okay." He nodded. "I'm with you on that."

Once outside, they walked to the outdoor seating area for one of the restaurants. Now closed, she chose a long bench and carefully brushed off the snow. "Sit."

Remy sat. She took a spot next to him.

They sat in silence for a few minutes, the cold seeping through her jeans and into her bones. Still she didn't move.

Finally, she turned to Remy. He sat as still as a statue, gazing off into the distance. "Where do you think Seth is now?"

He blinked and checked his watch. "By now I think he'll have arrived at the police station. They'll book him and put him in a holding cell until they decide whether to send him to the county jail. It depends whether the feds pick him up or not."

"It's so sad." She shivered, the cold finally getting to her. "Do you mind if we go back inside? My feet are numb."

Immediately he jumped to his feet. "Of course I don't mind. Let's go. We can always take Decker up on his offer to use his office, if you still need more quiet time."

"I think we both do," she said.

After they walked inside, the lobby still a chaotic mess of people and police and reporters, Remy led her through a door marked "Employees Only" and then down a long, carpeted hallway.

Her cell rang. Glancing at the screen, she didn't recognize the number, or the caller ID. Stepping away from Remy and Trey, she answered.

"Van, don't hang up." Seth's voice, sounding desperate. "I insisted on my one phone call and since right now they're keeping me locked up in the Roaring Springs jail, they let me. I called you."

Her chest hurt. Closing her eyes, she took a deep breath. "Why?"

"I wanted to let you know I'm sorry." He sounded so young and afraid that, despite everything, her heart went out to him. "I didn't mean to hurt anyone. I just wanted to get your attention."

She steeled herself. "What about Sabrina? Did you kill her?"

"It was an accident," he said. "I swear to you. We'd both been partying pretty hard and we started arguing. She pushed me and I fell and hit my head."

"And then what?" she asked. "You strangled her?"

"She'd gotten too clingy and threatened to tell you about us. I lost it and I strangled her. Just like that Avalanche Killer. I'd just watched a news story on him, so that might have been in the back of my mind."

She realized Seth always had an excuse for everything. Nothing was ever his fault. "What about Remy?" She couldn't help but bring him up. "He's devastated by what you've done."

"The hell with Remy. It's bad enough that he's got everything." The viciousness of his tone revealed his rage.

"That rich, snooty family of his thinks he can do no wrong. He never got tired of rubbing my face in his good luck."

Speechless, she didn't know how to respond. Was Seth actually putting the blame on Remy for his own bad behavior?

"Are you listening?" Seth had dialed down his tone. "Because I've got more to say. Remy always had more than me. Always. The final straw was when he got you, Van. I just couldn't take that. It broke me. That's why I went crazy there at The Lodge."

Now Seth was blaming *her*? "Seriously?" Unwilling to hear any more, she ended the call.

When she looked up, both Remy and Trey were watching her. "Everything all right?" Remy asked, putting his arm around her shoulders.

She gave a tight nod. "That was Seth."

"What?" Both men appeared shocked.

"He's in custody," Trey said. "How did he gain access to a phone?"

"He said he demanded his one call and they let him have it."

Trey cursed under his breath. "I need to have a talk with my men. Did he threaten you?"

"No." She inhaled deeply, still trying to digest the awfulness of Seth's claims. "He wanted to let me know that his behavior was all my fault. Not his."

Remy shook his head. Trey laughed. "If you believe that, I've got oceanfront property in the mountains to sell you."

"You know that's not true, right?" Remy growled, pulling her closer.

"Of course I do. It just hurts that he apparently believes that."

"Seth believes whatever he thinks will paint him in a better picture," Trey volunteered. "Sorry, Remy. He's always been envious of our family. You just couldn't see it."

"That's true." Vanessa relayed the rest of what Seth had said. "Apparently he's been eaten up with envy."

Remy nodded. "I need to find Decker. I should participate in the press conference."

Trey's cell phone pinged. He checked it and jerked his thumb toward Remy. "Well then, you're up. The mayor just arrived and is waiting for you. You'll need to put your heads together for a minute to collaborate your statement."

The absolute last thing Remy felt like doing right now was dealing with the press, but since Seth had been responsible for all this mayhem, he felt obligated to do his part. Squaring his shoulders, he thanked Trey and asked him to keep an eye on Vanessa.

"What for?" Vanessa asked. "I'm going with you. Don't worry, I promise to stay in the background."

Sensing she needed a distraction, he agreed.

Mayor Dylan waited near the yellow tape that marked the crime-scene area where Trey's men were still working. He grunted when he saw Remy. "Helluva mess, isn't it?"

"It is." Briefly, he outlined the facts, sparse as they were. Decker walked up, pivoting when Remy waved him away.

"You know they're going to ask if he confessed to killing Sabrina Gilford," the mayor said.

"We're not going to let them dwell on that." Remy kept his voice firm. "All we're going to talk about is what happened here today."

"I'll let you take the lead then," Mayor Dylan said.

"I'll wrap things up with a brief speech about keeping Roaring Springs safe."

"Perfect. And we're not taking any questions."

Though the mayor raised his eyebrows at that, he agreed.

When they stepped outside, the number of reporters present surprised even Remy. There was Ben, from the Roaring Springs paper, of course. But Remy didn't even recognize the seven others, some of whom had brought camera crews with them. In retrospect, he figured the Denver and Colorado Springs stations would want to send a few of their people, but considering the massive amount of snowfall and the road closures, he had no idea how they'd managed to make it up here.

As soon as Remy and the mayor stepped up to the group, video cameras started recording. Remy outlined the events, beginning with the fact that there had been only minor injuries and no fatalities. "We have the suspect in custody," he continued, bracing himself. "His name is Seth Harris."

Ben jerked up his head at that revelation and he began writing furiously in his notebook. Ben believed in reporting the old-fashioned way. He didn't carry a tablet or even a smartphone. Remy supposed he must use a computer somewhere, but if so, he didn't know where. He'd never seen Ben with even a laptop.

Remy stepped back, gesturing to the mayor. Mayor Dylan stepped forward and launched into a practiced speech lauding the safety of their town and ski resorts.

As soon as he'd finished, both he and Remy turned around and hurried back inside, ignoring the reporters' shouted questions.

The rest of the day passed in a blur. Remy knew at

some point he needed to go talk to his brother, but right now his own emotions were too high. Instead, he and Vanessa packed up their bags and moved back to his house. The snowplows had done a great job clearing the roads and downtown Roaring Springs had sprung back to life.

That night, Remy and Vanessa sat together in front of the fireplace and held each other. Remy didn't feel much like talking and either Vanessa got that or she felt the same way. The crackling of the fire was the only sound and provided the only light. He felt cozy and warm and...loved. He'd finally found the one woman who completed him—his other half—and the circumstances surrounding his brother tarnished what otherwise would have been a joyous time.

Seth blamed Vanessa and Remy for everything. Remy would much rather Seth blame only him. The only thing Vanessa had done wrong was coming here and trying to gain closure on the end of what she'd regarded as a friendship. *Closure.* That term seemed to be something women valued more than men. Either way, he was glad she had. Otherwise, he might not have ever met her.

But he couldn't keep from worrying that he'd been the one who'd caused his little brother to finally snap. That guilt was something he knew he'd have to live with for the rest of his life.

As the evening wore on, they dozed. Vanessa finally roused them to go to bed, asking him if he needed to eat anything since they hadn't had dinner.

Remy wasn't hungry, though he told her to go ahead and eat if she was.

"I'm only hungry for you," she said, tugging him into the bedroom with her.

They made love and fell asleep holding each other. Maybe because they were both so exhausted, but the next thing Remy knew, it was morning and the insistent sound of his doorbell ringing over and over and over woke him.

"What the…?" He glanced over at Vanessa, with her tousled hair and drowsy eyes. She shook her head and pushed him toward the edge of the bed. "Whoever it is, either get rid of them or stall them until I get some clothes on."

Despite his gnawing despair, he couldn't help grinning as he hopped out of bed and pulled on his pants. Barefoot, he padded out of the room, trying not to think about what he'd like to do when he got back in bed with Vanessa. Which he would. As soon as possible.

Whoever stood on his doorstep wasn't giving up. They kept pressing the doorbell, again and again. Remy knew only one person that tenacious. When he yanked open his front door and saw Trey standing there, he knew he'd been right.

"Did I wake you?" his cousin asked innocently.

"What?" Remy growled. "Don't you think Vanessa and I deserve to sleep in after the day we had yesterday?"

Trey dipped his chin. "Sorry. I guess I could have called, but I thought I might as well check in and see how you both were doing."

"Are you going to make him stand out there in the cold?" Vanessa chided, coming up behind Remy and nudging him with one hip. "Come on in, Sheriff. Would you like a cup of coffee?"

Trey pushed past Remy, grinning as his cousin reluctantly stepped aside. "Thanks," he said. "I never turn down coffee."

After closing and locking the front door, Remy followed everyone to the kitchen, unable to keep from admiring the sway of Vanessa's backside as she strolled along. He blinked, realizing she'd put on one of his sweatshirts over her leggings. She looked so sexy, for a moment he couldn't think.

Until he caught Trey looking at him, a knowing smile playing on his cousin's lips. Trey had recently gotten engaged to Aisha Allen, who'd been his best friend since grade school, and Remy had never seen him so happy. Until now, Remy had never understood the kind of blissful fog newly betrothed men seemed to walk around in. Now he completely got it, even though he wasn't engaged. *Yet.*

Reining in his thoughts, Remy took a seat at the kitchen table. He thanked Vanessa as she placed a steaming mug of black coffee in front of him, and waited for the sheriff to tell him what warranted a personal visit. He figured if it had something to do with his brother, Trey would have already spit it out. Since he didn't appear to be in a hurry to do that, Remy guessed it wasn't anything urgent. Still…waiting for Trey to speak felt like torture.

"Is Seth all right?" he asked, unable to take it any longer.

"Last report I got, he was fine," Trey answered, taking a drink of his own mug of joe. "But that's not why I'm here."

Smiling, Vanessa moved one of the chairs and sat down next to Remy, nudging him with her hip. "We just woke up," she explained, ducking her head shyly.

"I kind of got that." Trey grinned. "Both of you deserved it."

Remy cleared his throat. "And you're about to tell us why you're here?"

Vanessa groaned. "Remy…"

"It's okay." Trey's grin widened. "I'm used to it."

Unrepentant, Remy leaned back in his chair and crossed his arms.

"Fine." Trey sighed. "We're calling a family meeting. Bree's going to let us use her gallery since we don't want to meet anywhere public. She's closing it for the evening."

"Why not have it somewhere public?" Remy scratched the back of his head. "Wouldn't it be nicer if we could all sit down and talk over a meal and a beer?"

"Nicer, yes. But we can't take the chance of anyone else overhearing. I'm sorry, Remy, but we need to get together and talk about Seth."

Though he privately winced, he agreed. "Is this in the nature of a formal police investigation?" he asked. "I mean, he's already in custody, so I don't see the point."

"Of course not. I'd never discuss something like that with the family. It's just a lot of people have been contacting me, putting two and two together and figuring out that Seth might have been behind a lot more mischief before he attacked Vanessa and then shot up The Lodge lobby. If so, I'd have to say he had a definite bone to pick with the Colton family. We want to compare notes."

The idea that his brother would have acted so spitefully toward Remy's family should have come as more of a surprise. Instead, he found himself asking how he could have missed it.

"Seven o'clock tonight," Trey said, rousing Remy from his thoughts. "Family only. Will you be able to make it?"

"I wouldn't miss it."

Vanessa looked from one man to the other. "I'm sorry," she finally said.

Trey reached over and squeezed her hand. "Not your fault." He pushed to his feet. "See you later, Remy. You both take care." He slugged back the last of his coffee and ambled toward the door.

Remy hurried after him, so he could see him out.

"Remember," Trey said quietly, glancing back toward the kitchen. "Family only."

"I got it."

When he returned to the kitchen, Vanessa eyed him over her coffee cup. "Are you okay?"

"Yeah. I'm just dreading whatever else I'm going to find out about Seth tonight. Apparently my entire family has been adversely affected by him in some way."

"Ouch. I'm sorry. Is there anything I can do to help?"

The concern shining in her pretty blue eyes touched him. Without thinking, he went over to her and kissed her. "Just be you," he drawled. "Will you be all right here while I'm gone?"

"Of course." She gestured at the television. "I'm sure I can find an old movie to watch. Don't worry about me."

At six thirty, Remy grabbed his keys and got ready

to head over to Bree's art gallery, Wise Gal. He'd only been there once or twice, not including her grand opening. Both times had been when she'd had a huge exhibit and wanted her family there to support her. And support was one of the things the Coltons did best.

As he turned to go, he walked over to where Vanessa sat in the living room, comfortably ensconced in the recliner, remote in hand. He bent down to kiss her goodbye, meaning only to brush his mouth lightly against hers. Instead, he found himself kissing her as if he might never see her again.

Finally, he reluctantly broke away, half-aroused. Judging by the smoldering lust in her blue eyes, she felt the same.

"I'll be back before you know it," he promised. "Keep the doors locked—even though Seth is behind bars—and call me if you need anything."

She grinned. "Will do. Don't be surprised if I call you and tell you how badly I want your body."

This made him laugh out loud. Damn, he loved her.

On the drive over, he reflected on how much his life had changed in such a short time. Vanessa had made everything richer—each day seemed more vivid. If not for the apparently escalating situation with Seth, he'd have to believe he'd never been happier.

When he arrived at the Wise Gal Gallery, even though he was ten minutes early, he saw that several others had gotten there ahead of him. Since Bree had prominently displayed a Closed sign on the front door, he had no trouble finding a parking space.

"Here he is." Blaine clapped him on the back, managing, as usual, to appear both rough around the edges and amiable. "Trey has some news."

Remy glanced across the room and met the sheriff's eyes.

Trey nodded, one quick dip of his chin. "He confessed," he said, his voice carrying across the suddenly quiet room. "Sabrina Gilford's death has finally been solved, along with the other strange occurrences surrounding the Colton family. Seth hated what the Coltons had so much, he set out to sabotage them whenever he could, even starting rumors to disparage the family in town. He felt Vanessa was his ticket to something better—that when they married, he'd have her millions and be just as wealthy as his brother and wouldn't need some management level job at The Lodge."

Trey looked down before resuming. "Seth figured out that Shruggs was the killer and secretly followed him, taking Bianca's body and dumping it on Wyatt's property. It was Seth, not Davis, who set off the avalanche that uncovered the bodies to cause even more havoc for the family. And he framed the Avalanche Killer for Sabrina's murder—she'd gotten too clingy and threatened to tell Vanessa about them."

Remy inhaled, his throat burning. As if he suspected, Trey paused, giving Remy time to compose himself.

"The FBI is now involved, too," Trey continued. "Stefan Roberts is handling the case. Not only has Seth been charged with terroristic threats, but he's also been charged with murder. He's being held without bail. They'll be transferring him to the Federal Correctional Institute, Englewood, once he's sentenced. For now, we'll be keeping him here."

Chapter 13

The instant Remy walked through the door, Vanessa saw the defeat in his posture. The idea that this self-confident, vital man had been knocked so low made her hurt with a visceral ache.

"That bad?" she asked, trying for a lighter tone even as she braced herself.

Slowly, Remy nodded. He swallowed hard. "At least I now have a pretty good idea why my brother chose to keep his relationship with Sabrina secret. Apparently, Seth has been harboring resentment toward the Coltons for some time now. My family can be overwhelming sometimes. Seth didn't really like to be around them much. If they'd gone public, my family would have wanted Sabrina to bring him around to family events. She would have insisted on it, too. She might have been a party girl, but Sabrina was proud to be a Colton." He looked down and swallowed again. "We all are."

"I'm sorry." She didn't know what else to say, so she squeezed his shoulder in commiseration. If she could, she would have done anything to take away his pain.

"Though no one has actual proof—like video or witnesses—all of a sudden, my family now realizes he was behind what they previously thought were random acts of violence or vandalism. He recapped a list of Seth's dirty deeds, from trying to run family off the road, to throwing a brick through the window at Bree's art gallery. When he ended with Seth doctoring books and imitating the Avalanche Killer, she shook her head. "I have no words," she finally said. She'd seen how badly Seth had deteriorated, but this...

"It's a lot to take in," Remy admitted.

Still trying to process all this, Vanessa tried to make sense of Seth's actions.

Murder, attempted murder, stalking and embezzling. So hard to believe the man who'd held her hand through her parents' funeral had done all that. Heartsick, she shook her head. "It's like I didn't really know Seth at all."

"You and me both." Remy sighed. "I keep asking myself how it was possible that I hadn't known. I talked to Seth at least once a week, sometimes more." He met her gaze briefly before his own skittered away. "I feel responsible."

"You're not." She understood Remy's internal struggle. She needed to help keep him from going someplace really dark. She got up and went to him, wrapping her arms around him and holding on tightly.

"You can't blame yourself. I understand the raw guilt you feel, but stop it. No one suspects their brother is a killer. No one."

"I should have seen something. Some clue." Clearly not hearing her or believing her words, Remy moved away, rejecting her attempt to comfort him. "He murdered Sabrina. She was part of my family, even though she wasn't related by blood to Seth." Gaze tortured, he glanced at her. "And finally, he tried to kill you."

True. She managed to suppress a shudder. "Remy, Seth and I were friends for a long time. Not once would I have even remotely suspected he was capable of any of this. Never mind murder, but even the petty things like throwing water on someone or a brick through their window. You've got to stop torturing yourself."

"I'm trying." Still, he shook his head. "I'm still attempting to come to grips with the notion that my little brother is a psychopath."

So much anguish, so much pain in those words.

She had no words, hurting for him, with him. "Clearly, he needs professional help."

"I'm not sure anyone could help him," Remy finally said. "Though I'll leave that to the professionals to diagnose."

Again, she tried to comfort him and again, he shook her off. "I need to be alone." Then, clearly seeing the hurt flash across her face, he reached up and caressed her cheek. "Don't take it personally, Vanessa. I'm going to change and then go down to the basement gym and work out. Exercise is the best way for me to relieve tension."

Since she could understand this, she nodded, managed a smile and waved him away.

After he'd left, she thought about going for a run. But the sidewalks weren't all cleared and she wouldn't feel safe running in the street in the dark.

Instead, she decided to watch a Hallmark movie—exactly the kind of sweet, romantic escape she'd need to try to get in a better mood.

But thoughts of Seth kept running through her head. The *old* Seth, not the man he'd become now. The Seth who had gone skiing in Vermont with her, the Seth with whom she'd picked apples and done a 5K. That Seth—the man who'd been her friend—seemed like a completely different person.

She could only imagine what memories Remy had. He'd done his best to take care of his brother since Seth had been a teenager. Nothing but pain, all the way around.

The movie helped, somewhat. She tried earnestly to get into the emotional love story playing out on the screen.

An hour later, Remy walked into the room. She sat up, slightly groggy, hoping he'd been able to purge himself of some of the demons that haunted him.

When he crossed over to her, hair damp with perspiration, her breath caught. He looked at peace, relaxed and more at ease than he'd been since Seth had gone off the rails. When she met his gaze, he smiled. Love and heat blazed from his hazel-green eyes.

He crossed the room and dropped down next to her, pulling her into his arms. "I'm sorry," he rasped, lips against her cheek. "I needed to pound the punching bag for a bit. It helped me come to terms with everything."

If she turned her head just slightly, his mouth would

capture hers. But she had something she wanted to say first. "Remy, I want you to always remember that we're on the same team."

He nodded. "I know. I'm not alone. Neither are you. We'll work through this together."

Relieved, she turned her face toward his. Happiness bubbled up inside her as she met his lips.

They moved from the couch to his bed, shedding clothes as they went. They made love, Vanessa losing herself in him. When she finally drifted off to sleep, he held her tight in his arms.

The next morning, Remy opening the blinds woke her. She blinked against the sudden onslaught of sunlight and at the naked, gorgeous man smiling down at her.

"You're finally awake!" he commented, as if that somehow surprised him.

"I am," she murmured. "Now that you let the sunlight in." Squinting at him, she sighed. "You look extremely…energetic."

Maybe he could expend some of that energy with her. Her entire body tingled at the thought.

He shook his head, even though she hadn't voiced the thought out loud. "We can't. Not right now. We have plans."

"We do?"

"Yes. Dress warmly," Remy ordered. "We're going out."

Eying him lazily from the warmth of his bed, Vanessa considered. "Going out where?"

"To buy a tree."

For a second, she wasn't entirely sure what he meant. "A tree? Like a Christmas tree?"

"Yep." His hot gaze caressed her, making her ache for his hands. "You said you'd never had one of your own. There's a big lot at the north end of town. And the hardware store downtown sells lights and decorations." He smiled at her. "We can stop for coffee and breakfast on the way."

The idea enticed her. Even better, Remy seemed almost himself again. "Okay." She pushed back the covers, immediately intrigued. "I'm in. I'll just need a few minutes to shower and get dressed."

"Take your time," he said, though his impatient glance at his watch said otherwise.

His excitement must have been contagious. She hurried through her shower, blow-dried her hair and applied minimal makeup. Proud that she'd gotten ready in twenty minutes, she rushed into the living room. "I'm ready!"

He smiled, the heat in his gaze making her reconsider her earlier plan to get tangled up in the sheets with him.

"That was quick," he commented. "You look beautiful, as always."

Tongue-tied, she nodded. "Thanks."

Once in his Jeep, she buckled up while he backed out of the garage.

The brilliant white of the landscape warranted sunglasses, so she dug in her purse until she found them. Briefly, as she gazed at Pine Peak in the distance, she thought longingly of taking a couple of runs down it, but she pushed away that idea. She could always ski tomorrow. Today, she'd make new memories with Remy.

They had a hearty breakfast at a small coffee shop off the beaten path, which meant only the locals went there. The place only had about ten tables and a long breakfast bar, so they had to wait twenty minutes. The heady scent of bacon and pancakes and coffee was intoxicating. "Best hidden gem in town," Remy said.

Her stomach rumbled. "Good. Because I'm starving."

"After we eat, we're headed to a hardware store that has a huge Christmas section. Think about what kind of colors and theme you want," he advised her. "Of course, if you want something eclectic, I'm down with that, too."

How she loved this man. The idea of them decorating their first Christmas tree together sounded amazing.

By the time they were seated, the line stretched outside and down the sidewalk. Despite the cold, no one seemed to mind. Instead, those waiting appeared at ease and chatted happily.

They were shown to a high-top table near the front window. From there, Vanessa could see the residential area to the east and the mountain to the west. "This reminds me a little of Boulder," she commented. "Though more down-to-earth."

This made Remy grin. The waitress brought them menus and coffee, promising to return in a few minutes.

He pounced on his coffee. Shaking her head, Vanessa doctored hers up and took a small sip. "Wow," she said. "That's a good cup of java."

"Just wait until you try the food."

Opening her menu, Vanessa decided on pancakes and eggs, with a side of bacon. She glanced up to find Remy watching her, his menu unopened in front of him.

"I already know what I'm having," he confessed. "I'm a creature of habit. Whenever I come here, I get the same thing. It's called the Old South breakfast. Eggs, bacon, hash browns, grits and biscuits and gravy."

"Yikes. That sounds like a lot of food."

"It is." He grinned again before taking a long drink of his coffee. "Yet somehow I manage to finish it all."

The waitress returned and took their orders and refilled their mugs. Once she'd left again, Remy reached across the table and took Vanessa's hand. "Which would you rather do first? Buy the ornaments or pick out the tree?"

Stirring another bit of creamer into her coffee, she shrugged. "I think the tree. Once we've chosen that, I'll know better how much decoration to buy."

"Sounds good."

When their food arrived, Vanessa ate until she couldn't manage another bite. Everything tasted delicious, especially the fluffy pancakes.

Finally, pushing her plate away, she sipped coffee and watched Remy devour his breakfast. Somehow, she found the way he single-mindedly ate with a determined purpose sexy as hell.

Bemused, she mentally shook her head at herself. The waitress winked at her as she took away Vanessa's plates. "Clearly, he's still working on his," she said, dropping the check in the middle of the table.

Vanessa smiled and agreed.

Finally, Remy had cleaned his plates—all three of them. With a self-satisfied sigh, he drank the last of his coffee. "Are you ready to go pick your tree?"

"Yes." And she was. Though she'd never had the

experience of choosing a live Christmas tree before, she figured Remy had and would help guide her.

They drove to the end of Main Street, where it turned into a two-lane road. She recognized it as the one she'd taken on the way into town. Instead of turning right, they veered left, driving into a residential neighborhood with beautifully restored old homes.

"This is part of the original Roaring Springs," Remy told her. "These houses were here long before the town became a ski resort. The original owners got rich off the mines."

While she knew many Colorado mountain towns had mines, she hadn't heard anything about Roaring Springs. "Are any still open? I know I've been on a few mine tours in other places."

He shook his head. "No. They've long been boarded up."

They traveled a few more blocks down, then Remy slowed down. "There it is." He pointed to a huge parking lot with a few cars and one big, white tent. A large sign proclaimed Fern's Christmas Trees.

"They don't look too busy," she commented, not sure if she should be disappointed or not.

"Christmas is only a few days away," he reminded her. "Most people already have their trees."

She grimaced. "I hope they still have a few decent ones left."

For whatever reason, this comment made him laugh. "Oh, they will, I promise you."

Once he'd parked and gotten out, he took her arm. "You'll see," he said, leading her down a path and around a large boulder that shielded the place from the parking area and road. They went around the tent, which surprised her, but she followed his lead.

As soon as they scooted past the tent, she stopped and looked around her in awe.

A virtual forest stretched out in front of her. There were more trees than she ever could have imagined. Tall trees, fat trees, pines and firs and trees that had been flocked to look white. Hand in hand, she and Remy roamed the lot, which felt more like getting lost in a forest than anything else. Now she was glad there weren't many other customers. She had the strangest urge to commune with the trees until she found the right one. They were all different and each beautiful. Any one of them would look perfect in Remy's living room.

"Let's take a look," he said. "Come on."

Hand in hand, they began strolling down the rows of trees.

"I can't decide," she murmured. "They're all so magnificent."

He glanced down at her, the tenderness in his gaze warming her. "Take your time. I'm a firm believer in finding the perfect tree. When you see the right one, you'll know it."

They'd reached the edge of the row and she turned to make her way down the next one. Three trees down and she saw it. A blue spruce, maybe six-feet tall, perfectly formed, not too wide and not too thin. "This one," she breathed, stopping in front of it. "I don't know how no one chose this tree, but I'm glad. Because it's coming home with us."

Her enthusiasm earned her an adoring look from

Remy that turned her insides to mush. "Are you sure?" he asked.

"Yes." She nodded. "I've never been more certain of anything in my life."

"Perfect." He kissed her, long and deep. When the salesperson found them, he stood back and eyed them as if he thought they were crazy.

"There." Still wrapped in Remy's arms, joy and love darkening her blue eyes, Vanessa pointed at the tree she'd chosen. "We'll take that one."

Later, with the tree all wrapped up and tied to the top of his Jeep, they drove to Race Hardware and chose the ornaments and lights and tinsel for their first tree together. Remy mostly stood back and watched as Vanessa loaded up her basket, his expression amazed as she laughed and sang holiday carols under her breath. She got it, because she would never have guessed that such a simple thing could make her so happy. *He* made her happy. Though she had a home in Boulder, a life there, she knew she planned to enjoy every second of her time with him.

Once they were back in his Jeep, all the holiday decorations stowed in the back, Vanessa glanced at him and smiled. "I can't wait to get back to the house and get all of this put out."

"Me, either," he said. "Though I helped my father choose a showpiece tree once or twice, this will be the first Christmas tree I've had at my house."

"What?" Eyes wide, she studied him, not quite certain if he might be teasing her. "Are you serious?"

"Yes." He shrugged. "I've been a single guy. Putting up a tree seemed like a lot of trouble just for me. There's a tree at the office and at Colton Manor, not to mention every single store, restaurant and bar in town. Including The Chateau and The Lodge. Anytime I got an urge to feel in the holiday spirt, I just had to venture out of my house."

"That means you and I aren't so different." She touched his arm, smiling big and wide. "That makes this even more special. It's not only our first tree together, but our first tree, period." Who knew? Maybe this would be the first in a long line of them. Dared she allow herself to hope for a future with this wonderful man? He kissed her once more before releasing her and opening his door. "Now let's get this tree unloaded and set up so we can get it decorated."

After she helped Remy get the tree off the top of his Jeep, she escaped to the bathroom to freshen up. Excited to share what hopefully would become a yearly ritual, she hurried back out to the Jeep and started carrying in the bags of lights and ornaments. Part of her wished she'd been able to do this in her new home in Boulder. One of the first things she'd decided when she'd purchased it had been where she'd planned to put her Christmas tree.

But no, she reminded herself. For now she'd live in the moment and enjoy this time with Remy. She inhaled deeply, breathing in the scents of fir and pine, and smiled.

Once Remy sawed a bit more off the bottom, he had her help him put the tree in the stand. Then they spent the next several hours turning the living room into Christmas Central. Remy streamed holiday music and made them hot cocoa, then helped her string lights and garlands on the beautiful tree. For the first time that year, she felt in the actual holiday spirit.

When "Rockin' Around the Christmas Tree" came on, Remy grabbed her hands and began dancing around the living room in time with the music. She found herself laughing as he twirled her and hip-bumped her.

By the time the song ended, they were both out of breath. He pulled her in for a long, deep kiss. "This is fun," he murmured, resting his forehead against hers. Smiling, she agreed, the tree twinkling merrily in the background.

"It's beautiful and magical, too," she said.

Kissing her once more, he agreed and released her. "Let's get it done."

"Okay. Next up, ornaments," she declared, handing him a box of red glass balls. Grabbing a similar box of gold ones, she put hooks on them and began placing them on the tree. This precious moment—decorating her very first Christmas tree with the man she now knew in her heart she loved—would forever be etched in her memory.

By the time they'd arranged every single ornament on the tree, singing along to "Rudolph the Red-Nosed Reindeer" and a few other classics, she felt happier than she'd felt in years. This might be only temporary, but she couldn't help but feel a bit optimistic.

Side by side, they stepped back to survey their handiwork. Remy had placed the tree near the floor-to-ceiling windows that looked out over the backyard. He walked over and turned out the lights, so that the tree lit up the room and reflected in the windows. Vanessa inhaled, again blinking back tears. "It's beautiful," she breathed, leaning her head on Remy's shoulder.

"So are you," he said, kissing her temple.

Remy cooked them dinner, a delicious lasagna with salad and garlic bread. He opened a bottle of red wine while he cooked. Watching him, she realized she needed to buy Remy a gift. This might be a bit challenging since he already seemed to have everything. She'd figure it out. They still had a few days before Christmas.

The next day, Remy went to work and Vanessa went skiing. When she'd finished her morning runs, she stopped by The Lodge intending to do a little Christmas shopping and have lunch.

"I know you!" a voice exclaimed. Vanessa turned. Daria Bloom, the woman who'd been carrying the rifle when Seth had gone crazy in The Lodge's lobby. She wore her Bradford County Sheriff Department uniform, though her demeanor was a lot more relaxed, understandably.

"Vanessa Fisher, right?" Daria asked, holding out her hand. She had long, elegant fingers with short, unvarnished nails. No-nonsense, capable hands. Liking her even more, Vanessa shook her hand.

"Yes. And you're Deputy Daria Bloom."

"I am." The other woman grinned at her. "Did you just get in from skiing?"

"I did. And now I'm thinking about having lunch. Would you care to join me?"

"I would love to," Daria answered promptly. "I've been dying to get to know the woman who—" She bit back the words.

"Who what?" Vanessa asked.

Daria shrugged. "Managed to get Remy Colton to focus on something other than work." Her easy smile put Vanessa at ease.

They walked to the café and were seated immediately. After ordering—they both wanted salads with grilled chicken—Vanessa discovered she and Daria had something else in common. They both were involved in brand-new relationships.

"Stefan—you'll meet him at the family Christmas party—just moved in with me." Daria's warm brown eyes glowed with affection. "He has the most adorable five-year-old son named Sam. I've never been happier." She took a drink from her water, eying Vanessa. "Are you and Remy living together?"

To her surprise, Vanessa felt herself blush. "Not officially," she said slowly. "At first, it was more of a thing where he was helping me out because I had no place to stay. But we realized pretty early on that we wanted more, so we'll make it official soon."

Daria laughed. "When you know, you know."

Their food arrived and while they ate, talk turned to the upcoming holiday. "I have no idea what to get Remy," Vanessa confessed. "He seems to have everything."

"Not everything." Daria's thoughtful tone matched her faraway expression. "Ever since Remy was small, he's always wanted a dog. Of course, Whit would never allow something as messy as a pet inside his pristine dwelling, so after a while, Remy gave up. He's only mentioned it in passing a few times since growing up." She took a deep breath. "Now normally, I don't advocate giving animals as Christmas gifts, but Remy has talked about this for so long. I think the only reason he held off was because he considered himself too busy."

A dog. Vanessa considered. The more she thought about it, the more she loved the idea. She, too, had longed for a dog of her own. In fact, she'd planned to get one once this year's ski season had ended. Now, with two people able to help take care of it, she realized there was no longer any reason to wait.

"I think you just helped me decide what to get Remy for Christmas," Vanessa said slowly. "I don't suppose you happen to know what kind of dog he would like?"

Daria never even missed a beat. Brown eyes sparkling, she leaned in. "I don't think he cares. He's talked about rescuing some poor shelter pup. And you wouldn't believe how full the shelter gets around the holidays."

"That's sad." Vanessa shook her head. "And rescuing a shelter dog has long been something I wanted to do, too. But before I take such a big step, I have to make sure he's on board with it. I'd also kind of like for the two of us to choose our dog together. That might ruin the surprise, but I think it's a fair trade."

"I have an idea." Daria's infectious grin invited Vanessa to smile back. "Let me know what you think of this plan…"

Listening, Vanessa grew more and more excited. "That just might work," she said. "Why don't you see if you can get that set up, and I'll take care of the rest."

After her lunch with Daria, Vanessa felt like she could skip all the way home. Of course, she drove, but she realized she'd just made her very first friend here in Roaring Springs. As an extra bonus, Daria was part of Remy's family.

Trey called later in the day. "How is Remy?" he asked. "I've phoned him a few times but he doesn't pick up. And even though I've left him a few messages, he isn't returning my calls."

"Seriously?" Surprised, Vanessa wondered what was going on. "He's seemed pretty happy, considering. I mean, all the stuff with Seth hit him pretty hard, but he seems to be handling it okay."

"I don't think he is." The thread of worry in the sheriff's voice alarmed her. "I'm going to stop by his office before the end of the day, so he'll have no choice but to see me. But I thought I'd better check out his state of mind first."

She frowned. "As far as I know, Remy is fine." But now she wondered. He certainly seemed to have taken pains to stay away from even mentioning Seth. She'd actually thought avoidance might be helping him cope. But what if she was wrong? What if Remy still blamed himself, so much so that he couldn't face Trey, who had Seth locked up?

"He's avoiding everyone," Trey continued. "I've gotten a few calls from some of the others. They're all worried about how he's handling Seth's arrest."

He had a good point. She'd allowed Remy to keep her attention directed toward the bright and shiny new relationship they were forging together. *Was* he okay? Or was the situation with Seth tearing him up inside? She needed to find out.

"Keep me posted," she told Trey. "I'll talk to him tonight and make sure everything is all right with him."

"Will do," Trey promised. "And thank you."

When Remy got home, Vanessa watched him for any signs of internal distress. He acted completely normal. In fact, when she told him she'd had lunch with Daria, he grinned. "Due to some convoluted family shenanigans, she's technically my aunt," he said.

"You are fortunate to be part of such a large and

supportive family," she said warmly. "How's everyone else doing?"

He eyed her. "I'm sure they're all doing great. We'll see them in a few days at the Christmas party."

"Does all of your family attend?"

"Seth never went, so not all..." he began and then choked up. She understood. Because no matter what he'd done, Seth was still his brother. His *family*.

Though she watched him closely, Vanessa saw no signs he meant to reveal his inner thoughts or emotions. She took a deep breath. "I'm glad you brought that up. Speaking of your family..."

Slightly nervous, she twisted her thumb ring around on her finger. "I hate to be the one to bring this up, but Trey called me earlier. He's worried about you and he thinks you're avoiding him. He said he was planning to stop by your office this afternoon. Did you see him?"

"No." Remy frowned. "He must have gotten busy. As far as I know, he didn't come by."

"If he had, would you have seen him?"

"Maybe." He barely looked up, as if afraid of what she might see in his expression. "What does it matter?"

"You love your family," she pointed out. "And you and Trey seem close. Trey is worried about you. He says you've been avoiding everyone else, too, so I'm guessing others have reached out to you, too."

He got up, pretending to be occupied with putting another log on the fire. With his back to her, he spoke. "I've been to visit Seth twice. Both times, my brother refused to see me."

Shocked, she struggled to find the right words to

comfort him, but there were none. She settled on saying she was sorry.

"And that's why I've been avoiding Trey...and everyone else. Because of Seth. I failed him and I failed them. I need time." Though he attempted a casual shrug, the defensive tone in his voice made her ache.

"Remy." She kneeled down in front of him, lifting his chin and forcing him to look at her. "They care about you. No one blames you for Seth's behavior."

He sighed. "I know. I just can't get past my own guilt."

"Talking about guilt..." She took a deep breath. "I know. I have the same problem. I keep thinking of what I could have done differently. If I hadn't come to Roaring Springs, if I hadn't met you. Would that have changed anything?"

"This started long before we even met," he said, then gave a startled laugh. "You know what? Hearing the words spoken aloud actually makes me feel better. Still, finding out that he'd killed Sabrina blindsided me. If I'd known, could I have somehow saved her?"

"There was nothing you could have done to stop it. Don't you think Trey must ask himself the same question? Seth's a grown man."

"You're probably right," he admitted gruffly. "But I did everything I could to help my brother. Everything. I scrimped and saved so he could go to a better school, to rehab. I bought him clothes, his first car. I was always there for him, no matter what. He has to know how much I loved him."

"I'm sure he does." She hesitated. "Remy, you know Seth is troubled. Between that and his addictions, he's going to need a lot of help. All you can do is be there for him when he needs you."

"That will be kind of hard to do since he flat-out refuses to see me." Now, when he raised his face to hers, she saw the raw anguish in his eyes.

Her heart aching for the man she loved, she wrapped him in her arms and held him close. "Give him time," she said. "He's facing some serious charges."

"I know." He sighed. "He's made his choices and now has to suffer the consequences. And I've come to the realization that at this point, there's nothing I can do that could help him."

Since she'd come to a similar conclusion, she simply nodded. "He has his own journey he must make," she said. "All you can do is love him and be there if he ever asks for help."

Though the days leading up to Christmas were typically the slowest of the year, at least as far as public relations were concerned, Remy found himself fielding a lot of questions from various media outlets about the Seth hostage situation. He'd even gone so far as to type up a statement, which he read verbatim on every phone call. He and the rest of the family managed to keep a lid on all the other things Seth had done.

Most of the staff had taken personal or vacation days, and the normally bustling office was quiet. After the New Year began, they'd begin taking meetings with various advertising agencies, but right now there was very little to do.

He'd thought going to work might help him come to terms with what happened with Seth, but to his surprise, Remy had reached a sort of peaceful place on his own. He'd come to understand how wonderful his life had become. Because of Vanessa, because of love.

And that made him realize he didn't want to hide out in the office any longer. Basically, the PR department was closed for the holiday season. He might as well take himself home and enjoy his first Christmas with Vanessa.

But first, he'd try to talk to Seth one more time. He just needed some sort of understanding as to what had made his brother do the awful things he'd done. Despite the long drive, he headed to the federal penitentiary where Seth was being held.

Third time's a charm, Remy thought, both relieved and apprehensive as the guard told him that Seth had finally agreed to see him. After divesting himself of all his personal belongings and being patted down, Remy was led into a small, colorless room with only a table separated by a glass partition, with a chair on either side. It appeared he couldn't be alone in the same room with his brother—instead, all communication would come through a phone with receivers placed on both sides of the glass.

Remy swallowed when Seth walked into the other half of the room. Gone was the urban, well-dressed sophisticate he'd gotten used to seeing around Roaring Springs. Instead, the savvy street rat Remy had found in that filthy, awful apartment had returned. Noticing him staring, Seth smirked. When Remy met his brother's gaze, he didn't bother to hide his disgust. "Seth." Then, remembering, he picked up the phone and motioned for his sibling to do the same.

"Why haven't you posted bail?" Seth demanded belligerently. "I want out of here."

"The judge denied bail," Remy replied, his chest aching. He felt anger, true, but also that same tangled mess of love and confusion and pain that seemed to swirl around Seth like a storm cloud.

"That's ridiculous." Swearing, Seth dragged his hand through his dirty blond hair. "Do something. I know you can. You Coltons have connections, influence. Use them."

"We don't—" Remy began, interrupted by a spate of virulent cursing.

"You won't, you mean," Seth snarled, his eyes slits in his once-handsome face. "Because I'm not one of you, not a Colton. That's why I've always hated you, all of you. Entitled, condescending pricks, each and every one. Acting like I'm not good enough to shine your shoes. Well, I guess I showed you, didn't I?"

Stunned, Remy needed every ounce of self-control he possessed not to recoil from his brother in horror. Not just to the virulent rancor, but his logic, which made no sense. "Seth," he pointed out, keeping his own voice flat and emotionless. "You killed someone. Hurt people. You did a lot of horrible things for no discernible reason. How is that in any way showing anyone anything?"

"I should have killed Vanessa, you know." Voice low, eyes crinkled with amusement, Seth leaned as close to the glass partition as possible. "It would have been fun to watch her die, slowly and painfully, just like Sabrina did."

Remy hung up the phone. Stomach roiling, he battled back nausea, aware that Seth wanted a reaction, would clearly take pleasure in getting one. So instead, he kept his face expressionless and merely shook his head. He'd wanted answers, hoped for an explanation, but instead this visit had only confirmed that his brother had become a monster. Seth would surely go on trial and be convicted; hopefully, hopefully the justice his crimes deserved would be meted out. And Roaring Springs would be a better, safer place without his brother.

Despite the certainty of that knowledge, as Remy turned to go, he felt sorrow settle like a stone inside his gut. Clearly, for far too long he'd seen Seth with blind eyes, chose to believe his brother could become someone he was not. It hurt. A lot. But finally he understood Seth was where he belonged, where he couldn't hurt anyone else.

The long drive home helped him reach a place of calm. He realized he had no more room for bitterness in his life. He could no longer look back, but keep going forward. After all, he had a future to plan, with a wonderful woman.

When he finally got home, he decided not to mention his visit to Seth. Not yet. He'd tell her later, once he'd had time to process everything.

Vanessa hugged him close when he walked in the door, almost as if she knew. While he didn't want to lie, he couldn't bring himself to talk of it yet. "I'm glad you're home," she said, her gaze quietly searching his face. "I didn't want to interfere with your work, so I'd been planning a couple of solo shopping trips and maybe a few more runs down Pine Peak."

"We can do all those things together," he said tenderly. "And more. There's a Christmas light-sleigh-ride tour that's really popular this week." He dug in his pockets and extracted a pair of tickets. "We go tomorrow night."

She kissed him then, thanks turning to heat. They made love there on the sofa in the afternoon, and afterward, simply held each other since neither was in any hurry to move.

This, he understood, was contentment. And the time had come to let her know about his brother.

Bracing himself, he casually mentioned that he'd been to see Seth. Vanessa nodded, watching his face. "He's unrepentant," he told her. "Still blames everyone else but himself."

"That's sad," she said, snuggling close. "Are you all right?"

"I am," he replied, meaning it. "I really am." The next few days passed quickly. For the first time that he could remember, Remy actually got the Christmas spirit.

"Me, too!" Vanessa exclaimed when he told her. "The last time I felt like this, I was too young to know better."

His heart squeezed. "Never again," he promised. "As long as I'm alive, you'll never spend Christmas alone."

"Right back atcha," she replied.

They went skiing—twice. The cold air and snow put a flush on her cheeks and a shine in her eyes. Once, he actually waited at the bottom of a run so he could watch her come down. When she skied, she was poetry in motion. Superbly confident and very skilled, she drew the eye. He wasn't the only one watching her.

"Hey!" She skied up to him. "What are you doing?"

"Watching you," he replied, kissing the tip of her cold nose. "Are you ready to go Christmas shopping?"

"Sure." They headed back to the ski lockers, where they'd stowed their shoes and her purse, grabbed their stuff and traipsed out to his Jeep.

Hand in hand, they wandered down Main Street, stopping for a cup of hot cocoa. He watched her as she shopped, taking pleasure in the tactile way she shopped, touching some things, almost caressing others.

She bought a few things, smiling at him as if shopping in downtown Roaring Springs might be the most fun ever. With her, he reckoned it was.

When they got back to the house, he put on Christmas music—amazingly, he hadn't gotten tired of it yet—and changed into sweats. Though lately they'd been going out every night, tonight they'd both agreed to stay in.

"I can't believe it's nearly Christmas." Smiling shyly, she put a brightly wrapped gift under the tree. There were a few others already there, one of them being a pair of sapphire earrings he'd bought her because they matched her eyes. "I know you said your family doesn't do gifts except for the children, but I got this for Daria. She's been really kind to me and I wanted to get her something."

"What did you get her?"

"A bracelet. I saw it in the shop and thought it would suit her."

He nodded. "She'll like that." This generosity of spirit was one of the many things he loved about her.

"I love the way Roaring Springs embraces the holiday season," she continued. "Not just the decorations, but the festivities. They seem to have something going on every night."

She should know. He'd accompanied her to just about every single event, often reluctantly. To his amazement, he'd enjoyed himself every time. He hadn't realized how much of a hermit he'd been until she'd come along.

"I love you," he told her, nuzzling her neck. "Thank you for being you."

Her grin made her eyes sparkle. "I love you, too. I can't believe we're finally saying that to one another, given everything that's happened."

"I know," he admitted, his voice husky. "Our love story is just beginning," he added, holding her closely.

"What are we doing on the actual holiday?" she asked. "I mean, shouldn't we discuss it, since it's only two days away?"

For a moment he stared at her, confused. Then he realized he must have forgotten to tell her. What he took for granted since it was a long-standing tradition, she had no way of knowing.

"Well, on Christmas Eve, I thought we'd have our own private celebration here." He gestured at his living room and the beautiful tree she'd decorated. "We can go out to eat or eat in, whichever you prefer."

"Hmm." Her grin widened. "That sounds heavenly. And on Christmas Day?"

"My family has a long-standing tradition. There's a big meal on Christmas Day at Colton Manor. Everyone comes and brings their significant others. The youngsters get gifts, and we eat. There's so much food it's ridiculous."

To his relief, she cocked her head and seemed interested. "Is it a potluck-type thing? Will we need to bring something?"

"No. Mara and Russ have their cooks prepare everything. Sometimes, one of the guys brings a cooler of beer. But there's a full wine cellar that's opened up to everyone, plus top-shelf liquor for those who prefer that."

"You seem to have a large family." She toyed with a lock of her dark hair. "Is it crowded?"

He couldn't tell if she was asking because she would find it overwhelming or if she had hopes of blending in with the crowd. "Yes." He kissed her again, this time on the lips. "But don't worry. They'll love you. I promise."

One corner of her mouth twitched before she kissed him back. "I guess I'll have to take you at your word for it. Tell me about their house."

He eyed her, wondering how to best explain the overstated opulence known as The Manor. "The Colton home is huge, but stark. I honestly don't see how anyone can love living there."

"Oh." She grimaced. "I've been to a few houses like that. Where everything seems designed to impress and awe rather than for comfort or real life."

"You nailed it." Then he remembered her parents had been wealthy, too.

"I take it that wasn't your childhood home?" she asked, watching him closely.

"No. My family had it built about ten years ago. Before that, they lived downtown near The Chateau.

The house I was raised in was a much more normal place."

A shadow crossed her face. "I have no idea what normal is," she admitted. "My parents were well-off, but as I mentioned previously, I spent my childhood in boarding schools. Their main home was in Boston, in the Seaport area."

"I've never been," he replied.

"You can come with me next time I go, if you'd like," she offered. "I actually have to go sometime after Christmas. I'm still in the middle of settling my parents' estate."

"I'd love that," he said. "I've never been to Boston. We'll figure out dates so I can make sure to take off from work."

The excitement in her eyes made him smile. Just then, he realized he wanted to make their relationship permanent. But would she? Not only had she recently lost her parents, but she'd been engaged to Seth and broken that off. She'd just bought her first home in Boulder. Maybe she wasn't ready to chuck all that to build a life with him.

Remy had always been a confident man, certain he knew the right course of action. Around Vanessa, he couldn't see a clear path. He knew what he wanted, without a shadow of a doubt. But he also wanted to make sure to do what was right for her.

Even if that turned out to be letting her go.

Just the thought made his chest hurt.

Unaware of his thoughts, she smiled at him. "You know what? For the first time since my parents died, the prospect of flying back to New England doesn't seem daunting. I'm actually looking forward to showing you around. It's a beautiful city, even in the winter."

Grabbing his laptop, he powered up a travel website. "Let's check out tickets," he offered.

Chapter 14

"It's Christmas Eve," Remy murmured in her ear, before kissing her awake with slow, languorous presses of his mouth to her neck and collarbone. Vanessa tried to burrow back under the covers, though she actually craved his attention as much as she craved sleep. When his touch became a caress and the press of his fully aroused body an invitation, she let herself get lost in the lovemaking.

Afterward, they lay together and held each other close. "That's what I'd call a perfect start to a holiday," he teased, kissing her once more before getting out of the bed and heading off to the bathroom.

She stayed in the bed, stretching, feeling as lazy as a sated cat. When she heard the sound of the shower starting up, she closed her eyes and reflected on how much her life had changed. If anyone had told her, even as recently as a couple of months ago, that she would have found her one true love, she would have rolled her eyes and refused to believe it. Even now, she fought the worry that their happy bubble could burst at any moment. Christmas Eve. Despite the awesome way the day had started, right now it didn't feel any different than any other day. No surprise there, since it never had. All her life, she'd heard of people who claimed to have had magical Christmas Eves. Whether spiritual or simply joyous, surrounded by family and friends, she didn't know. Either way, she'd always been slightly skeptical and maybe a bit envious.

In primary school, she always felt like the child standing outside the candy store, always separate, always looking in. Her classmates' excitement had been palpable—the tree shopping and decorating, the Christmas cookies baked, the pile of brightly wrapped gifts under the tree. They'd all fly home to be with their families the instant the holiday break dawned, but she didn't have many good childhood holiday memories that she could look back on, except for Christmas. The other holidays, she'd waited for those phone calls as if they were the most precious gift she could have been given, always wondering why they couldn't take her with them. She'd grown up unwanted and unloved, always feeling that if she could only somehow be better, do more, then maybe, just maybe, her parents might love her.

Now they were gone, taking with them any possible opportunity for a better relationship. This, she suspected, is what she mourned the most. The opportunities that would forever be lost.

She'd felt ashamed admitting this to Remy. But

once she had, he'd said he understood, reminding her his childhood hadn't been a picnic, either, so he got it. He'd made her feel better, holding her close, and murmured endearments in her ear until she turned her head and kissed him. Those deep, drugging kisses drove everything else from her mind.

"Your turn." Emerging from the bathroom, toweling his hair dry, the brilliance of his smile filled her with love. "We've got a big day today, so we might as well get started."

"A big day?" She tried to remember. "I know we talked about starting our own tradition and having a special Christmas Eve meal, but what else do we have planned?"

His smile turned mysterious. "Wait and see. Now go get ready, before I'm tempted to join you in that bed one more time."

That made her laugh. And then, because she'd never been able to resist a surprise, she jumped up and ran for the shower.

When she emerged thirty minutes later, hair and makeup done, the smell of cinnamon rolls and bacon drew her to the kitchen. "Here you go." Remy handed her a cup of coffee, made exactly the way she liked it. "You're just in time for breakfast."

He brought over a plate of cinnamon rolls and another plate of bacon.

"Wow." She grinned. "I'm seriously impressed."

"New tradition," he said, his expression serious. "Cinnamon rolls and bacon on Christmas Eve morning, made by yours truly. Then I thought we'd head downtown and take in the parade."

"Parade?"

"Yep." Taking a seat, he helped himself to two rolls and four slices of bacon. "Every year Roaring Springs has one. It's a really big deal. There are floats and bands and horses and vintage cars—all the same stuff you'd see at any other parade anywhere else."

She thought for a moment. "I don't believe I've ever been to a parade."

"Seriously?" He eyed her skeptically, as if he wasn't sure if she might be joking.

"Seriously." Shrugging to show it wasn't a big deal, she took a huge bite of her cinnamon roll. "Mmm."

Shaking his head, Remy made short work of his food. Then he drank his coffee, watching her eat. "You really lived a sheltered life," he teased.

"I did." Blotting her mouth with her napkin, she eyed him. "Does that bother you?"

"Not at all. I think I'm going to look forward to being the one to introduce you to so many new things."

A lot of firsts, she thought, nodding. She couldn't think of a better person to share them with.

They got to the parade route early. Downtown Roaring Springs had already been blocked off and onlookers had begun to assemble. Remy led her to a café with outdoor seating and waved to another couple, who waved back.

The tall and muscular man stood as they approached. "About time you got here," he commented. With his dark brown hair in a crew cut plus the way he carried himself, Vanessa guessed he was either current military or former.

"Blaine Colton," he said, grabbing her hand with his large one and shaking it. "And this is my fiancée, Tilda."

"Hi there," Tilda greeted them softly. Her eyes were striking and she wore a knitted ski cap over her long, wavy, dark brown hair.

Remy introduced Vanessa, holding her left hand. "Blaine's in charge of the extreme-sports division at The Lodge," Remy reminded her as they took their seats.

"That's right," Vanessa murmured. "So…what kind of sports do you guys consider to be extreme?" She smiled. "I know which ones I do. I'm a competitive skier."

Blaine grinned. "We have quite a selection, depending on the season. Since it's winter now, we have ice climbing, snowboarding, skiing, of course, snowmobiling, monoskiing and snowblading."

Intrigued despite herself, Vanessa nodded. "And in the summer?"

"There are too many to list. But we do a lot of rock climbing, bouldering and free climbing, plus caving, slacklining, and the biggie, white-river rafting. The Lodge offers tours for just about anything."

"Vanessa's an amazing skier," Remy added proudly.

Blaine studied her. "Are you looking for a job? We can always use skilled snow athletes."

She laughed. "Thank you, but no. I've got more than enough to keep me busy between settling my parents' estate and practicing my skills on the slopes."

While they waited for the parade to start, she learned Tilda was a teacher, though she was off for winter break. She and Blaine had a thirteen-year-old son, who was there but had wanted to watch the parade with his friends instead of his parents.

"You'll meet him at the party tomorrow," Remy said, still holding her hand.

His offhand comment had Blaine regarding him with renewed interest. "Are you two serious?" he asked. "You must be, if he's dragging you to the family get-together on Christmas Day."

"Blaine." Tilda swatted his muscular arm. "Quit."

Instead of answering, Remy merely smiled a mysterious smile. Vanessa's insides twisted as she realized she'd allowed herself to believe they had something permanent, with a real future.

"Look." She pointed. "I think the parade is about to start."

"I'd better go get our drinks then," Blaine said. "Coffee okay for everyone?"

For the next hour, Vanessa watched high-school cheerleaders, braving the cold in their cute outfits and cowboy hats, band members toting instruments who looked as if they wished they'd had their jackets, floats made from fake flowers and glitter, and tractors pulling wagons full of people. There were restored hot-rod cars and an entire group of kids on horseback carrying a 4-H banner. Santa and his elves and even Mrs. Claus passed out candy, while a dancing Frosty the Snowman and a green Grinch rode on their own float.

It was all very festive and fun.

When the last group finally passed, all of the people lining the street began to move. The café instantly became packed.

"Time to go," Remy said, standing. He handed Blaine some cash and kissed Tilda's cheek. "See you two at the party tomorrow."

Vanessa slipped her hand into his. "Wow," she commented. "So far every single person I've met in your family is super nice."

"We try." Remy squeezed her hand. "I'm glad you got to meet a few before the get-together tomorrow. There's so many people, it can be kind of overwhelming."

When they got back to the house, Remy went straight to the tree and retrieved something from underneath.

She had a moment of panic when he handed her a small, elegantly wrapped gift. "I'm giving you your present tomorrow," she said. "Maybe I should wait."

"It's okay." He kissed her, nuzzling her neck. "You really didn't have to get me anything. Having you in my life is gift enough."

Though she wanted to swoon at his words, she shook her head instead. "Same here. But still, I feel weird accepting a gift from you when I don't have one to give you in exchange. Yet."

"Don't." He kissed her again, his lazy tone matching the heat in his eyes. "It's not a competition. Plus, I want you to wear this tomorrow. Humor me, please."

Trying not to feel bad—what if the plan she and Daria had cooked up turned out to not go over well?—she slowly unwrapped the gift.

Inside, nestled in a black velvet box, was the most exquisite pair of sapphire earrings she'd ever seen. "My birthstone," she said, marveling. "How did you know?"

"I didn't. I got them because they match your eyes."

"They are beautiful," she breathed. "I love them. Thank you so much, Remy."

Keeping her gaze locked on his, she slowly put

on the earrings. Then she stood and stripped off her
clothes and helped him do the same. Once they were
both naked, she made love to him wearing only his gift.

Afterward, wrapped in each other's arms, they
dozed.

When she opened her eyes again, Remy had pulled
all the covers off her. Seeing her awake, he grinned.
"Nap's over! We've still got a lot more Christmas Eve
celebrating to do."

Though she couldn't imagine what else they could
possibly do, she was game.

After they'd gotten cleaned up and dressed again,
he checked his watch. "Are you hungry?"

She had to think about it for a moment. "You know
what? I think I am."

"Good." He grinned. "We have reservations at a
special Christmas Eve dinner in an hour."

Though that seemed kind of early, she didn't mind.
They hadn't eaten since the cinnamon rolls and bacon
earlier that morning. "Special?" she asked. "Does that
mean I need to dress up?"

"Nope, not at all. This dinner is the most antici-
pated even of the holiday season. Luckily, I was able
to snag a pair of tickets."

"Tickets?"

His smile turned enigmatic. "You'll see. Just wear
comfortable—and warm—clothes."

Intrigued, she peppered him with questions, but
all he would say was she'd have to wait and see. By
the time they were ready to get into his Jeep, she felt
like a little kid at Christmas, full of excitement and
anticipation. Which, come to think of it, might have
been the point.

* * *

Vanessa's exuberance made Remy happier than he would ever have thought possible. He'd guessed he'd been living in Roaring Springs too long, because in years past attending the annual holiday feast and charity talent show had been more of a chore than a joyous event. Even though it certainly could be pleasurable, he'd been more focused on customer relations, making sure all of the well-heeled guests had a good time.

This year would be different. For one thing, he wouldn't be attending in an official capacity, but just as one of the guests. For another, he felt certain Vanessa had never seen anything like the frequently raucous fun. The decorations were over-the-top festive and the food extraordinarily delicious. Everyone who knew about it wanted to go, which was one of the reasons the tickets sold out weeks, if not months, in advance. He always was given two tickets, paid for by Colton Enterprises, due to his position as head of public relations of The Chateau. This year, he'd actually been grateful.

The organizers purposely held the event early, so that people could do midnight church services or family get-togethers after. Usually, a large group went caroling. Remy had never been part of that, but this year, if Vanessa was willing, he hoped to be.

He wanted to pull out all the stops and make this Christmas Eve one that they'd always remember.

Once they pulled into the very crowded parking lot, he told her what was taking place. "A talent show?" she asked. "Are you performing?"

Since the thought had never occurred to him, he

laughed and shook his head. "No. But all the acts have to be Christmas-themed. It's really a lot of fun."

"As long as there's food," she replied, smiling. "I'm starving."

"Wait and see."

They got into the line, which snaked around the front of the building and down one side. Luckily, it moved quickly, as the sun had begun to set and the breeze turned chilly. Walking behind and close to Vanessa, Remy sheltered her from the wind.

After handing over their tickets, their hands were stamped and they stepped inside. People milled around, laughing, talking, holding drinks. There were bars at each end of the building, and rows of white-tablecloth-covered tables, each seating six.

"We have assigned seats," Remy said, checking the numbers on his ticket stubs. "Do you want to sit or walk around a bit?"

"Let's get a drink and then find our seats," Vanessa responded. "There's Daria!" She waved. From the other end of the room, the deputy sheriff waved back.

"Is there any chance we could trade seats and sit with Daria and Stefan?" Vanessa asked.

"I wish we could, but a lot of careful planning goes into the seating chart," he told her. "They try to put a Colton at every table. In the past, I've never been able to sit with my family."

Clearly disappointed, Vanessa nodded. "Maybe we can get together with them after the show. I really like Daria. I think with time, she and I will become good friends."

Once everyone was seated, the buffets that had been set up at each side near the bars were opened. The array of food choices—everything from seafood to steak to vegetarian fare—was astounding. The dessert tables were separate, but from past experience Remy told Vanessa to grab what she wanted before she sat down, because certain delicacies vanished quickly.

After everyone had gotten their meal, the lights dimmed somewhat and the talent show started. Many of the acts were musical, from local bands rocking out to Christmas classics, to country crooners. There were a few magicians, one act with trained dogs and Mrs. Pauly's entire third-grade class playing bells.

As the talent show went on, Remy found himself watching Vanessa. Her rapt attention, her earthy laugh and the way the lights caught her cheekbones made her far more enjoyable then anything on stage.

When the show finally ended, everyone jumped to their feet and clapped. Eyes sparkling, Vanessa jumped up and down, applauding before turning to Remy and throwing her arms around him. "So. Much. Fun."

Though they looked around for Daria, she and Stefan must have left as soon as the show ended, because they didn't see them again. Vanessa said she was up for Christmas caroling, so, hand in hand, they joined the others and began trekking through the snow to all the downtown houses.

By the time they'd finished, they had wet feet, cold hands and warm hearts.

Vanessa hummed all the way back to his Jeep. "That was amazing," she said. "Thank you for a wonderful night." And then, right there, right in front of his Jeep, Remy slowly lowered himself to one knee in the snow.

Eyes wide, Vanessa tugged on his hand. "What are

you doing?" she asked. "Get up. It's too cold to be playing in the snow."

"Wait." Remy shook his head. "I'm not getting up just yet. There's something I need to say, something I need to ask, and this is the right way to ask it. Vanessa, I love you. I don't have a ring—I thought if you'd like, we can pick one out together—but I want to make this permanent. Forever. Will you do me the honor of becoming my wife?"

Now he had her full attention. She lowered herself so that they were on the same level and gazed deeply into his eyes. "I love you, too," she whispered. "And yes. My answer is yes. And I'll relocate to Roaring Springs, to be here with you."

Full of joy and the certainty that he and Vanessa were meant to find each other, Remy kissed her right then and there, with the two of them both on their knees in the cold, wet snow.

Right then and there, he came to a decision. "We have one more stop to make on the way home," he said. "This might be the most fun of all."

"Really?" She shook her head. "I doubt you can top this. But I'm game. Where are we going?"

"You'll see." That's all he'd say, right up until he pulled up and parked in front of Mountain Luxe Jewelers. A sign on the window proclaimed them to be *the* ultimate fine jewelry destination. In fact, they were the only jewelry store in town, if one didn't count the sterling-silver-and-turquoise shop at the other end of Main.

Reading the sign on the marquee, she turned and eyed him. "Now?" she asked. "Today?"

"Why not?" Though he tried to sound casual, he

saw the steady love in her gaze and leaned over and kissed her. "Every woman should have a ring on the day she receives a proposal."

Her husky laugh warmed him to his toes. "Well, when you put it that way…"

Sinclair Jones, owner and frequently the sole employee of the shop, looked up when Remy and Vanessa entered. He squinted at first, as if having trouble placing why they might be there. Then, he pushed up his round glasses on his nose and beamed. "Remy Colton. What brings you and your lady friend to MLJ today?"

Putting his arm around Vanessa's waist, Remy drew her forward. "Sinclair, this is my fiancée, Vanessa Fisher. Vanessa, Sinclair is the owner of this fine establishment."

"Fiancée?" Sinclair's entire face lit up. "Congratulations, you two. I'm guessing you'd like to see some engagement rings or bridal sets."

"Yes," Remy agreed. "Though I need to ask you to keep this between us until I get a chance to tell my entire family."

"Of course," Sinclair answered with great dignity. "Your confidence is safe with me."

Curious to see what Vanessa would choose, Remy took a seat next to her as Sinclair brought out trays of his finest diamond rings. He watched as Vanessa perused them, not touching anything. She searched as if she had a particular style in mind.

Apparently, Sinclair noticed this, too. "I have a large inventory," he said. "Not bragging, just stating a fact. If there's a particular style you're looking for, why don't you describe it to me and I'll see if I can locate it for you?"

She nodded, sitting back in her chair. "I'm not good with words, but I'll try. All of these—" she waved her hand at the trays of glittery rings "—are flashy. Showy. And while they're absolutely beautiful, I'd prefer something a little more...understated. And elegant. If you have a pen and paper, I can sketch out what I mean."

Immediately, Sinclair handed her a small pad of paper and a pen. Both men watched as Vanessa began to sketch a thick band, with elegant, scrolled Celtic knots and a total of three diamonds, a larger round one in the center and two smaller gems, one on each side.

"That's beautiful," Sinclair commented, his tone surprised. "Though that might be more of a custom-designed ring, I think I just might have something similar." He slid the trays they'd been viewing back into the display case, which he then locked. "Give me a moment," he said, disappearing into the back.

When he returned, he carried a single diamond ring in the middle of a black velvet box. The instant she saw it, Vanessa's face lit up. "That's it, exactly!" she said excitedly. "White gold, Celtic design and the perfect diamond."

"We'll take it," Remy informed Sinclair.

"Don't you want to know what it costs first?" Vanessa asked, still unable to tear her gaze away from the ring.

Smiling, Sinclair wrote something on a slip of paper and handed it to Remy. Reading the number, Remy nodded and got out his credit card.

"Thank you." Turning back to Vanessa, the jeweler removed the ring from the box. "Would you like to try it on? If it doesn't fit, we can have it resized."

When she nodded, Remy took the ring from Sinclair and slipped it on Vanessa's finger. The instant he did, he realized it fit as if it had been specifically designed for her. Maybe it had, Remy thought. Maybe the world still had a few miracles left for people who were in love.

Alternating between staring at the stunning ring on her finger and the wonderful, sexy man driving them home, Vanessa battled an inexplicable urge to cry. Though her parents hadn't been the loving, caring types, they'd been hers and she suddenly missed them. She'd finally met The One and they were engaged to be married, and not only did she not have any family to tell, but she also wouldn't have her father walk her down the aisle. Until this moment, she hadn't even realized she wanted a traditional wedding.

Maybe she had once. Now, she just wanted to be married. A simple ceremony, no fuss. Just vows and love.

"We'll make our own family," Remy replied, once she'd vocalized her thoughts. "I'm with you on the simple ceremony, though I should tell you as a Colton, it's my duty to have an elaborate and ornate ceremony." The dry tone of his voice told her he wasn't serious. "Though they're going to want us to have a traditional wedding, with so many other engagements and weddings on the horizon, I'm thinking we might be able to pull it off. My family will just have to get over it."

Though she nodded, she still found herself blinking back tears. Noticing the look of concern on Remy's face, she shook her head and waved him away. "It's nothing," she began. "And it's everything. So much raw emotion today. I'm sorry, I'm not usually so weepy." She sniffed. "Tears of happiness, I promise you."

"I get it," he said softly. Glancing sideways at him, she could have sworn she saw an answering sheen of tears in his eyes. "I love you, Vanessa. That's what's most important."

"I love you, too," she said, before she found herself weeping in earnest.

He let her cry, tears running silently down her face. Though she felt slightly foolish, she couldn't help it, so she simply gave in and let her emotions have full rein. Beyond his declaration of love, he didn't comment or ask for reassurance, though she figured he had to be worried she was about to change her mind. "I'm not, you know," she sniffled.

"Not what?" Parking in front of the garage, he shut off the ignition and pulled her into his arms.

"Changing my mind."

"I never thought you were," he replied, holding her tight. "I have confidence in our love."

Yet one more thing she adored about him.

Once she'd gotten herself under control, he handed her a tissue and she wiped at her eyes. "I'm not the weepy type," she muttered. "I have no idea what just came over me. You must think I'm a mess."

"I don't. It's not every day that a woman gets a proposal of marriage. I get it. It's a lot to process." He kissed her, still holding her close. "But know this—I love every aspect of you."

He kissed her again. "Whether you're laughing or crying, I'll always be there for you."

How had she gotten so lucky? She kissed him back. "Thank you. And the same for me. Though maybe," she teased, "I should have you write that into your wedding vows."

That made him chuckle. "I have just one request. Like I mentioned to Sinclair at the jewelry store, let's keep this engagement quiet until we can announce it to my entire family together, okay? People tend to get their noses bent out of shape if someone finds out before someone else."

"Of course."

"Perfect."

"The first Christmas Eve for the rest of our lives," he replied, making her so happy it hurt.

The next morning, Christmas Day, when Remy woke with Vanessa in his arms, he realized for the first time ever, he didn't dread the big get-together at Colton Manor. He still felt a deep twinge of sadness over Seth, but because he had this beautiful woman by his side, everything became better.

He made coffee and mimosas, along with Belgian waffles, strawberries and whipped cream. Accepting her mimosa, she shook her head and grinned. "You are spoiling me. I had no idea you were such a chef."

"You're not the only one who knows their way around a kitchen," he replied, kissing her on the neck.

They spent a lazy morning eating and drinking coffee and, later, snuggling in front of the fireplace. Finally, they knew they needed to shower and get ready for the family party.

"The main event," Remy called it, something he'd always done privately in the past.

When Vanessa put on her form-hugging, designer red dress, Remy thought he'd never seen her look more elegantly beautiful. She also wore her new sapphire earrings and several bracelets and a pair of sexy black stiletto boots. He wanted to devour her.

As for himself, he wore his usual black slacks, white shirt and red tie. Despite Whit's constant prodding, Remy never wore a jacket. It was, he argued, a holiday, after all.

"You look breathtaking," he told Vanessa.

"Right back at you," she replied, smiling. Dropping Daria's gift in her purse, she walked ahead of him to the garage, hips swaying. For a brief moment, he entertained a fantasy of skipping the party and taking her back to bed.

Of course, he did no such thing. They got in his Jeep and headed off, Christmas music playing on the radio.

Vanessa seemed unusually pensive as he drove.

"Are you nervous?" he asked.

"A little," she admitted. "I'm sure I'll get over it."

"I love you," he told her.

A slow smile lit up her face. "I love you, too."

"We're almost there." Deliberately taking the last curve in the road slowly, Remy watched for her reaction.

"Wow." She gazed up at the mansion perched high on the hill. All angles and glass, the modern-style mountain home had been designed to blend into the landscape. "You weren't kidding. That place is monstrously huge."

He grinned. "Just wait until you see the inside. It's so pretentious, it's almost tacky." He glanced sideways at her. "What was your parents' house like?"

"Old-school Boston. Elegant and restrained. The kind of place that almost felt like a church, where you were afraid to laugh or play or make noise." Her quick shrug didn't fool him. "I always told myself I was glad they didn't want me to live there with them."

Covering her hand with his, he squeezed. "I know it might not have seemed like it at the time, but you were probably lucky."

"Maybe. I'll never know now. But—" her expression brightened "—at least I had skiing."

"True. And now you have me." He placed a quick kiss on her neck, inhaling the light, feminine scent of her. "Here we are."

He pulled up the drive and stopped under the portico, where a line of other vehicles waited. Taking his place, he watched as one group of cousins exited the car, carrying bagged gifts and brightly wrapped parcels. As soon as they entered, their vehicle was driven away and another promptly took its place.

"They have valet parking?" Vanessa asked, her eyes wide. "For a family get-together?"

"Yep. Just wait until we get inside. There are servants tripping over each other. It's insane. But you'll get used to it."

Vanessa rolled her eyes, making him chuckle. "This is going to be interesting," she said. "Hopefully, even fun."

"It will be," he promised. "As long as you focus on the people rather than the pomp and circumstance. My family—your family soon—is really great. Oh, and I should warn you. I intend to announce our engagement this afternoon."

Waving her ring, she smiled. "I'm sure they'll figure it out once they see this."

"True." He pulled her close and kissed her. "But you deserve a formal announcement."

Finally, their turn came. When the young man opened the door for her, Vanessa swung out her shapely legs, tugging down her skirt at the same time. Her long legs and high-heeled black velvet boots drew the kid's gaze and Remy couldn't blame him.

She took his arm. "Let's do this," she said bravely.

"It's going to be all right, honey," he replied. "Relax. You've gone all tense."

Leaning into Remy, she exhaled and then shook her head. "I downplayed it earlier. To say I feel nervous would be an understatement. For whatever reason, I'm terrified."

"You have no reason to be, I promise. Look at it this way. At least you've already met a few members of my family."

"True," she mused, relaxing slightly. "Trey and Daria have both been nothing but kind. I have no reason to suspect the rest of the Coltons will be any different."

"Exactly."

At the front door, a uniformed servant took their coats. Smiling, Remy put his hand at the small of her back as they moved forward, her heels clicking on the marble floor.

The huge foyer led to a long hall, which opened out into the great room. This would be where the family gathered.

"Let's do this," he began. But before he could take another step, his cell phone rang. Caller ID showed the Bradford County jail. His heart skipped a beat. "It's Seth," he told Vanessa. "I have to take this."

She nodded. "Of course."

Taking a deep breath, he answered the call.

A robotic voice informed him that an inmate was placing a collect call and asked if he wanted to accept the charges. He replied yes without hesitation.

Click. "Seth?" Remy might have sounded too eager. Or maybe too cautious. He didn't care. "Seth, is that you?"

"Who else would be calling you from jail?" Seth said, the bitterness in his voice making Remy swallow. "I just wanted to call and see what you could do to get me out of here."

Stunned, Remy couldn't find any words. No "Merry Christmas" or "Happy Holidays." Just Seth, seeing what angle he would work.

"Hello?" Seth demanded. "Are you there? I hate it here."

"Seth, we've been over this already. You're in federal custody and bail has been denied. Not only are you a murderer, but you held a teenaged girl hostage with a gun against her temple. All of the horrible things you did hurt a lot of people." He took a deep breath. "You've got to pay for what you've done. There's nothing I can do to help you. It's time you learned how to help yourself."

"You're a sanctimonious jerk," Seth spat. "Where do you get off giving me advice? You've always had everything handed to you, just like all those other Coltons."

Not true, but damned if Remy would argue t'
now. Suddenly tired, he rubbed his aching
hope you get some help, Seth. Maybe onc

some time to reflect on what you've done, you can apologize to some of the people you hurt."

Silence. Then Seth laughed. "You always were such a sap, Remy. So desperate for love that you believed anything I told you, no matter how much evidence you had to the contrary."

"I'm going to hang up now," Remy warned, his chest tight, his heart aching. Anger mingled with sorrow, all twisting up his insides. "Merry Christmas," he said, before doing exactly that.

Dropping his phone back in his pocket, Remy eyed Vanessa and shook his head. She held out her arms and he walked into them, letting her hold him while he tried to sort out his chaotic emotions.

Chapter 15

Entering the room packed full of strangers, the first thing Vanessa noticed was the children. There were several, some racing about, others sitting quietly, enthralled with a tablet or a phone. They ranged in age from infant to teen. This instantly made her feel better. She liked kids. For the most part, they were honest and down-to-earth. She knew if she started to feel out of place, she could always talk to one of the children.

Dragging away her gaze, she looked around the room.

Everyone had dressed up, most in festive colors. She spotted one woman whose style she instantly admired, loving the artsy, new-age flair to her flowy skirt and layered blouse. "Who's that?" she asked.

"My cousin Bree. She owns that Wise Gal Gallery I told you about." He looked around. "Her little dog should be here somewhere. She never goes anywhere without him."

Dog. Looking down, Vanessa hid a smile.

"How are you at remembering names?" Remy asked, his voice tender.

She raised her head to look at him and shrugged. "I do okay." Scanning the room, she grimaced. "Though with this many people, I'm thinking I'll have some trouble. I'll try my best, though."

Some of her nervousness must have come through in her voice. "Don't be scared. Everyone is going to love you, because I do."

That made her smile. "Lead the way. I'm ready."

"Good. Let's do this."

After the first group of couples, Vanessa abandoned all hope of keeping up with the names. She met matriarch and patriarch Russ and Mara Colton, and Fox and Kelsey, along with their adorable adopted baby named John, who was eight months old. They met Fox's sister Sloane, her husband, Liam, and their brother Wyatt, a handsome cowboy, plus his wife, Bailey, and their infant son, Hudson.

Moving on from that group, Remy introduced her to Rylan and Bree, Skye and Leo, and Skye's identical twin, Phoebe, along with her fiancé, Prescott.

She already knew Blaine and Tilda and Daria and Stefan, though she had the pleasure of meeting Sam. Trey came over and greeted her, introducing her to Aisha, his fiancée.

After that, Vanessa simply smiled and nodded, especially when Remy introduced her to his father, Whit. The older man looked her up and down, his manner flirtatious, until his grandfather, Earl, rapped him sharply on his arm, which made Remy chuckle.

Vanessa slipped Daria her gift. Daria's eyes filled with surprise. "You didn't have to do that."

"I wanted to," Vanessa assured her.

"I'll open it later," Daria promised, dropping it into her purse. "Thank you so much."

Finally, they filed into a large dining room with a long, polished wood table, the size of which Vanessa had never seen. There had to be at least thirty chairs. Huge holiday centerpieces adorned the middle, one strategically placed about every four seats. Christmas plates and gold silverware, along with red wine and water glasses, completed the place settings. In two of the corners were smaller tables, most likely meant for the children. Even so, they were equally decorated, with slightly smaller flower arrangements.

"Assigned seating," Remy muttered. "Let's see if we can find our place cards."

Other couples roamed past them doing the exact same thing.

"Here." She pointed. "Remy Colton. Since the one right next to you says only 'Guest,' I'm assuming that's me."

This made him shake his head. "I'm sorry. I did give them your name. I'm not sure what happened."

His obvious concern touched her. "No biggie. Don't worry, I'm not taking it personally."

"Good." He kissed her cheek, which earned them several curious looks, though thankfully no one commented.

The room got noisy as everyone found their seats. Vanessa watched, grateful that so many of them had been kind and accepting. This would soon be her family, too. She suddenly realized the truth of what Remy had said. She'd never be alone again.

This in itself felt like another sort of miracle. She felt like the luckiest woman in the world.

"Are you ready?" Remy whispered, his warm breath tickling her ear and making her shiver. "I'm going to do this before we eat."

She nodded, her heart full of so much love it ached.

"May I have your attention?" Remy stood, tapping on his water glass with his fork. "Everyone?"

The room got quiet. Looking around, Vanessa caught Daria's eye. The deputy sheriff grinned and winked, as if she knew exactly what Remy was about to say.

"I wanted to let everyone know that Vanessa and I are going to be married," he said. "She has graciously consented to become my wife."

Everyone started talking at once, offering congratulations. Only Whit, Remy's father, said nothing. He sat stone-faced, eying his son with a narrow-eyed gaze. But he didn't seem angry, merely thoughtful. Finally, when the furor died down, the elder Colton stood and raised his glass.

"A toast," he said, finally smiling. "To my son and the beautiful Vanessa. May they have many years of happiness."

Everyone cheered.

"When's the wedding?" Kelsey asked. "If it's next summer, you'd better get with Blaine and Tilda. They're planning to get married in June."

Remy and Vanessa exchanged a look. "We haven't

worked out the details about the ceremony yet, but as soon as we do, we'll make sure to let everyone know."

Several of the women came over and asked to see her ring. Vanessa showed them, glad when Mara ordered everyone back to their seats so the first course could be served.

The eight-course meal made the feast they'd enjoyed yesterday seem positively meager. There were actual servants, standing behind the chairs after they'd brought the food, which reminded her of a few occasions at her grandparents' Boston mansion. Because she'd been to a few of these types of shindigs as a child, she took small bites of each offering, aware that was the only way she'd make it through to the end.

Watching some of the others, she noticed many of the women did the same thing.

The men, on the other hand, appeared to be doing some serious chowing down. Watching Remy devour his entire prime rib, she wondered where he put it. Catching Daria's eye, she exchanged an amused smile as she noticed Stefan eating just as much as Remy.

As they slowly made their way through courses, Vanessa felt more and more jittery. Something big was coming after this was all over—Remy's gift. Assuming, of course, that what she and Daria had planned worked out and that Remy was on board if it did.

When the last dessert plate had been cleared away, Russ Colton stood, cleared his throat and made a toast. "To our Colton family," he began, his tone mellow after a few glasses of wine. "To our engaged couples— Rylan and Bree, Phoebe and Prescott, Trey and Aisha, Blaine and Tilda and, of course, now Remy and Vanessa."

Everyone politely clapped. Russ waited a moment for silence before he continued. "To our newlyweds Skye and Leo, as well as Fox and Kelsey, and to new arrivals like baby John and Hudson, and of course Stefan's young son, Sam. To Blaine and Tilda's Josh." He raised his glass, grinning. "To animal sanctuaries and art galleries, ranches and farms, The Lodge and The Chateau, and most of all, to our town Roaring Springs!"

He cleared his throat. "Mara and I are talking again and I've officially decided to retire after the New Year." Everyone went quiet at this. When they started to speak, Russ held up his hand. "Decker will be co-CEO with Blaine. Remy, I'm placing you on the board of directors along with Mara and Phoebe. We finally have a new little dynasty in the making. This year has been a tough one for our family but we've emerged stronger than ever before. Merry Christmas to all of you, with love!"

"Hear! Hear!" those assembled responded, raising their glasses high before taking a sip. "To the Coltons!"

Touched, Vanessa met Remy's gaze as she drank her champagne. So much emotion blazed in his eyes—love, contentment and joy—that she teared up.

When the time came to leave the holiday gathering, Vanessa caught Daria's eye. She'd managed to keep her excitement under wraps for the entire get-together, so much so that she felt confident that Remy didn't suspect anything. Daria dipped her chin in a casual nod and then tugged on Stefan's arm. He raised one eyebrow, then bent down and scooped up his son, Sam.

The three of them would leave right after Remy and Vanessa and follow them to their destination.

Suddenly nervous, Vanessa asked Remy if he'd mind making a quick detour before going home.

"Sure," he replied, his gaze quizzical. "Where to?"

"It's a surprise," she promptly told him. "But I think you might like it." At least she hoped he would. Self-doubt momentarily plagued her. Their relationship was so new. What if she assumed too much?

Deciding Remy would surely let her know, she decided to make it clear that in the end, the choice would be up to him. "Remy, before we go…" Swallowing, she tried to find the right words.

Brow furrowed, he waited. "Should I be concerned?"

That made her laugh. "No. I just realized, though, that you might not feel you have a choice. I want you to understand that you don't have to worry about hurting my feelings. I can't say more without ruining things, but keep that in mind, okay?"

Slowly, he nodded. "That sounds ominous."

"It's not, I promise." She kissed his cheek. "Let's go."

As they drove, following the directions on Vanessa's phone's GPS, she wondered if Remy noticed Stefan and Daria following them.

"Here we are," she said, at the exact moment her GPS told them that they'd arrived at their destination.

"Bradford County Animal Shelter." Pulling up into the empty parking lot, Remy read the words aloud. He turned to face Vanessa, his expression puzzled. "You know they're closed, for Christmas, right?"

She nodded, unable to resist glancing in the mirror

for Stefan and Daria's car. She didn't see it yet, but knew they'd be here soon.

"Then why are we here?" Remy asked, clearly still puzzled.

"I wanted to give you your Christmas gift," she said softly. "So if it's all right with you, I thought we could give one of the shelter dogs a true Christmas miracle." She took a deep breath, watching him closely. "Daria got special permission to let us in today. I've already filled out the paperwork and signed it, so all that's left is choosing a dog. *Our* dog."

Remy opened and closed his mouth. "Are you serious?" he finally said.

"Yes. Daria told me that you've always talked about rescuing a dog. I've wanted to as well, but my life was too unsettled. It's not now."

"No, it's not."

Determined to finish, she nodded. "But this is why I told you earlier that in the end, it had to be your choice. If you're not ready or want to wait, then we will. A dog is a big commitment."

Remy shook his head. He grinned from ear to ear. "So is marriage. I've wanted a dog for so long and I love that we'd be getting one together."

"Are you sure?"

"Yes!" He hugged her, still smiling. "I'm sure if you are. Let's do this!"

Just then, Daria and Stefan pulled up. They got out and as soon as they'd unbuckled Sam from his car seat, he started running circles in the snowy parking lot.

"Hey there." Stefan greeted Remy. "I hear you're about to get a new family member. Congratulations."

A slow grin blossomed over Remy's handsome face.

"Thanks, man." He eyed little Sam, who'd stopped short and stared when he'd heard the word *dog*. "You know, I can think of someone else who might want their own pet," he said.

Stefan laughed at Daria's dumbfounded look. "I was just thinking the same thing," he said. "Sam's been wanting a dog for ages. Of course, if you're not on board, Daria, you'd better decide how you're going to dissuade him."

Daria stood on her tiptoes and kissed him. "We'll see," she said. "Now let's go get Remy and Vanessa their dog."

Unlocking the door, she flipped on the light. They stepped into a small reception area with a long counter. Daria pointed to another door leading to the back. "The animals are that way. The cat room is to the right and the dogs are past that. The shelter is full right now. Apparently, a lot of people dump their animals during the holidays."

As soon as she opened the door, the cacophony of barking began. High-pitched yaps and deep barks, some coming rapid-fire as if in desperation or alarm. Startled, Sam clutched his father's hand and drew back, unsure.

"It's okay," Stefan reassured his son. "I think we might have just woken all the doggies up."

"Go ahead, you two," Daria said, stepping back and motioning Remy and Vanessa to go past her. She wrinkled her nose. "It's a clean facility, but it still has that smell."

Gripping Remy's hand tightly, Vanessa swallowed. Together, they went through the doorway, walked down a short hallway and entered a room with concrete floors and tall, metal dog runs.

They both stopped, staring. "How are we going to choose?" Remy asked. "There are so many."

Though her heart had started pounding, she managed to shrug. "I have no idea. But I suspect when we meet the right one, we'll know."

Remy nodded. "I certainly hope so."

As they walked down the first row, dogs of every shape and size and breed greeted them. Long-haired and short. Broad noses and pointed. Ninety pounders and nine pounders. Many jumped at the bars. Most barked or pawed, seeming desperate for attention. One or two continued to lie on their cots, eying the humans with feigned indifference or disappointment, Vanessa couldn't tell which.

She stopped in front of a regal-looking golden retriever, considering, before moving along. Then she saw a beautiful, long-haired white dog and a cute hyper small terrier, and exhaled. "This is going to be more difficult than I thought," she said.

Remy had gone on ahead of her and stopped in front of the last cage in the row. "Vanessa, come here."

There, in the kennel, stood a medium-size, brown-and-white dog with huge brown eyes. He had a white flash around his neck and on his muzzle. He wasn't barking; instead, he twisted his entire body in apparent spasms of joy. "He's kidney beaning," Remy said. "Boxers are known for that."

Vanessa bent down and spoke to him through the bars, carefully holding out her hand for him to sniff. To her surprise—and joy—he licked her. And then he tilted his head as if to say "Come on, get me out of here, why don't you?"

"This one." The certainty in Remy's voice matched the feeling in her heart. "His name is Raider. He's a two-year-old boxer," he said, tapping the kennel card posted to the front of the pen. "Owner surrendered for constantly jumping out of his chain-link-fenced yard. Since we have a six-foot-tall wooden fence and don't intend to leave him out alone in the backyard, that shouldn't be a problem."

Vanessa dug in her pocket for the leash she'd purchased earlier. She hadn't gotten a collar, since she'd had no idea what size dog they'd end up getting. "I already paid and filled out the paperwork," she told him. "It's sitting on the front desk. All we need to do is let them know which dog we're adopting."

From the other row behind them, they heard Sam squeal. "Please, Dad? Look how much that puppy loves me. Can we take her home?"

Daria's voice joined Sam's. "What do you think, Stefan? I think she really needs us."

Stefan said something that sounded like agreement.

Vanessa and Remy exchanged a grin. "Looks like we're not the only ones giving a dog a home on Christmas."

Remy opened the kennel and slipped the leash around Raider's neck, using it as a collar until they could get a proper one. "Come on, boy. Let's get you out of here and take you home." He sniffed. "I foresee a bath in your very near future."

Watching Vanessa's beautiful face glow with love as she watched their new dog, Remy wanted to kiss her. But that would have to wait until later, since his hands were full right now with an excited flashy fawn boxer. Unlike most other women he knew, Vanessa didn't appear to mind the dog brushing up against her fancy dress with his nose.

The instant they stepped outside, Raider leaped into the air, jumping with joy. He did this over and over, like an end-zone happy dance. Amused, Remy watched him celebrate his freedom with gusto.

"Something tells me he's going to be a handful," Vanessa murmured, still smiling, clearly besotted. "In a good way."

"That's how boxers are," he answered. "I've read up on them because I've always wanted one. They do nothing half-heartedly, including love."

"That sounds perfect for us." Vanessa kneeled down. Immediately, Raider rushed her, licking her face and wagging his little nub of a tail so fast it looked like a helicopter prop.

She wrapped her arms around him and the dog leaned in, eyes half-closed, enjoying every second and absorbing the love.

"Our dog," she said. "I can hardly believe it. It's like a dream come true."

"*You're* a dream come true," he told her. "You and Raider both."

The shelter door opened. Daria, Stefan and Sam emerged. Daria held a tiny, fluffy dog in her arms while Sam ran circles around her, begging to be allowed to pet it.

Seeing Remy and Vanessa, Daria smiled sheepishly, letting them see her precious cargo. "Meet Xena, Warrior Princess. Her kennel card says she's a Cavapoo—half Cavalier King Charles spaniel and half poodle. She's eight months old."

"And I'm going to love her!" Sam announced.

"We're *all* going to love her," Stefan corrected. He eyed Raider, who'd caught sight of the puppy and was now wiggling his entire body in happy greeting.

"That one looks like a handful," Stefan said. His comment made Vanessa laugh.

"We were just saying that. But it's okay. He'll be *our* handful."

Daria handed Xena over to Stefan and went back to make sure everything was shut down for the night.

Overhead, a single bright star shone in the cloudless night sky. Remy caught Vanessa looking at it and pulled her close. "Christmas is full of miracles," he said.

"And love," she murmured back. "Always love."

He would have kissed her right then, a deep kiss that they both would have felt all the way to their toes, but Raider chose that moment to tug hard on the leash, sending Remy off balance.

He laughed and let the dog lead him over to the base of an evergreen. After Raider explored and marked his territory, he zoomed right back to Vanessa, who crooned baby talk to him and stroked his fur.

After Daria finished locking up the shelter, she joined them, once again taking little Xena from Stefan's arms. "I wish we could save them all," she mused. "There are so many dogs—and cats—who just need someone to love them."

Eying Raider and Xena, her expression softened. "The shelter is going to be running an adoption event right after the New Year. Drastically reduced adoption fees. Senior animals will be free. They're hoping to clear the shelter."

"Wouldn't that be perfect?" Still petting Raider, Vanessa smiled at her.

"For now, these two got their open happy ending," Remy interjected. "Let's go home."

"Merry Christmas to you both." Daria hugged Vanessa first, then Remy. Stefan followed suit.

Arms around each other, Remy and Vanessa watched the other couple climb into their car, Daria and little Sam now tenderly cradling their new puppy.

"I love my new family," Vanessa mused. "Thank you for that."

Trying to keep Raider from tangling his legs up in the leash, Remy laughed. "Thank you, too. Being with you has made me happier than I've ever been."

"Me, too." Smiling, Vanessa eyed him and their dog. "Come on, Raider," she said. "Time to go home."

They all loaded up in the Jeep.

Clearly Raider enjoyed car rides. He sat up in the back seat, tongue hanging out, alert and happy and at ease.

When they pulled up to Remy's house, he parked in front of the garage so it would be easier to get Raider out. Turning off the ignition, he met Vanessa's gaze.

"Merry Christmas," she murmured.

He leaned across the console and kissed her, putting all of the love he felt into the kiss.

Not wanting to be left out, Raider poked at them with his wet nose, effectively breaking them apart. Remy laughed, feeling a lightness of spirit he hadn't felt in a long time. "Merry Christmas," he replied. "Let's get this boy in and show him his new home."

They let Raider out in the backyard first and stood on the back deck with their arms around each other watching as their dog checked out his new surroundings. Once he'd taken care of his business, Remy called him, curious to see if he'd come.

Of course, Raider bounded over immediately, short nub of a tail wagging furiously.

"I bought a bag of dog food, some dog bowls and a bed for him a few days ago," Vanessa announced. "I hid them under the guest bed so you wouldn't see."

This made Remy laugh again. He couldn't recall the last Christmas he'd laughed so much. "Full of surprises," he murmured, nuzzling his fiancée's neck.

She turned her head, just so, and kissed him. "And many more just like this," she promised.

The next morning, Remy woke up early to let the dog out. After a bath to get the shelter funk off him, Raider had spent the night curled up at the foot of their bed, ignoring the huge dog bed that Vanessa had purchased. After exchanging quick looks, they allowed it, drifting off to sleep to the sound of contented boxer snores.

Raider fit right in, so quickly he might have always shared their lives. They went to the pet store located on the same street as the Wise Gal Gallery and bought their dog a collar, harness, matching leash and some toys. The clerk who rang them up commented on what a beautiful dog he was, and how he was obviously very spoiled. Her words made both Remy and Vanessa grin like fools.

"Proud dog parents, aren't you?" Bree said, greeting them when they walked down the street to her gallery. "I heard from Daria all about your Christmas-night adventure."

"You're one to talk," Remy said, pointing. Her little dog, Jekyll, sat up on a chair and surveyed them all with disinterested disdain.

Bree laughed. "Dogs rock. That's why I never go anywhere without mine."

Raider woofed quietly, wiggling his nub and straining to be allowed closer to the small dog. "Should I?" Remy asked.

"Not today. I wouldn't bring your big boy close to him," Bree answered. "He's having one of his off days. That's why I named him Jekyll. He has a split personality."

This made Vanessa chuckle. "It's a whole new world, isn't it?" she asked. "Being dog owners, that is."

Bree concurred, exchanging a quick look with Remy and giving him a thumbs-up in approval once Vanessa turned away to look around at some of the paintings.

"I'm really going to enjoy being part of your family," Vanessa commented on the way home. "Not only will I gain relatives, but I think I've made a couple of new friends. Soon, they'll be my in-laws."

Once they were married. A thought occurred to him. A radical, yet sensible thought.

"We should talk about the wedding," he ventured. "I don't want to wait."

A slow smile curved her mouth. "I don't, either. Are you saying what I think you are?"

"Yes. As long as you haven't been harboring a secret dream of a big, fancy, formal wedding, let's just keep it simple and quick."

She gave him a long look. "Won't your family be upset?"

"Yes," he admitted. "We'll have to allow them to throw us a big celebratory party to pacify them, but it'll all work out in the end. That is, if you're agreeable."

"I am." She kissed his cheek since he was driving, which made Raider bark and both of them chuckle. Their happiness must have been contagious, as their new dog spent the rest of the day amusing them with his antics.

They decided to put her Boulder house on the market as soon as possible, with her parents' Boston home to follow as soon as she finished cleaning it out. Remy offered to sell his custom home too, so that they could choose a new one together, but Vanessa vetoed that idea.

"We'll just make it ours," she said, warming his heart. "There's so much of you in it already, and since I love you, of course I love your house."

"Our house," he corrected, smiling. "Neither one of us will ever have to be alone again."

The Friday after Christmas, Remy and Vanessa went down to city hall and got their marriage license. Since Colorado had no waiting period, blood test, or residency requirement, they walked over to the justice of the peace and quietly got married.

Then they went home and celebrated with Raider. Later, Remy would make phone calls and let his family know, but right now he wanted to enjoy the moment with his new bride.

"Vanessa Colton," he said, loving the sound of it. "My wife."

"My husband." Smiling, she kissed him, and this time their dog paid them no mind, too intent on romping in the snow.

* * * * *

Don't miss the previous volumes in the
Coltons of Roaring Springs *miniseries:*

Colton Cowboy Standoff *by Marie Ferrarella*
Colton Under Fire *by Cindy Dees*
Colton's Convenient Bride *by Jennifer Morey*
Colton's Secret Bodyguard *by Jane Godman*
A Colton Target *by Beverly Long*
Colton's Covert Baby *by Lara Lacombe*
Colton's Mistaken Identity *by Geri Krotow*
The Colton Sheriff *by Addison Fox*
Colton on the Run *by Anna J. Stewart*
Colton Family Showdown *by Regan Black*
Colton's Secret Investigation *by Justine Davis*

All available now from
Harlequin Romantic Suspense

WE HOPE YOU
ENJOYED THIS BOOK!

⬥HARLEQUIN®

ROMANTIC suspense

Experience the rush of thrilling adventure, captivating mystery and unexpected romance.

Discover four new books every month, available wherever books are sold!

Harlequin.com

The memories flooded back so fast and hard, slamming
into him like a physical blow, that he stumbled behind
Anna, and had to catch himself with a hand against the
wall.

How could he have forgotten all of that stuff?

Anna stopped abruptly in what looked like a dining
room and turned to face him, tipping up her face
expectantly to the light. The curve of her cheek was
worthy of a Rembrandt painting, plump like a child's and
angular like a woman's. How was that possible?

"Well?" she demanded.

"Uh, well what?" he mumbled.

"Are my pupils all right?"

He frowned and looked into her eyes. They were
cinnamon-hued, the color of a chestnut horse in sunshine,

with streaks of gold running through them. Her lashes were dark and long, fanning across her cheeks as lightly as strands of silk.

Pupils. Compare diameters. Even or uneven. Cripes. His entire brain had just melted and drained out his ear. One look into her big innocent eyes, and he was toast. Belatedly, he held up a hand in front of her face, blocking the direct light.

She froze at the abrupt movement of his hand, and he did the same. Where was the threat? When one of his teammates went completely still like that, it meant a dire threat was far too close to all of them. Without moving his head, he let his gaze range around the room. Everything was still, and only the sounds of a vintage disco dance tune broke the silence.

He looked back at her questioningly. What had her so on edge? Only peripherally did he register that, on cue, the black disks of her pupils had grown to encompass the lighter brown of her irises. He took his hand away, and her pupils contracted quickly.

"Um, yeah. Your eyes look okay," he murmured. "Do you have a headache?"

"Yes, but it's from all the sanding I have to do and not from my tumble off your porch."

Don't miss
Navy SEAL's Deadly Secret by Cindy Dees,
available January 2020 wherever
Harlequin® Romantic Suspense
books and ebooks are sold.

Harlequin.com